THE KYDD INHERITANCE

In Regency England, Nell Kydd is at her wits' end and it's easy to see why. Her father is dead, her brother, Kit, is missing and her loathsome uncle, with his mismanagement, is wrecking the family estate. She must contend with a perturbing lack of funds, an unwelcome proposal of marriage and a mother who lives in a reality of her own. Cue the arrival of the unsettling Captain Hugo Derringer: an old schoolfriend of Kit's who blows hot then cold, and is discovered at odd times — in odd places — asking very odd questions. How far can Nell trust him?

Books by Jan Jones
Published by The House of Ulverscroft:

FAIR DECEPTION
FORTUNATE WAGER

Jan Jones fell in love with Jane Austen, Georgette Heyer and the 1800s aged twelve, and the love has never left her. She likes to think her Regencies are 'in the Heyer tradition, with a dash of Mary Stewart', another favourite writer.

A multi-genre author living in Suffolk, Jan's novels, serials and short stories are written whilst organising events for the Romantic Novelist's Association. She is immensely proud that her Newmarket Regency *Fair Deception* was shortlisted for the Love Story of the Year in 2010.

There is more about Jan on her website: www.jan-jones.co.uk She also blogs at http://jan-jones.blogspot.com and is on Twitter as @janjonesauthor.

JAN JONES

THE KYDD INHERITANCE

Complete and Unabridged

ULVERSCROFT
Leicester

First published in Great Britain in 2011 by
Robert Hale Limited
London

First Large Print Edition
published 2012
by arrangement with
Robert Hale Limited
London

British Library CIP Data

Jones, Jan, *1955 –*
The kydd inheritance.
1. Great Britain- -History- -George III, *1760 – 1820*
- -Fiction. 2. Love stories. 3. Large type books.
I. Title
823.9′2–dc23

ISBN 978–1–4448–0959–6

Published by
F. A. Thorpe (Publishing)
Anstey, Leicestershire

Set by Words & Graphics Ltd.
Anstey, Leicestershire
Printed and bound in Great Britain by
T. J. International Ltd., Padstow, Cornwall

This book is printed on acid-free paper

For my lovely Lizzie, who read the first
three pages and wanted to know what
happened next

PROLOGUE

India: 1815

The heat was unremitting. Eight months in India still hadn't accustomed Kit to the on-slaught. Maybe a gallop would raise enough of a wind to cool him down. He strode across the yard and took the reins from the waiting syce, noticing that the man was unfamiliar but thinking no more about it.

Yes, a good gallop would do the trick. He set his foot in the stirrup and swung into the saddle — only for the horse to scream and Kit himself to be hurled into the thick, pungent air and slammed down hard upon the ground.

Shock flooded him, but instinct hurtled to his rescue, rolling him away from the horse's murderous, trampling hoofs, keeping him tightly-balled with his arms protecting his head.

The reverberations through the hard-baked ground diminished. Servants helped him up, exclaiming and brushing dust from his clothes. Others ran with soft, urgent footfalls to capture the maddened beast.

1

Kit's heart rate slowly returned to normal. A mischance, surely. The horse had been spooked. And yet . . . And yet . . . There had been that runaway cart last week. And the falling bale of silk in the warehouse that had only just missed him. Kit had never been accident-prone before.

The grooms had got the saddle off the horse now, were soothing him and examining the blanket. 'A thorn,' shouted one in relief. 'No need to destroy the animal. It was just a thorn. Do you still wish to ride?'

A house servant hurried up with mail. Kit recognized his sister Nell's writing and waved the grooms away. A clutch of letters from home was better than a gallop any day. His heart lifted at the thought of Kydd Court, just coming out of its winter hibernation. His business here was all but finished — in a few months he would be back in England's cool green lanes: teasing Mama, sparring with Nell, sipping Madeira with his father after a day's sport, throwing himself into all the doings of the estate. He couldn't imagine now why he had ever fancied himself bored.

He began to read avidly, and felt his blood turn to ice as one shocking sentence after another assaulted his senses. 'No,' he whispered. 'No!'

He strode out of the yard, his fist crushing

Nell's letter, his mind numb. Business was forgotten. Minor accidents were forgotten. He was intent only on booking a passage home without loss of time. His father was dead and his mother ill. The news had already been four months on the journey. He had to get back to Kydd Court. Nell was the best of sisters — brave, intelligent and determined — but she was still a minor for all that. God alone knew what straits she might find herself in before he arrived back.

★ ★ ★

Behind him, the new syce slipped from shadow to shadow.

1

Nell stared at her uncle in shock. 'I don't believe I understand you, sir.'

Jasper Kydd continued to sort through his mail. 'I fail to see how it could be plainer. Philip Belmont called whilst you were in town to ask if he might pay his addresses. My felicitations.'

'But I do not wish to marry Philip.'

'Immaterial. Belmont is a young man whose land marches with that of Kydd and he has known you long enough that your hoydenish disposition fails to excite in him any alarms. It seems an excellent arrangement.'

Nell reminded herself that she had sworn not to lose her temper with her hated uncle today. 'Have you forgotten Mama and I are to go to London in the spring? Papa was adamant that I should not marry until I had had at least one London season.'

'London? Ha! If my brother's purse had matched his ideas you might have a hundred such seasons. As it is, his uncurbed expenditure means Kydd Court will be hard pressed to remain solvent this winter, much less next spring.'

Her attempt to remain submissive exploded. Ever since her father's death in a riding accident the previous year, Uncle Jasper had been abusing his memory. Papa might have been more given to penning philosophical essays than reckoning household accounts, but he had *not* been profligate. If anyone was to blame for the estate's present financial straits, it was Jasper Kydd himself with his appalling notions of land management.

'Papa laid by a considerable sum for my season. I remember him discussing it with Kit. It is only because he broke his leg shortly after Kit went out to India that I was not presented eighteen months ago.' Her voice shook as she mentioned her brother. Kit had to be alive, he just *had* to.

Her uncle glanced at her coldly. 'You are arguing again, Helena. You know my views on ladies who argue.'

Not for the first time, Nell wished she and her mother had not been so numb with grief at Papa's death that they failed to notice Jasper taking over the ordering of Kydd Court. With no opposition, he had smoothly convinced the solicitor that in the absence of

6

the heir, he himself should act as his nephew's agent. Now it seemed to Nell that he was as often here as he was at his own estate of Windown Park, countermanding her running of the house and home farm, and imposing his joyless regime over all.

Jasper selected a cream-coloured packet from amongst the correspondence and broke the wafer. His complexion darkened as he read the enclosure. 'The Half Moon Street house is *still* not let. Last time it was haunted attics, now the agent reports the kitchen is damp! Another bad investment by your father. Would that I could sell the place and be rid of it.'

Nell burned with anger. Her uncle had said *I*. The Kydd estate was not his. Not yet. And if she could only trace Kit it never would be!

Her indrawn breath drew Jasper's attention. He looked up, his lips thinning as he observed her clenched fists. 'Enough of this folly. The subject is closed. A season in London without a sizeable dowry is an absurdity. Accept Belmont and be thankful. We dine there tonight. Be sure to wear something suitable.'

Nell dropped a seething curtsey. 'As you wish.'

★ ★ ★

The conversation pounded in Nell's head as her maid dressed her in a particularly ugly mulberry satin evening gown. If by 'wear something suitable' her uncle meant 'attractive enough for a man to propose marriage', then he should have left the commissioning of her wardrobe to her. No one knew better than Nell that the fussy greys and mauves he had ordered so high-handedly from his wife's dressmaker did not become her, but put off Papa's mourning a day earlier than the full twelve months she would not, especially for such a reason as this.

Marry Philip Belmont indeed, when he cheerfully admitted himself that he'd never been much of one for brains. Nell would be biting her tongue half the day for fear of making him unhappy. She couldn't imagine what had induced him to offer for her. It certainly wasn't love — only last week he had been asking whether she didn't think Charlotte Grainger's hair the exact colour of ripening corn. How Kit would roast her when he heard.

Oh, Kit! Nell wished with all her heart that her brother was here right now. Six years her elder, taller by a head and as well formed as he was carelessly intelligent, Kit would rout their uncle from Kydd Court without breaking stride. His continuing failure to show up and do that very thing was an acute source of worry. He had vanished eight months ago — on the very eve of his journey home from Bombay — and no explanation had been forthcoming.

Not that they had known he was missing at the time. With the sea crossing taking several months, Nell had simply been counting the days and doing her best against his return. Protecting her mother, whose reason had deteriorated with the shock of Papa's death. Bolstering the servants. Fighting her uncle's ill-judged schemes for Kydd Court.

'How much do you suppose a season costs, Annie?' she speculated now.

Her maid's adroit fingers coaxed the ostentatious lace trim around the neckline to fall evenly. 'We can figure it easy, miss. We know how much fabric a gown takes, and we know what cambric and silk and muslin are the yard . . . '

'So we do,' said Nell, turning an idea over in her mind. 'And I'm sure if Mama has itemized the wardrobe she assembled for *her* first season once, she has done it a thousand times. But even if we sewed everything ourselves and came only to a tenth the sum other households expend, Uncle Jasper will still say the estate cannot bear it. He positively delights in our misfortune.'

All her life, Nell had been accustomed to debating issues with her father and his friends. It would never have occurred to her to treat conversations with her maid any differently. Annie, a brisk no-nonsense woman approaching her middle years, had been her confidante on many occasions. Every time her uncle accused Papa of having run up debts or ruined the estate, Nell came to Annie to vent her anger safely. Indeed, with Kit overseas and Mama withdrawn into her own private world, had Nell not had the servants to talk to, she would likely have run mad.

Now Annie took up a silver-backed brush and attacked Nell's cloud of dark hair until it stood out like an aureole from her face. 'He's like to know about the accounts,' she said, pinning up the back à la Grecque, 'being as how he took over all the books when the master died.'

Nell's hazel eyes, more green than brown, met those of her maid in the mirror. 'No, I cannot believe the money is all gone. I know Papa was more careful than that and I know he arranged my fund with our solicitor. I *must* see Mr Tweedie without my uncle's knowledge and find out what is being done to locate Kit. Could I go to London with one of our friends? But that would mean leaving

Mama alone here.'

She clasped a simple gold chain round her neck and surveyed her reflection. 'Goodness, what a fright I look. The only consolation is that Philip cannot possibly be tempted into the folly of offering for me tonight. I will be amazed if I get so much as a partner for dinner.'

⋆ ⋆ ⋆

When Nell, her mama and her uncle were shown into the saloon at Belmont House, they found the usual neighbourhood families assembled. Mrs Kydd, still in the unrelieved black of deep mourning, was steered solicitously to the fireside.

About to follow, Nell was accosted by her host. Philip was thankfully not looking in the least lovelorn. He was with a tall, dark-haired stranger and, from his cheerful demeanor as he hailed her, she rather thought it had slipped his mind entirely that he had asked permission to address her only that morning.

'Nell! I hoped you would come soon! May I present my friend Captain Hugo Derringer? Hugo, Miss Kydd. Kit's sister, you know. Hugo arrived today, Nell, is it not capital?'

A new addition to their circle was always a matter of interest, but Nell was brought up short by the astonishment on the newcomer's tanned face. 'I am pleased to make your acquaintance, Captain Derringer,' she said pointedly.

He recollected himself and bowed. 'Your servant, Miss Kydd. Forgive me, I was expecting a younger lady.'

Nell's eyes narrowed. Although she had joked about her appearance with Annie, it was beyond the bounds of civility for a stranger to intimate that she looked haggard! 'I am eighteen, sir,' she said in dulcet tones. 'How much younger a bride would you expect your friend to seek?'

She had the satisfaction of seeing Captain Derringer's heavy eyebrows snap together. His utterance, however, was unexpected. 'Bride? How is this?'

'Forgot to say,' said Philip. 'M'mother's idea. She said I should get in quick now your mourning is nearly up.' He looked hopefully at Nell. 'Does that mean you agree? I didn't think you would.'

Nell bit her lips at this artless speech. 'No, dear Philip, I do not agree. We should never suit. I would tease you dreadfully.'

'Pity,' said Philip. 'I hadn't thought about you until m'mother suggested it, but it's a good idea. A fellow knows where he is with you.'

She patted his hand. 'Not for long, I dare swear. But I thank you for your offer and shall always think kindly of you for making it.'

Captain Derringer appeared to be struggling with amusement. 'It didn't appear to me that my friend *had* made you an offer.'

'That is because you have not known Mr Belmont so long as I have,' said Nell repressively. 'It was perfectly clear to me, I assure you.'

Philip wrinkled his brow, looking from one to the other. 'Yes he has, Nell. Known me for long, I mean. We were at Eton.'

Nell studied the guest with more friendliness. 'Then you must know my brother Kit.'

Confusion touched Hugo Derringer's countenance. 'I do, yes. I was sorry to hear of his disappearance. I suppose everything possible is being done to — '

'My dear, you are remiss.' Jasper Kydd's smooth tones issued from behind her. 'You have not yet made your curtsey to Mrs Belmont.'

Both young men stiffened and Nell felt a surge of irritation at the way her uncle never left her alone. As if Philip's mama would mind how long she took before going over to her. 'I am coming directly,' she said. Her chin lifted as she met Captain Derringer's dark eyes. 'Pray be easy. If you are acquainted with

Kit at all, you will know he has been falling into scrapes since the day he was born. I am persuaded that had any harm truly come to him, I would be aware of it.'

Approval flickered in his expression. 'Your sentiments do you credit.'

Her uncle cleared his throat. The unspoken remonstrance grated. 'As my manners do not, it appears,' she said. 'Allow me to present Captain Derringer, sir, a friend of Mr Belmont. Captain Derringer, my late father's brother, Mr Jasper Kydd.'

'*Captain* Derringer?' Her uncle's cold glance swept over the serviceable black cloth coat, cream waistcoat and buff pantaloons.

'I was invalided home some little time ago.' As Hugo Derringer turned, Nell realized that he held his left arm stiffly.

'Indeed? And how do you find Northampton-shire, Captain Derringer?'

'I was never in this part of the country before. Belmont tells me there is excellent shooting to be had.'

Commonplace dialogue but Nell sensed taut undercurrents, for all the world as if the two men were rival dogs circling a juicy bone. 'I should pay my respects to your mother, Philip,' she said. 'I hope you enjoy your stay, Captain Derringer.' As she moved away, she could feel his eyes following her.

14

Her uncle accompanied her across the well proportioned room, a stalking shadow at her shoulder. 'Does Derringer remain with Belmont long?'

'I do not know. We had but just been introduced.'

'I trust not for Belmont's sake. A half-pay officer with time on his hands will be the ruin of his coverts.'

Implicit in his disparaging words was that a half-pay officer with time on his hands would be equally ruinous to any young lady foolish enough to encourage him. Nell almost missed a step in astonishment. The juicy bone had been *her*? This was a most unexpected development. Jasper had never been solicitous about her future before.

Though they were not placed close enough to converse at dinner and were at different tables for the card play that followed, Nell found her eyes several times drawn to Hugo Derringer. He might dress plainly, but he did not give the impression of being an impoverished soldier bent on amusement. Rather, he had an air of quiet self-reliance. On the occasions when she discovered his watchful gaze to be fixed on her, she met his regard directly. She was not entirely surprised when it was he who tendered her merino shawl as the guests waited for carriages to be brought round at the end of the evening.

'Thank you,' she said. 'If your sport palls, I hope you will give us the pleasure of calling at Kydd Court.'

'The pleasure would be all mine. Are you at home to visitors tomorrow?'

Goodness, that was remarkably quick! 'I believe so,' said Nell, slightly taken aback, 'but do not make an engagement you might not keep. I understand Philip's birds are rising particularly well this year.'

Mrs Kydd looked up from arranging her own shawl. 'Where is Kit?' she said vaguely. 'I wish you would tell him we are ready.'

Nell felt hot colour flood her cheeks. Their friends all made allowances for Mama, but Captain Derringer was a stranger and wouldn't understand how badly Papa's death had affected her. He had been the lodestone of her life, the axis on which her world turned. Barely able to grasp that Robert Kydd had gone from her, the awful news of Kit's disappearance just when they were looking to see him home had caused Mrs Kydd's mind to recoil even further into a place of her own devising.

'Kit is not here tonight, Mama,' she said.

To her horror, her mother's mouth crumpled. 'Oh no, I was forgetting.' She laid a tremulous hand on the captain's sleeve.

'You'll go after him, won't you, sir. You'll bring my boy back.'

'Mama — ' said Nell desperately, but Hugo Derringer intervened.

He covered Mrs Kydd's hand with his own and said in a deep, comforting voice, 'I shall do everything in my power to help you, ma'am.'

'I knew you would. So kind, always.'

Nell was rigid with mortification as Hugo escorted them to the carriage, but before her uncle had even joined them he had nodded a brief farewell and returned to the house. Nell didn't blame him in the least.

★　★　★

That could have been awkward, thought Hugo, hurrying back to the house. He passed Jasper Kydd striding towards the Kydd carriage but made no salutation. Hopefully the man hadn't remarked him. He wondered at himself. Getting along with people was his stock in trade — never had he taken such an instant dislike to a person as he had to Mr Kydd. He felt sorry for Nell and her mother having to live in the same house with him. Nell herself, though . . . Hugo felt himself smile. What a personality! In spite of that appalling dress. He hadn't at all been looking

17

forward to coming up here, but just a few exchanges with Nell had done much to reconcile him. He had a very agreeable impression that spending time with her would be stimulating and challenging and no hardship at all.

★　★　★

Next morning Nell rose at her usual early hour. There wouldn't be many fine days left this autumn if she read the weather signs aright so she would make the most of them while she could. Slipping down to the stables in a riding habit of dull olive cloth, she met her groom emerging with their mounts.

Seth was part of the fabric of Nell's life. The product of a dull-witted maid and a visiting ostler, he had been adopted into Cook's family and had grown up on the estate. Nell had declared him to be her groom at the age of two when he'd first helped her scramble onto Kit's outgrown pony. Kit always said Seth had taken her so literally he'd barely let her out of sight on horseback since. Now he hoisted her into Snowflake's saddle and swung his leg over the only one of Kit's horses to remain unsold after Jasper Kydd's retrenchment campaign. Nell had fought her uncle more bitterly over this than anything else and had only managed to retain

Valiant because Seth needed a mount that could keep up with her in a gallop.

She loved the early morning. The wind streamed past as she gave Snowflake her head along the lane that cut through to the fields. At times like this she could easily understand Mama's withdrawal into her own world. For now there was nothing to think of bar the necessity of avoiding ruts and rabbit holes at speed. It was a shock when her concentration was broken by the sight of a mounted figure by the Six-Mile Acre.

'Captain Derringer!' She reined to a halt. Everything about him was ordered, from the dark locks under his brushed beaver to his gleaming top boots. Nell was uncomfortably conscious of her faded habit and escaping tendrils of windblown hair. Normal life was back with a vengeance. 'Whatever are you doing here?'

'I might ask you the same thing!'

'I am exercising my horse. You are trespassing.'

'Am I? Then I beg your pardon. I thought this was still Belmont ground.'

Seth came galloping up belligerently. 'Who's this, Miss Nell? What's he doing on our land? Will I see him off?'

Not again! Nell felt her cheeks flame. Mama last night and Seth this morning. Was she to be forever embarrassed in front of this man? 'Captain Derringer is a friend of Mr Belmont, Seth. He was at school with Master Kit.'

Seth went through an instant *volte face*. 'That's primer then. Nice horse, Captain. Fast, is he?'

Hugo Derringer took the groom's familiarity in his stride. 'Conqueror will go eighteen miles an hour all day if need be. When I call at Kydd Court, perhaps you would be good enough to tend to him.'

'I will,' said Seth with satisfaction. 'Master Kit don't let no one groom Valiant but me.' He patted the black stallion's neck fondly.

'He is fortunate that you remain to take care of his stable whilst he is away.'

Seth snorted. 'What's left of it after Mr Jasper sold 'em all!'

'Enough, Seth,' said Nell.

'But Miss Nell, you was mad as fire too when the hunters went. And the mares Master Kit was keeping for breeding. You said you'd like to — '

'Yes, Seth! It is of no interest to Captain Derringer, however.' She avoided looking at the betraying quiver around the captain's mouth and turned Snowflake to ride back.

He nudging his own horse to keep pace with her.

'I must apologize,' she said stiffly. 'Seth grew up on the estate with Kit and me. He forgets that other families view servants differently. I assure you Conqueror will be in safe hands.'

Hugo smiled. It quite transformed his expression, making him seem altogether more carefree. Nell's heart thudded in surprise. 'I would be simple myself not to perceive that,' he said. 'You look delightful this morning.'

His eyes were not black at all but a deep shade of green, much darker than her own. And his tan, once you were used to it, gave him a rugged, mature air. Nell coloured fierily, as much at being caught staring as at his words. 'I am afraid you must think me disrespectful to be dressed like this,' she said in confusion. 'My uncle's daughters rarely ride, so it did not occur to him to order me a black habit.'

'I do not suppose your late father would object. Green suits you. You should always wear it.'

A most peculiar sensation stirred in Nell's breast. Was he *flirting* with her? 'Always? But how singular I should look. And I cannot help thinking that I should become a trifle *jaded* with the colour after a while.'

Hugo Derringer's eyes danced in appreciation. 'A jest this early in the morning settles the matter. You would be wasted on Belmont.'

'Indeed, I would be very bad for him.' Alarmed at the way that neither her tongue nor her body were behaving with propriety, Nell changed the subject. 'Tell me, what were you staring at so intently before I arrived?'

His hands stilled for an instant on the reins, almost as if he was vexed at her query. 'It seemed to me the south-east corner of the meadow was in standing water. I was pondering the breach of etiquette involved in a guest mentioning to his host that his land was likely to become sour.'

Nell laughed. 'Then you should be grateful to me for putting you right.'

'But I have told *you* and it is your land.'

'Kit's. And I already knew it. I have been saying to my uncle for months that he should set the men to clear the ditches but he claims they can never spare the time. When I argue that the returns will justify the outlay, he begs me desist from such talk as ladies cannot understand.'

'It does not seem to me a difficult concept,' said Captain Derringer.

'Ah, but you are a man. Females, you must know, are notoriously deficient in comprehension.' Anger loosened Nell's tongue. 'It infuriates me! He will listen to nothing I suggest. Even when Old John supported me about replanting the hedgerow the bull broke, he would not agree, so the crops from both top fields are now spoiled due to the wind flattening them.'

'Odd, but you will admit such farming wisdom is not usually to be found in the fairer sex?'

And now he was laughing at her! 'I have lived here all my life and used to roam the estate with my brother. What he learnt, I learnt. Were I only of age to administer in his stead — ' She broke off, not trusting herself to continue.

They were passing a field in which heavy ears of corn rustled fatly, gilded by the morning sun. Nell's lips compressed. Every previous year these crops had been gathered in first. It was all very well for her uncle to say changes were long overdue at Kydd Court, but when a system worked, what profit was there in altering it?

Hugo scanned the empty landscape, his forehead creased, his thoughts writ plain upon his face. Nell felt her temper bubble over. Was he doing this on purpose? 'You are wondering where the harvesters are. As indeed would anyone. I warned my uncle how it would be when he let half the heavy horses go from the Home Farm and the men with them. The result of his *economy* is that good crops stand rotting in the fields whilst too few workers salvage what they may from bad! It is ridiculous!'

'I am sorry. Has your uncle no estate of his own to learn from?'

'Indeed he has, and it puzzles me to know how it comes to be as profitable as he claims if he runs Windown Park the same way he does Kydd Court! I cannot see that Northamptonshire and Wiltshire can be so different that the ill-thought methods he uses *here* work so well *there*!'

'No, it is very strange.'

A flight of birds rising from a distant spinney recalled Nell's attention. 'I beg your pardon,' she said belatedly. 'You should not have let me run on in so wild a fashion.'

Captain Derringer raised his eyebrows. 'There was a way of preventing you?'

At this outrageous remark, Nell had to remind herself quite strongly that one day's acquaintance was not long enough to answer him in kind. 'It distresses me to see the land my father loved mishandled,' she said in a controlled voice. 'Papa left Kydd in good standing for Kit. My uncle is likely to ruin it before ever my brother sets foot back on these shores.' She reined to a halt and pointed along a track to the left. 'Your road lies that way. It is muddy from last week's rain but not impassable. Beyond the spinney, you will find Belmont's East Wood. There *is* a fence between.'

'You do not go with me to see me off your property?' There was a teasing challenge in his tone.

'I would, of course, but when my uncle is in residence, I do not care to be late for breakfast. Naturally, if any reports reach me of kindling gone missing or game being startled, I shall know who to blame.'

Captain Derringer had been about to turn. Now he halted, deep green eyes sharply interested. 'When he is in residence? Mr Kydd does not live here always?'

Nell was unreasonably piqued at his ignoring her sally. 'I should be even more cross-grained, were he to do so.' But why did he always come when he could meddle to the greatest effect? Harvest time, for instance.

Captain Derringer held out his hand with a smile. 'Until later then.' He paused. Nell saw a gleam in his eyes. 'If I knew you better I would beg you not to return by the dairy; I feel sure you would sour the milk.'

'If you knew me better, you would not dare do any such thing,' she retorted. She hesitated before putting her gloved hand in his. What she was about to ask was embarrassing in the utmost. 'My uncle does not approve of my riding out this early. When you meet him next, I would appreciate your not mentioning our encounter.'

His eyebrows arched. 'And lay myself open to a charge of trespass? From my observations of Mr Kydd last evening, I cannot imagine he would take my transgression near so understandingly as you.' He let go her hand, wheeled away and cantered towards the spinney.

Nell watched him, conscious of an aroused interest in her breast. Was it just because he was unfamiliar, someone she had not grown up with since the cradle? He was the oddest mixture of infuriating and kind, and they had certainly fallen into rapport with indecent speed. She had said things to him that she had previously only raged about in private to Annie.

She frowned as she ran over their conversation. For a stranger he had been asking curious questions. Then she cursed as she realized how far she was from the house. She needed to make haste to get to the breakfast table before her uncle graced it with his presence. She touched her heels to the mare's flanks. 'You're going to hate this, Snowflake,' she said insincerely. 'I'm afraid we're going to have to gallop again.'

2

Nell changed rapidly into a dove-grey round dress and soft slippers before hurrying to the breakfast parlour and slipping into the place set for her next to her mother. With the ease of frequent practice, Olivant the butler provided coffee in less time than it takes to tell and Tom the footman, working equally fast, supplied her plate with buttered toast. A moment later the door opened and her uncle walked in.

'Good morning,' she said brightly. 'A fine day, is it not? Mama and I were considering a walk in the gardens.'

'It would be better to hold yourself indoors in readiness to receive Mr Belmont.'

'I should like to go outside, Nell,' said her mother, placidly emerging from wherever she was wandering to enter the conversation. 'The roses in the bowls are becoming sadly overblown.'

Nell smiled at her with great affection. 'Then you shall, Mama. We will gather our shears and defy Brimston together.'

Her uncle snorted contemptuously. 'It will be interesting to see how tyrannical your gardener is when he has to do some work himself for a change.'

There was a small, charged silence. 'What can you mean?' said Nell.

Jasper Kydd speared a piece of ham. 'I have been reviewing the household accounts. Fully a third of the Court staff are an unnecessary drain on Kydd's already extended purse. Fortunately, quarter-day approaches.'

Nell cast a horrified glance at Olivant and Tom, standing correctly by the sideboard. 'I am sure Kit would view any changes with disapprobation.'

Her uncle's smile did not reach his eyes. 'Christopher is missing. Should he return and prove as sentimental as you, he may re-hire at his leisure.'

Cook's excellent coffee turned to pond water in Nell's mouth. The havoc on the estate and in the Home Farm was already bad. If Jasper was now talking of turning away more Kydd people who depended on the Court for their livelihood, she would have to find a way of contacting Mr Tweedie well before the spring.

★　★　★

'The fox is in the poultry run now, miss, and no mistake!'

28

Nell took a hasty turn about her room, running her hands through her hair to the detriment of the confining riband. 'Annie, I could not speak I was so furious! What do they say in the Hall?'

'What don't they! All looking sideways at each other and counting in threes.'

'Truly I think Uncle Jasper must be addled. What sort of saving will one less garden boy or one fewer housemaid make? All it will do is to throw more work on the others. Oh, if only I was of age!'

'You're mussing your hair, miss. Sit still and I'll do it afresh.' Annie pressed her mistress firmly down before the glass and teased out the grey satin riband.

Nell glowered at her reflection. 'My uncle may hold the purse strings, but he is not master of Kydd. Kit is on his way home, I know he is!'

Annie briskly re-threaded the ribbon. 'Well enough if he arrives before Michaelmas. If he doesn't . . . '

Nell's hands went to her hair again, but at Annie's look she clasped them under her chin instead and tried to set her thoughts in order. 'I cannot write to Mr Tweedie about all that is amiss,' she said slowly, 'because last time all he did was to send back that, as my uncle stands next in the entail after Kit, the board

Papa appointed for just this eventuality have every faith in him.' She stood in order to let Annie slide her arms into a slate-grey velveteen spencer which they had rendered marginally less hideous by the removal of an upstanding neck ruff and quantities of purple braid. 'There must be *something* I can do!'

Annie gave a disparaging tweak to the folds of Nell's grey muslin. 'You can take the mistress outside and enjoy an hour of each other's company. Never fret about us.'

Nell smiled wanly. 'What nonsense. Who else is to fret if I do not? But it is good that Mama wishes to gather flowers. It brings her closer to the world when she focuses on domestic matters.' She sighed as she tied the ribbons of her straw chip. 'I never thought to be glad of the way she retreats into her mind, but at least it spares her the discomfort of knowing my uncle's maladministration.'

'I'm sure the whole household would wish to spare the mistress pain.'

Nell grinned suddenly. 'Not Mr Brimston. And if he has heard of my uncle's schemes, he will be surlier than ever.'

But Mrs Kydd, when Nell ran her and the despotic head gardener to earth in the rose walk, seemed to be holding her own quite satisfactorily. To be sure, Mr Brimston was keeping up a continuous grumble about lazy boys, mildew in the glasshouse and the deplorable habit that people had of choosing blooms just when they would be displayed to best advantage in the beds, but Mama was answering him back in quite her old way. Even the circumstance of her simultaneously discussing a wholly imaginary morning call couldn't mar Nell's delight.

'I didn't think Lady Norland in good looks this morning, did you, Nell?' Snip.

'Perhaps she finds the weather oppressive. It is often so before a storm.'

'You didn't want to pick that'n, ma'am. That'n'll die soon as ever it's indoors.'

'Nonsense, Brimston, it's a perfectly sound bud.' Snip.

'And if you was thinking of the *Nymph* for that bowl of yourn, they'm looking real ragged so they are.'

'Nothing a dressing of potash won't cure. I'm sure you've told me as much yourself.' Snip. Snip. 'And what did you think of Miss Sophia's extraordinary gown, Nell? Cherry-red flounces with her complexion!'

'Very few people can carry off cherry-red, Mama.'

'Them yaller'ns is covered with the blackfly. Can't have none of them today!'

'White, then. The scented white that Master Kit likes so much. By the by, Nell, I do wish Sophia wouldn't make such sheep's eyes at Kit. I quite felt for him. Do you think I should have dropped a word in Lady Norland's ear?'

'It would be one way to prevent them calling again.'

'The *Albas* is all gone over, ma'am. Now if you'd only a-gathered of 'em last week . . . '

'How provoking. We shall have to send to my old home at Hadleigh for a few sprays. They are always quite splendid there. Webb has such a way with roses.'

'As to that, I've always understood the Hadleigh gardens to be wunnerful sheltered which I've asked for time and again here, it being more northerly in these parts, not that anyone listens. Howsumever, if you'm set on 'em I daresay I could find one or two blooms still right-side up . . . '

Nell chuckled and sauntered behind, parrying Mama's observations on Lady Norland (whom in reality they had last seen in London some two and a half years previous) and allowing one or two thoughts about newly-arrived Dragoon officers to stray agreeably across her consciousness.

'And bronze chrysanthemums for the stairs. What do you think, Nell?'

'Very elegant,' said Nell promptly. Then, as the gardener looked daggers at her, 'Unless

Mr Brimston has something else to suggest?'

'Michaelmas daisies. We'm plenty of they, and they're a good *respectful* colour.' He eyed Mrs Kydd's black dress meaningfully.

'Against the oak panelling?' Mama's peal of laughter was as joyous as it was unexpected. Brimston looked quite as taken aback as Nell. He led the way to his precious chrysanthemum bed without further demur.

Perhaps Mama was getting over Papa, thought Nell. The year was up in October. Would her mother come out of mourning? Black might not be such a trial with her flaxen hair and blue eyes as it had been to Nell, but it was still a dreadfully sobering colour.

They were returning to the house when the sound of hoofbeats was heard from the sweep. Mrs Kydd tutted. 'Visitors. How provoking. Go and meet them, my love, and bring them *slowly* up from the stables that I might have time to arrange these. Brimston will never forgive me if, after persuading him to let me cut them, I do not get the blooms immediately into water.'

Nell laughed and turned back to the autumn sunshine. She distinguished Philip Belmont's sturdy roan horse easily and when, on her approach, both riders dismounted, she saw with a pleasurable flutter of confirmation that the rangy brown gelding with him bore Captain Derringer. 'How is this?' she said. 'I made sure you would be decimating the population of the East Wood today.'

Philip saluted her cheerfully. 'Hugo took a fancy to see some of the country hereabouts first.'

The captain was dressed in the brown riding coat he had worn earlier. Its plain lines fitted his form admirably. 'So as not to be confounded by further questions on Northamptonshire, perhaps?' teased Nell. 'Or merely to establish your bearings?'

Hugo Derringer raised her gloved hand in his and levelled a deep green glance along the length of it as he touched it to his lips. 'Both. I dislike being at a disadvantage.'

Nell withdrew her fingers, feeling a quite ridiculous tingle where he had kissed them. 'I have often observed military gentlemen to be uneasy when they find themselves at a standstill,' she said. 'It is the habit of command in you, I suppose.'

Philip's roan picked up his pace towards the stables, anticipating Seth and the apples that were invariably stowed about his person. Hugo looped Conqueror's reins over his hand and strolled alongside Nell. 'You have a wide experience of my profession?' he said with a lift of his eyebrow.

A bubble of laughter built up in Nell's throat. 'Kit has several friends in the Dragoons and the Light Bobs. And the Duke of Wellington always says — '

Her companion stopped dead, causing Conqueror to snort in mild surprise. 'The Duke of Wellington?' repeated Hugo.

Nell peeped up at him demurely. 'He was most put out when I captured his Queen. Positively *threw* his knights into the attack.'

'Miss Kydd, are you telling me you are on chess-playing terms with the Duke of Wellington?'

'No,' sighed Nell regretfully. 'But I should dearly like to be.'

'She beats me every time,' called Philip over his shoulder.

Captain Derringer's mouth worked. 'You hoyden!' he said at last. 'I was near believing you!'

'Plausible, ain't she? Always has been. Ho, Seth! Where are you, rogue?'

'He's not the only rogue hereabouts,' said Hugo with feeling. 'I should have remembered.'

Nell frowned. 'Remembered?'

He scrubbed at a spot of dried mud on his coat. 'Your brother used to say you were the most complete hand at telling bouncers.'

'And he was not, I suppose? And I did

meet Sir Arthur Wellesley once, in Hyde Park the season before Kit went to India. A friend of Papa's introduced us. Are you acquainted with his Grace?'

'Junior officers unhandy enough to catch sabre cuts in their upper arms do not tend to move in the same circle as commanders of armies.'

Nell chuckled. 'I suppose not. Was it very dreadful, the Peninsula?'

'Very.' His mouth closed in a grim line. Then, as they entered the stable yard and a beaming Seth came forward, 'Did I mention the Peninsula?'

Nell ticked the points off on her fingers. 'Tanned complexion, sabres, your reaction to the Duke's name . . . '

'Told you she was up to snuff,' said Philip, rejoining them. 'Which reminds me, Nell, m'mother says I must offer for you properly. Says I must have muffed it.'

'If you wish to,' said Nell obligingly. 'I am under instructions from *my* mama to take you both up to the house by the longest route possible so as to give her time to arrange some flowers. She has had such an invigorating passage of arms this morning with Brimston that she seems almost her old self which is why you find me in unprecedented spirits. So we will stroll around the shrubbery and the lawn and you may seize the day, Philip.'

'I will!' He frowned in concentration for a moment. 'Miss Kydd, I — '

Amusement danced in Captain Derringer's eyes. 'Am I not in the way? An offer of marriage is generally held to be a matter of some delicacy.'

'Lord, no. Where was I? Burn it, Hugo, you've made me forget m'speech now. No, wait, I have it.' Philip cleared his throat. 'Miss Kydd, I have long admired your beauty and vivacity and think that we should deal very fairly together. I am aware of your lack of dowry — just a couple of thousand from your father and that manor in Hertfordshire from your mother when she's gone — but Belmont's as snug a place as you'll get anywhere and you won't find me ungenerous. Will you grant me the honour of your hand in marriage?'

'Philip,' said Nell, awed. 'Did you learn all that just for me?'

'Pretty good, ain't it?'

'*Extremely* good. But my answer is still the same. You are a good friend and I like you very well but I am not in love with you. You deserve someone far more restful. I am not going to wed anyone until Kit returns.'

'M'mother says your uncle told her that's

looking more doubtful every day. That's why she had me offer for you. Said it was my best chance. Said it would be more comfortable for you than stopping here with Jasper Kydd in charge.'

'My uncle said that!' Nell's bosom swelled indignantly. 'You don't believe it?'

'What, Kit stick his spoon in the wall before his time? Never!'

Nell looked sideways at Captain Derringer. 'And you?'

'I confess I find it unlikely.'

'Good.' But all the same, the day had lost its light-heartedness. And Nell had remembered something. 'I have not thanked you, Captain Derringer, for your kindness to Mama last night. I think you realize by now that she does not always . . . that is, sometimes she thinks — '

A touch of colour under his tan belied Hugo's stilted words. 'I spoke no less than the truth. I should be very glad to render either of you any service necessary. I trust your absence this morning went unremarked?'

'Thank you, yes. My uncle abandoned his early walks towards the stables some time ago. I believe he only used to go there in order to complain of my lack of femininity to Papa over the breakfast table.'

'Foolish thing for him to get in such a

pother about,' said Philip. 'Thought so at the time. What's it to him when you ride? Anyone would think you hadn't been on horseback since before you could walk. Bruising rider to hounds, Hugo.'

Captain Derringer's voice shook. 'And you wonder why she didn't accept you? Good God! The tree house!'

The change in his tone was startling. He was staring at a venerable oak, into whose spreading boughs a rough platform had been irreligiously wedged and crazy walls nailed up to give a semblance of privacy.

'My brother and his friends built it some ten or a dozen summers ago,' said Nell, chuckling at his thunderstruck air. 'He was forever bringing boys from school to stay. Were you never of their number?'

'My guardian lived abroad. I used to go to him for the holidays.'

'The tree house was not their only project,' said Nell. 'One year they dammed the stream for a bathing pool, another time they created a camp in the woods. Those were the only occasions on which I found Kit at all tiresome — when his friends insisted little girls had no place in their grown-up schemes.'

'Never stopped you as I remember,' said Philip. He wrinkled his brow at the tree house. 'That was the year I had measles. Got sent home with them and then m'mother wouldn't let me out of the house all summer. Missed all the fun.'

Captain Derringer had started moving again. Nell glanced at him. 'Are you quite well? You look pale.'

He smiled. 'It is of no moment. It was a strange thing to find in a tree is all. Twelve years, you say? I should not have thought it would survive so long.'

Nell laughed. 'I see we will have to divert towards the woods to show you the bathing pool. Whole schools of trout live there now as well as perch and roach and I know not what. When Kit sets his mind to building something, it lasts!'

Mrs Kydd was just finishing the last container when Nell brought their guests into the hall. The scent filled the elegant oak-panelled space. 'Lovely, Mama,' she said approvingly, 'and here are — ' There was a disturbance behind her. Looking around she saw Tom, very red in the face, picking up Captain Derringer's hat and gloves from the floor.

'I beg your pardon, sir,' said Tom. 'I don't know how I came to — '

'My fault. I handed them to you clumsily. Think nothing of it.'

'Here,' said Nell firmly, 'are Philip and his

friend Captain Derringer to sit with us a while.'

'Oh yes,' said Mrs Kydd at once, holding out her hand to Captain Derringer. 'I remember you very well. You *have* grown up smart. I declare it only seems like yesterday, does it not?'

A look of alarm crossed Hugo's face, but he answered civilly, 'As to that, ma'am, I can safely say you look only a day older than when I saw you first.'

Nell choked on a laugh. Hugo looked at her sidelong with a reproving quirk of his lips and she felt the delicious soft tug of an insensible bond between them. 'Philip is showing his guest the countryside, Mama,' she said, leading the way into the saloon. 'Where have you been so far? Which picturesque ruins? Or have you, as I suspect, confined yourselves to the hunt?' She smiled her thanks to Olivant, arranging a decanter and glasses on a side table. 'Would you care for refreshment?'

'I should say,' said Philip. 'Thirsty work, sightseeing.'

'By which he means the Cross Keys and the smithy in the village, the road to town and another to some tumble-down castle, distance unspecified,' said Hugo, crossing to the tray. 'You have the right of it entirely, Miss Kydd.'

He paused, his heavy brows drawn together at its lack of non-alcoholic contents.

'Mama and I will both take a small glass of Madeira, thank you,' Nell said demurely.

A glimmer of amusement showed in Hugo's eyes. 'You add an educated palate to your other attractions?'

Other attractions? Nell felt her face heat. 'Oh, nobody taught me,' she said airily. 'I tried some one day and liked it.'

'But you did not like cider,' said her mother in a thoughtful voice.

'Cider?' said Philip. 'You don't want to drink that rotgut, Nell. Fanshawe brought a gallon to Eton once. Lord, were we ever sick as cats! Remember, Hugo?'

'I endeavour *not* to!'

'And what must Kit do but tell the story at home,' said his fond mama. 'And what must Nell do the very next time we were visiting in the West Country but — '

'Mama!' Nell's shriek caused Philip to go into whoops and brought Captain Derringer's transforming smile to his face.

'Margaret, Helena, you should have sent Olivant to apprise me of visitors.'

The gaiety in the saloon was extinguished as abruptly as a snuffer puts out a candle. Jasper Kydd's gaze rested briefly on Philip before flicking to Nell. She felt besmirched by the cold assessment. 'Do you stay to luncheon, gentlemen?'

Philip shifted uneasily. 'No — er — that is — '

His friend cut in. 'Most kind of you, but I fancy Mrs Belmont is expecting us back.'

Nell's intellect received a sharp prod. Captain Derringer was taking her uncle on as smoothly and naturally as if there was no other course to follow. Why?

'Yes, that's it. M'mother don't like her arrangements upset.' Philip drank down the rest of his Madeira. 'Best hurry, Hugo, if we're to get any sport in later.'

'So soon?' But Jasper made no effort to detain them. 'Helena, you may escort our guests to the stables.'

'No, no,' said Philip. 'Talk to Nell any time. No need to trouble her.'

'Then you must bear us company at dinner. Tomorrow, perhaps?'

Philip's easy-going countenance began to look harried. ' 'Fraid I can't say what m'mother has planned. I know I'm to drive her some-where or other in the morning.'

Hugo spoke, his voice indifferent. 'I don't believe we are engaged, Philip. Mrs Belmont was saying only at breakfast how vexed she was that she had not arranged more amusements for us.'

He *wanted* to put himself through an uncomfortable evening? How very intriguing. The least Nell could do was facilitate it. 'Then you can all three come,' she said. 'That will be delightful. Mama was wishful of repaying your mother's hospitality, Philip.' She was aware of her uncle seething. He hadn't at all intended including Captain Derringer in the invitation. There would be little chance of a tête-à-tête between her and Philip with an unattached friend in attendance.

'Such a nice boy,' said Mama placidly after the visitors had gone.

'Very suitable indeed,' agreed Jasper Kydd, pouring himself out another glass of Madeira.

Nell said nothing. The firm pressure of Hugo Derringer's parting handshake remained on her fingers. She wondered just which 'boy' Mama had meant.

★ ★ ★

Hugo had to endure much blunt astonishment on Philip's part that his aim was so unsuccessful that day. He pleaded the same lack of concentration that had led to them now having to put up with an evening at Kydd Court. Philip was justifiably aggrieved on that subject, so Hugo offered himself as a

44

conversational sacrifice for the duration of the dinner. They finished the shoot in a more amicable accord.

Remembering that he was a guest, Hugo pushed aside any further abstraction, encouraging Philip and Mrs Belmont to talk of the area so that he would follow what the neighbours he might meet would be discussing. As soon as he retired for the night, however, Nell Kydd's lively face and occasionally pensive looks filled his mind.

'Enough,' he said to himself, and with immense determination, fetched out pen and ink from his pack and began to catch up with his correspondence.

3

Sadly, Mrs Kydd had withdrawn into her own world again by the next day. A quarter of an hour into breakfast, she jumped up with a muttered, 'Goodness, I'll see to it at once,' and hurried from the room. Nell sighed. It had been too much to hope that one morning with her gardener followed by a lively visit from two personable young men would effect a cure. *Personable?* Nell caught herself. Philip was comely enough, but Hugo Derringer's heavy black brows and foreign tan would not win him many admirers amongst the ladies of the district. Until he smiled.

'Something is amusing you, Helena?' said her uncle.

Nell set her teeth. 'Nothing of any import.'

'What do you do this morning?'

Always the same ritual. She would tell him, and then he would criticize. 'The marketing, naturally. Have you any commissions?'

'You are taking the barouche, of course. Does Gray drive you?'

She gripped her butter knife rather tighter. 'I am *not* taking the barouche. I am driving

46

my curricle. Seth will accompany me as he always does.'

'I wonder that no one has ever told you what a singular appearance you present jaunting about in this fashion. A young lady sitting beside a male relative and occasionally handling the ribbons is acceptable, but a sporting curricle is a most unfeminine vehicle for everyday use.'

'Papa disagreed. He encouraged me to learn and said it was quite the done thing for ladies to tool about the London parks. He *approved* of Kit making the curricle and bays over to me before he set sail.'

Her uncle snorted. 'You had best hope that if Christopher returns, he does so plump in the pocket, or you are likely to lose your toys. He will want them back.'

Nell's voice pulsated with anger. 'Kit *never* breaks his word!'

'A paragon of virtue. Strange that he should have vanished so comprehensively without a single reassuring line to his nearest and dearest.'

It was fortunate that Olivant chose that moment to refill the cups, or Nell might have let fly. She took a deep breath and said in a tolerably steady voice, 'As we have mentioned before, I daresay Kit was forced at the last moment to take a different ship. Likely he is travelling as fast as his letter.'

She caught a glimmer of approval on Olivant's face and felt heartened. Every time she did not rise to her uncle's bait it was a victory won. She finished her roll, drained her coffee and crumpled her napkin. 'I had best make a prompt start. With company tonight, I should not be surprised if Cook has a long list.'

As she left the room, Tom's eyelid flickered in a surreptitious wink. He was the Olivants' son and had been very thick with Kit when they were both madcap boys who cared little for difference in class. He would have been burning just as hot as she at Jasper Kydd's disparaging comments.

In the kitchen, Nell found her mother seated at the long scrubbed table whilst Cook kneaded bread and the work of the establishment went on around them. 'So this is where you got to, Mama. I wish I had followed you, it would have been by far more comfortable. Good morning, Mrs Olivant. What needs to be fetched from town today?'

Cook was a substantial woman, wife to their butler and as warm hearted as she was ample. She nodded to a scrap of well-worn paper on the dresser. 'List's there, Miss Nell. I was just discussing dinner with the mistress.'

Nell surveyed her mother, who was sipping her tea and wearing the earnest look of one who was certainly discussing something with somebody, but whether it was tonight's menu was another matter entirely. 'Will you come with me, Mama? I promise not to overturn you.'

She got a look of vague surprise. 'But I do not believe Mr Kean is playing tonight, my love,' said Mrs Kydd.

Cook shook her head. 'Leave her be, Miss Nell. She'll come to no harm here and the bustle will do her good.' She eyed her subordinates. 'Leastwise, it would if there *was* any!'

In her room Nell sighed as she donned a grey, pleated-silk bonnet and a drab pelisse, over-embellished with black frogging. She sometimes wondered if twelve months was fixed on as the limit for mourning because folk would themselves expire if they had to wear such atrocious colours any longer.

There was a heaviness in the air suggesting autumn storms on the way. Seth beguiled the journey with observations on when they might expect rain, how well the bays were pulling and the nonsense Gray had spouted yesterday about Captain Derringer's horse never having seen war work. On their way past the top field they waved to the harvesters. Over the ridge, the bull glowered in his solitary kingdom.

Nell swung the curricle wide to avoid a gaggle of urchins stravaging along the lane. Up to mischief, she deduced, and smiled to see a dusty figure toiling in their wake. Like Nell in her younger days, little Jenny Copping wasn't about to let her brother find amusement without her.

* * *

They had done the marketing and left town when they were overtaken by a rangy brown gelding.

'I trust I find you well, Miss Kydd. May I ride with you?'

Nell's heart betrayed a pleasurable agitation. 'There is but one road, Captain Derringer. It would be difficult indeed for you if I refused.'

'What for you want to do that, Miss Nell? Captain's primer, he is. Didn't see Conqueror at the Lion, Captain. You didn't oughter leave him at the Three Tuns. Ostlers there don't know one end of an animal from t'other.'

'I was dispatching a letter, so had no need for livery.' Hugo Derringer's dark green eyes rested thoughtfully on the groom. 'I wonder,

Seth. Might you like to try Conqueror's paces if I were to take your place beside your mistress?'

Seth's round face shone. 'I'd like that fine,' he said, never doubting that he was being offered a treat.

'Are you so light in hand with everyone you meet?' murmured Nell, her pulse beating faster once the exchange had been effected.

Hugo was justifiably smug. 'My guardian is a diplomat. Some of his ways couldn't help but rub off on me.'

That accounted for his self-possessed air. Nell glanced sideways at him. He was wearing his brown riding coat again with buckskin breeches and very muddied top boots. Ahead of them, Conqueror's legs were likewise splattered. 'Do you generally ride cross-country when there is a perfectly sound road to town?'

He shot her an amused look. 'By no means, but my horse feels himself ill-used if he has not at least one gallop a day.'

'Well for him that you did not accompany Philip and his mother. Mrs Belmont believes that an escort should conduct himself with dignity and propriety.'

'I offered to do so, but was excused. Two maiden aunts, I was told, whom the sight of an unknown gentleman would send all of a-twitter.'

'Ah, that would be the Misses Standish.' Nell chuckled as she visualized the local geography. 'And afterwards it would be natural to call at the Graingers on their way home. I understand Mrs Belmont letting you off.'

'As I do not. Who are the Graingers?'

'Charlotte Grainger is the young lady with golden ringlets who was failing to engage your attention over the teacups at Belmont House the other night. Philip must have informed his mother that I declined his hand. Miss Grainger has seven thousand pounds which, in default of sensible conversation, I imagine Mrs Belmont would rather see attached to her son than to his friend.'

Captain Derringer stared at her, shaken out of his calm. 'What? Does Mrs Belmont think I am hanging out for a bride?'

'Philip's mama has had but a single thought in her head since Philip came of age. It is difficult for her to see another motive in anyone.'

'She may acquit me at least! I have no wish to become leg-shackled!'

Nell was slightly disconcerted by the energy in this statement. His attentions to *her* on so short an acquaintance had not led her to suspect him of misogyny. And yet he did not seem the sort to trifle. 'There is an easy solution,' she said, rallying. 'Let it be known you have no prospects. I promise you will be properly shunned by match-making mamas. It should not take much effort, my uncle already has you tagged as a half-pay officer with time on your hands.'

She had certainly given him to think, judging by his knotted brow. They travelled perhaps half a mile in silence before he threw off his abstraction and said, 'Belmont is a tidy manor. It will be a sad blow to your uncle if my friend succeeds in attaching Miss Grainger.'

Nell snorted. 'Uncle Jasper is less concerned with my well-being and more with saving the estate the expense of a season. He thinks I should be content to remain in society I have known all my life without hankering for aught else.'

'Do you dislike it here, then?'

'I love Kydd dearly, but there is more to the world than this corner of Northampton-shire. We used to always go to London in the spring which was exciting even for a child, and Kit has written to me of such wonders that it makes me long to travel.' Nell smiled ruefully at her companion. 'I daresay with living abroad and having been in the army, you are blasé about new places and different ways of going on but *I* should think it splendid. Where is your guardian based?'

'Vienna.'

'How marvellous.'

'You are not worried at the thought of sea crossings?'

'According to Kit, the discomfort is over in a couple or three days.'

'You have a sanguine nature, Miss Kydd. I cannot help but think, however, that you would do better to bide in Northamptonshire for the nonce.'

'That, sir, is a craven answer because you do not wish me to recruit you into pleading my case with my uncle for a London season.'

Captain Derringer's smile made her doubt his misogyny even more. 'Tell me about him so I do not founder tonight,' he said. 'Does he stay with you long?'

'Longer than I would like. I cannot think why. He has no feeling for Kydd, for all he grew up here. He and my father held each other in great dislike, and until Kit went abroad we were not wont to see him or his family above once a year for which we were all very grateful. He disapproved of the freedom in which Kit and I were raised and never scrupled to tell us so. *His* children were confined strictly to the nursery and school-room and never even saw visitors, let alone entered into serious discussions with them as

Kit and I were encouraged to do. I am a sad trial to him.'

Hugo's brow wrinkled. 'I do not perfectly understand his hold over you.'

Nell chose her words carefully. 'Mama and Kit are my legal guardians, but when the report came that Kit had not joined his ship home, the interim board appointed by Papa decided Mama was not — that is, they acceded to Uncle Jasper's proposal that he continue to manage both Kydd and me.'

There was now a heavy frown on Hugo's face. 'By my reckoning, you must have been some eight months into your uncle's misrule by then. Why did you not make representations to this board?'

'I did! I sent letters! Would you like to hazard a guess how much notice men of business take of young unmarried ladies?' It hadn't stopped her trying though. Not until one bitter argument when her uncle's eyes had slid to where Mama was having a murmuring conversation with herself. Jasper's expression had made Nell's blood run cold. She had known at that moment that her mother's precarious sanity, possibly even her freedom, was a hostage to Nell's own obedience.

As they approached the road to Kydd, Captain Derringer cleared his throat. 'You handle the ribbons very well. I wonder if — '

But Nell was distracted by a tangle of scrawny arms and legs pumping down the hill. 'What is it?' she called.

The cluster of lads looked terrified and defiant all at the same time. 'The bull, Miss Nell,' panted William Copping. 'We was only looking at him from the next field and him broke out and come for us.'

One of the other boys snivelled. 'Didn't mean no harm, we didn't.'

Nell turned the curricle without thinking twice. Only looking indeed! When did boys ever just *look?* She'd have to fetch the men, persuade the bull back into — Wait! She half-stood, scanning the lane, concern hammering at her chest. 'Where is Jenny?'

William Copping's mouth opened and closed. 'Up-up the road a-ways.'

'Are you telling me you maddened the bull to such an extent that he broke through the hedgerow and then you ran to save your own miserable hide without even checking on your sister? Seth, get the men! You boys, I want you back up that hill now!' Nell whipped up the horses and as soon as the stile was reached, she thrust the reins at Hugo and scrambled over.

'Come back! What are you about? *Nell!*'

Nell ignored him. Looping up her skirts,

she pelted through the long grass towards the crouching dot that was Jenny Copping. Thank God she was safe. She forced herself to speak calmly. 'Don't be scared, Jenny. I'm here.'

'I ain't afeared, Miss Nell,' said the white-faced girl. 'Only my ankle won't work proper an' it's all swole up.'

'Then it needs a cold compress and a bandage as soon as we have got Mister Bull back in his proper place.'

'Yes, Miss Nell. Only him gets main angry whenever I tries to move.'

The bull was indeed swinging his head and pawing the ground, as if waiting for an excuse to let off more of his temper.

Nell lifted her chin, her mind already three steps ahead. 'Well now, see how things turn out. Only this morning I was bewailing the dreadful colour of this pelisse, but now I perceive it is the very thing. If I were to have been wearing my red coat, I should have had to take it off and leave it lying in all this dirt.'

She walked steadily across the field as she spoke, keeping her voice low and pleasant. The baleful eyes of the bull followed her, but either because the grey of her attire was indeed sufficient to calm him, or because he recognized her authority over all things Kydd or, as Hugo afterwards maintained, he was too stunned at her abysmal stupidity in approaching him to take advantage, he allowed her close enough to grasp the ring through his nose.

Relief pumped through her. 'Now, sir,' she continued, 'is this your pasture? Is there a trough here? Water? Shelter?' She led him to the gap in the hedgerow and his own domain. On the ground she noticed, with a compression of the lips which bode extremely ill for the boys, a stick with a grubby red rag attached to its end.

'My gawd, Miss Nell. Whatever's 'appened?' Into the field had run some four or five panting and blowing estate workers.

Nell pushed back through the gap and stood with her fists planted firmly at her waist. 'Your son happened, Bill Copping. Your son and his cowardly cronies.' She snatched up the rag-bedecked withy and brandished it. 'I doubt they'll think it such good sport to taunt a dumb animal again however.'

One of the men guffawed. Nell looked at him icily. 'Furthermore, every last one of them turned tail to save his own skin and left Jenny alone up here!'

'My Jenny? Where is she? So 'elp me, I'll kill 'em!'

A grim voice answered. Hugo Derringer had hitched the bays to the stile and was striding across the field. 'Your daughter has sprained her ankle but is otherwise unharmed. I have carried her to the curricle.'

Nell got the feeling not all of Hugo's anger was directed at the men. 'What manner of sons are you raising?' she said, grappling for the initiative. 'Never once would my brother or his friends have run off and left me in mortal danger like that.'

'None of 'em will again,' said Bill Copping, his broad hand fingering his belt.

'I am glad to hear it,' said Nell. 'But before you render them unable to walk, I want them in here mending the hedgerow under your eye. Indeed I cannot imagine why they were not at work in the fields already. Lest it occur to them to vent any lingering aggression on the bull, you will transfer both their energies and your own to the crops by the Six-Mile Acre. *That* will keep them busy!'

'Master won't like it,' drawled the man who had guffawed earlier. 'Told us to do up here, he did.'

Master? Never! Never as long as she had breath in her body! Nell turned a look of blazing fury on the speaker. 'I don't believe I heard you aright, Walter Harvey. Would you care to repeat that?'

'Nay, Miss Nell, we'll shift all right,' said Bill Copping hurriedly.

Herded by Conqueror, the youths sidled

into the field, casting looks of acute dislike at Jenny Copping, perched in state on the curricle. 'I could 'elp an' all with harvest,' she said to Nell. 'I'm as good as them.'

Nell unhitched the bays and settled herself, breathing hard, on the seat. She viewed with a kindling eye Hugo's waving on of Seth and the hard set to his mouth as he swung up beside her. 'Naturally you are, but not with a sprained ankle. And this way you get to ride in the curricle and I am the one who tells your mama so you will not be accused of tattling.'

It took less than two seconds for Jenny to assimilate the wisdom of this. 'So when they all gets walloped, it won't be my fault!'

'Just so.' Nell could wish the curricle was wider. A male thigh pressed against hers, even rigid with disapproval, was not what she had been used to.

'But I won't get no half-borde for helping.'

'Nor will they, today. They should have thought of that before playing truant.'

'They didn't play truant. Mr Jasper said he didn't hold with letting lazy, good-for-nought urchins go messing up his harvest.'

Nell stiffened. 'Did he now?' Beside her she felt Hugo's jolt of interest.

'An' he told them not to go bothering the bull an' all.'

Which had no doubt put the idea in their heads! What a nodcock!

Hugo Derringer's thoughts evidently matched hers. Nell felt his muscles ease as he mulled over this nugget of information. 'Did he tell them not to do anything else?' he enquired.

'Dunno. There's Ma! And Granfer sitting outside! Ma, look at me! Look at me, Granfer! Ain't I smart?'

Betsy Copping took one look at the grandeur in which her youngest daughter was being conveyed home and let out a shriek that set the hens scuttling to the furthest corner of the yard.

Nell relinquished the reins to 'Granfer', otherwise known as Old John Farley, who had been foreman at Kydd before he was forcibly retired. She explained the sorry tale as Captain Derringer carried Jenny into the cottage.

'Oh, Miss Nell, what am I to do? William's not a bad boy, but he's easy led, and ever since Jack was turned off with the horses and his Johnny went to be a soldier our Will's got no one but his pa to tell him how to go on, and you know what boys and their pas are like!'

Nell turned to Hugo. 'Jack Farley is Betsy's older brother. Mr Belmont was very glad to take him.'

'And who wouldn't be, as fine a worker as he is? Oh, but when I think of how Mr Jasper let him go and kept on that nasty bit of work Walter Harvey, my blood boils so it does.'

Captain Derringer interrupted. 'Farley, you say? Your nephew is a soldier? What company?'

'The 28th Foot, sir, the North Gloucesters.'

'You should be proud. Wellington commended the 28th at Waterloo.'

Betsy sniffed. 'That's as may be, but Johnny didn't oughter be in the middle of a war. And it's a line regiment which cuts us clear to the heart, him having been with horses all his life.'

'I have a friend in the 5th Division. I could write requesting a transfer to groom work.'

Betsy was voluble in her thanks. She pressed refreshment on them, but Nell said they must be going.

'I am minded to accompany you all the way to Kydd Court,' said Hugo as they left. 'You are not safe to be abroad. Running into that field was the most imbecilic thing it has ever been my misfortune to witness!'

'Fustian,' said Nell. 'You are cross because I got there before you did. Would you have done aught else?'

She got a speaking look from beneath his

heavy brows. 'I am something over six foot tall, twice as heavy as you and unencumbered by skirts! Furthermore, I am a trained soldier.'

'I do not see how that would have helped unless you planned to put a bullet through the poor creature? Do go on your way. How many enraged bulls does one meet in a day? Anyway, Seth will be with me. Here he is now.'

Hugo helped her up to the curricle seat. 'That relieves my mind tremendously. Anyone less likely to keep you out of trouble I have yet to meet!' As he twitched the folds of his riding coat straight, some papers fluttered to the ground. 'I beg your pardon, I appear to be carrying off your secrets.'

Nell took them, smiling. 'Oh, very secret! The accounts from the butcher and the fishmonger — 25/- and 18/6 respectively, expended on your dinner tonight.'

He raised an eyebrow. 'Your uncle thinks to flatter us with such largesse.'

'He treats all company so. His economy takes strange turns. He begrudges every groat spent on the estate, yet he refuses to give a dinner that is not as lavish as our neighbours.' Nell flicked a finger at her pelisse. 'It is the same with my mourning clothes. The material must be the very best, though from the design and cut the dressmaker is likely the cheapest in Wiltshire. Certainly my maid and I doubt her continued solvency.'

Hugo smiled at this sally and Nell experienced a flicker of triumph. 'I will see you later,' she said, holding out her hand. 'Thank you for your assistance.'

He shrugged ruefully. 'It was little enough. I daresay you could have managed the whole without me. I believe those boys would rather have met St Peter at the Gates of Heaven than you at that precise moment.'

She laughed. 'If they try any such mischief again they will wish they had!'

He lifted her fingers to his lips and held them a space longer. 'These kid gloves you wear are misleading. They are by far too soft. I am beginning to think nothing less than worked steel runs through your veins.'

She looked archly into his face. 'You have not given the matter sufficient consideration. They are *Kydd* gloves, Captain Derringer. There is a difference.'

* * *

Kydd gloves, indeed. But Hugo's smile faded as he watched her out of sight. She should not have to be this brave. She should be arranging flowers or sewing a more fetching gown or . . . Hugo gave up. He didn't know exactly what Nell should be doing, just not this.

He had always been aware that his friend Kit's upbringing had been rather less conventional than his own, but why had no one apparently even told his sister how to go on? He had never felt so much genuine fear in his life as that moment when — half a field away and out of his reach — she walked over to the deranged bull. He was furious that none of the menfolk in her life had stressed the necessity of never putting herself in danger. And to cap it all she had laughed when he attempted to remonstrate after the event.

And yet . . . and yet there was something beguiling about her unconcern. She was as quick and clever as a sackful of monkeys, that was for sure. Out of the whole tedious company at the Belmont party the other night, she was the one he had wanted to spend time with. Unfortunately he had an agenda which was tricky enough in the first place and which certainly didn't include half-hours wasted in intelligent banter.

Just as well, really. He came over sleet-cold again at the realization that the neighbour-hood matrons weighed up single men's prospects as a matter of course. It would be appalling conduct in him to give rise to expectations. Nor did he want anyone looking too far into his antecedents and affairs.

My uncle already has you tagged as a half-pay officer with time on your hands.

Nell's words floated through his head. Silently, he thanked her.

4

Nell finished her journey largely preoccupied with thoughts of Hugo Derringer, but as soon as Tom Olivant helped her down from the curricle, she snapped back to the real world.

'I'm to go at the end of the quarter,' he said.

For a moment, she was stupefied with shock. Tom? Tom to be turned off? 'Nonsense,' she said. 'It's unthinkable!'

'Lizzie as well, and Emma and Hannah. Beth, Mary, gardeners, gamekeepers, Hicks from the stables — and Seth, though he don't know it yet.'

There was a roaring in Nell's ears. 'God in Heaven, it cannot be possible!' She gripped the curricle body to steady herself, staring at him in horrified disbelief. Lizzie was his older sister, the senior housemaid. With Emma and Hannah gone too, all the work of the Court would fall on very junior maids indeed. And then there was the kitchen — Mary was Cook's chief assistant! The loss of Seth she refused even to contemplate. 'This is monstrous. I will speak to my uncle. There must be a way. However pinched we may be, Kit and I would rather dress in rags than see any of our people suffer.'

'It's about time he was home, so it is.'

'He will be,' said Nell. *Wouldn't he?*

For the next hour she did her best to comfort the staff, promising that if her intercession with her uncle failed, she would find them new positions just as she had with the farm workers.

'I'll write one more letter to Mr Tweedie and if that has no effect I shall take the stagecoach to London myself!' she vowed to Annie later. 'Oh, not that dreadful mulberry satin again. Have I nothing more passable?'

'The pale grey silk? If you wore it with your paisley shawl?'

The dress was hardly alluring, being high-necked and too fussy with frills for Nell's taste, but at least it didn't fight her complexion every inch of the way, and the paisley shawl was really quite pretty.

Annie helped her into it and began to dress her hair. 'Have you changed your mind about Mr Belmont, then?'

In the glass, Nell saw pink tinge her cheeks. 'I have not.'

Annie twisted Nell's hair into a half-knot and secured it with a pearl pin, letting the remaining curls fall to her shoulders. 'Some people would hold Captain Derringer to be a fine looking gentleman.'

Nell pretended not to hear. 'What is in the case, Annie?'

'Your mama's pearls,' said Annie, clasping the string round her mistress's throat. 'She said you were to have them, though they could really do with a good clean. There. You'll do. Keep Mr Jasper sweet and you'll likely have more fortune when you talk with him tomorrow.'

'Amen to that,' said Nell.

With such a small party assembled, the conversation was less formal than at Belmont House. Not, however, informal enough to include the episode with the bull, for which Nell was grateful. Either Philip was being uncharacteristically discreet or his friend had neglected to mention all his doings that morning.

Hmm. His friend. She admitted to a feeling of pique regarding Hugo Derringer. She hadn't expected him to address her with familiarity, but she had envisioned rather more conversation between them than a bare half-dozen sentences. He took no more notice of her restrained grey silk than he had the mulberry satin (though as he was wearing the same black coat and cream waistcoat as before, clothes may not have interested him). All his attention was directed towards her uncle and when he took her in to dinner his arm was as remote as if he had been that gentleman. His expression was very nearly as glacial. Strongly put out, Nell wondered why he had wangled the invitation to dine at all.

Fortunately for her sorely-tried sensibilities, the emotions below stairs had not affected the food. Nobody eating the boiled fillets of sole, the green goose, the haunch of venison, fricassee of sweetbreads or any of the other delicacies on the table could have guessed that Cook was currently bewailing the savage reduction of her empire and the imminent unemployment of her children. Tom handed round clear soup and whipped syllabubs with a steady hand. His father refilled glasses in his customary stately fashion. Nell was proud of them.

'I was wondering,' said Hugo Derringer, making considerable inroads on every dish in front of him, 'what you would recommend I see in Wiltshire? I have a friend near Salisbury who has been inviting me for a visit this age. Mrs Belmont tells me your estate is in that county.'

Jasper Kydd looked sharply at him, but evidently seeing nothing more in the question than a desire of not being bored whilst taking advantage of a friend's hospitality, answered with details of the cathedral at Salisbury, various castles and picturesque ruins, and the

70

hunting to be found thereabouts.

Next to Nell, Philip said in a low voice, 'I've told m'mother.'

'So I understand. And how did you find Charlotte today?'

'Well enough, but I do wish m'mother would let me alone.'

'She desires to be a grandmama and have the succession assured.'

'But how is a fellow to decide when all the girls simper and flatter so? It's deuced embarrassing, Nell. And it's interfering with my hunting.'

Nell choked back a laugh. Poor Philip. 'Charlotte Grainger is a lovely pea-goose,' she said. 'You and the estate would do better with Emily Caldwell.'

Philip rubbed his nose awkwardly. 'She's not a looker.'

'For shame! Stand up with her at the next assembly and take her into supper. I will be amazed if you do not find her good sense and placid manner a great deal more to your taste than corn-gold ringlets which, however beautiful, you would soon grow tired of.'

The conversation around them had swelled to include the Lake District where Mrs Belmont had taken a tour one year. Mrs Kydd (briefly and most wonderfully in the present) fondly recalled her home county of Hertfordshire and in particular the roses to be found in all the gardens. Encouraged by this, Nell began to hope they might yet come through the evening without mishap.

The gentlemen did not linger over their port. It appeared that after quizzing his host on the state of the game in the Kydd Court preserves, Captain Derringer had been moved to tell over the Peninsular campaign and had got so very detailed that Jasper Kydd had suggested an abrupt removal to the drawing room.

'Never saw a man more turned up,' confided Philip to Nell with a chuckle.

Hugo Derringer, happening to catch Nell's eye for one of the few times that evening, lifted his shoulders in an innocent shrug. Certainly her uncle took the earliest opportunity to settle his stomach with a cup of tea and it was at this point that Mrs Belmont's genius for saying exactly the wrong thing at the wrong time asserted itself.

'Margaret has been telling me about going to London for the season. Perhaps Nell will find suitors there more to her taste than my poor Philip.'

There was an awful silence.

'Margaret is mistaken,' said Jasper Kydd in a clipped voice. His eyes rested on Nell with chilling malevolency. 'It is by no means fixed.

I will be surprised if by the time the year has turned, she and Helena do not have other plans entirely.'

'I remember my first season,' said Mrs Belmont comfortably. 'The gowns I had! The girls today would stare to see them I daresay. But they served the purpose, for I took Mr Belmont's eye and was settled here by the summer.'

'I'm sure no one could be surprised,' said Nell warmly, 'if all your dresses were as fetching as the one in the painting in your dining room.'

Mrs Belmont preened. 'Why, I don't think it anything out of the ordinary, I assure you.'

So the subject was averted and the guests drank their tea and departed. Almost before they were through the door Nell hurried her mother upstairs in order to escape her uncle's temper. Tomorrow was likely to be most unpleasant.

★ ★ ★

Nell had been dreading her first encounter with Seth, but to her amazement her henchman led the horses out next morning whistling in sunny unconcern.

'Did Mr Jasper not speak to you yesterday, Seth?'

Seth's face darkened. 'Aye, an' I was main angry, so I was! Going to draw his cork for him! But Tom said as how you was going to speak up for us, an' then the captain said he'd make it all right.'

Nell was so startled she jerked the reins and had to regain control of her jibing mare. 'When did you see Captain Derringer, Seth?'

'When he came to stables to say as they was ready for carriage.'

'And you told him about being turned off and he told you not to worry? Does he think to take on a groom, then?'

Seth shrugged. 'He said as how Tom and Lizzie needn't fret, neither.'

It made no sense. Judging by his limited wardrobe, Hugo Derringer was scarcely in a position to offer people work. What could he mean by giving such cruel assurances?

She sat down to breakfast quite out of charity with him. She was still vexed at his ignoring her last night and thought it would serve him right if she bullocked Mama into paying a morning call at Belmont House, forcing him to acknowledge her. One thing though, she must do first. She waited until her uncle's plate was supplied with food, and his cup freshly charged with coffee, before saying, 'Might I have a talk with you this morning?'

'I have visits to make.'

'When you are at leisure then.'

'Leisure? What leisure is there to be found with this mouldering pile to run?'

Any other day, Nell might have pointed out that had Jasper not dismissed the Kydd agent and taken the whole of the business of the estate on himself, he would have plenty of leisure to discuss the welfare of the staff. Today, however, she gripped her temper tight and said she would await his convenience.

Thus instead of flooring Captain Derringer with choice phrases on the subject of empty promises, she spent the morning figuring where economies might be made in the running of the Court which did not involve turning people off. She was hampered by having none of the bills, Jasper keeping the household accounts locked away in the study, but with much pulling of brains, consultations with Olivant and Cook and sums on scraps of paper, she came to several encouraging conclusions.

Olivant had just entered the saloon to announce luncheon to Nell and her mother (presently shopping in Bond Street if her occasional disjointed phrases were to be believed) when Jasper Kydd arrived back at the house. The sound of his booted feet stamping angrily down the passage, the timbre of his voice as he called for refreshment *now*, told both Olivant and Nell that he was in a towering rage. Olivant trod hastily towards the decanter.

The door was flung open. 'So,' thundered Jasper. 'There you are, Helena!'

Nell widened her eyes. 'I said I would await your convenience. Where did you expect me to be?'

'Silence!' He tossed a glass of Madeira down as if it had been small-ale and demanded a second. With an oath he ripped off his gloves and curly-brimmed beaver, thrusting them at Tom with enough force to make the footman stagger. 'Your meddling has gone too far, niece. I discovered this morning that not content with disobeying my instructions and rejecting Mr Belmont's hand, you have also seen fit to interfere with the running of this estate!'

Nell's chin went up. 'If you mean I set the boys to work on the harvest with their fathers, that is the way things have always been done at Kydd. Kit and I both used to help in our younger days. If you mean directing the men to the Six-Mile Acre, it is only what you yourself would have suggested had you seen what little there was left to be gleaned in the top fields. Last week's downpour was not an isolated event. It is of the utmost importance to harvest as much as we may before the storms begin in earnest.'

His countenance darkened with anger. 'Weather lore, now!'

'Only in that I have lived here all my life and have paid attention to the pattern of the seasons. With respect, I believe you are likely now more attuned to the West Country climate than that of Kydd.'

At this Jasper stepped towards her and slapped her hard across the face. 'Insolent girl! You would be well served if I married you off to a man thrice your age who would teach you your place with the buckle of his belt!'

Olivant had started forward. Tom's fists were clenched. Shocked and shaking with rage, Nell spread a hand to halt both men. 'I have known Philip too long and think too well of him to accept. I would not make him as happy as he deserves.'

'Undoubtedly,' said her uncle. 'But as *he* did not seem to realize the fact, it was over-scrupulous of *you* to point it out. I hope you are not forming expectations of his friend? Even if yesterday's unwomanly exploits were not enough to give him a distaste of you — I know *everything*, you see — I should have no hesitation in forbidding that connection, none at all!'

'I assure you I am not considering

matrimony at all.' Nell gave him back stare for stare, her cheek stinging, her thoughts furious. Hugo Derringer had told her uncle about the bull? How dare he!

'Then explain to me why Mrs Belmont labours under the delusion that your mother is to take you to London. Did I not make my feelings plain?'

'What you make plain and what Mama comprehends are two different matters.' In a flash Nell saw her opening and went for it. 'But I still cannot see that it would be so very expensive. I daresay the whole season could be done for a thousand pounds.'

Jasper gave a coarse laugh. 'Impossible. Why, the coming-out ball for my daughters cost five hundred guineas alone!'

And wasn't it just like him to have delayed Amelia's presentation and brought both girls out together to save money. 'Then give me a thousand pounds and see what a hash I may make of it,' challenged Nell.

'Are you mad? Waste a thousand pounds on a venture I know must fail? You must think me as crack-brained as your father!'

Nell's temper rose to a new peak. The pain in her cheek fuelled her anger. 'You shall not say such things of Papa!'

'I shall say what I please. My brother was as foolish as he was spendthrift. His liberal, woolly-minded ideas led him to employ too many servants at too high a wage. His dilettante habits caused him to neglect his heritage and made it impossible that his daughter will ever take in the polite world. You should thank me for not putting you through the shame of a ludicrously unsuccessful season.'

'I would take that risk.'

'*I* will not!' He turned suddenly to Olivant. 'What the devil do you mean by listening all this time? Are the servants in this house insubordinate as well as lazy?'

'Luncheon awaits, sir,' said Olivant stiffly.

'Then why did you not say so? Take care you do not find yourself at point-non-plus at the quarter's end too!' Jasper slammed down his empty glass and turned on his heel out of the door.

There was silence in the room.

'Mrs Olivant would be happy to put together a tray for you both in the mistress's sitting room, Miss Nell,' said Olivant.

'Thank you, Olivant, but I am not finished yet. Come, Mama, it is time for luncheon.'

Mrs Kydd looked vaguely towards her. 'Is it, my love? So noisy here, I believe I will not come again.'

Olivant offered Nell a glass of Madeira. Full of steely determination, she drank down the contents as quickly as her uncle had done. Fire exploded along her veins. She was ready.

Her uncle was helping himself as they took their places. Tom served Mrs Kydd, his eyes flicking to Nell's cheek in mute sympathy. They widened in horror when after a mouthful of game pie, Nell said, 'I still do not see how living in London should be so expensive. It is not as if we have to pay extra wages, for we always take the servants with us, do we not, Mama?'

Mrs Kydd gave her a bright smile.

'You have forgotten the necessity of entertaining, Helena. Also of clothing your-selves suitably. Such gowns as you wear in the country will never do in town.'

'But there are warehouses where you may buy fabrics very cheaply. Bedford House, I remember, is one. Also Grafton House. And the Pantheon Bazaar, where I used to spend my pin money, had a vast quantity of — '

'Enough! I will have no more of this foolishness at my table! Neither your mother nor yourself is fit to run a town house. You would need to employ a housekeeper and they, Miss Insolence, do not come cheap!'

'I manage very well here with Cook and Olivant,' said Nell, ignoring Tom's indrawn breath behind her. 'Indeed, that was what I wanted to talk to you about. I believe it may be possible to retrench considerably, without turning away the staff.'

'Nonsense!' shouted Jasper, crashing both fists down on the board so hard that the dishes jumped. 'When I dismiss servants, they stay dismissed!'

'The losses will place too much work on inexperienced shoulders. You must see that necessary tasks will not get done, such as lighting fires to ward off the damp, or airing unused rooms to keep them fresh. Such a state of affairs cannot be good for the Court.'

'So,' he snarled, 'you think to hold house better than me, do you?'

She had done it! She had worked him up to such a pitch that he was hardly aware of what he was saying. 'I believe I am fit to do so if you would only let me.'

'By God, I will!'

Nell's heart leapt. 'You will keep the staff on and let me manage Kydd?'

'Good God no. Do you take me for a blockhead?'

'Then — Mama and I may go to London?' It was too good to be true.

Jasper Kydd sat back in his chair and signalled Olivant to refill his glass. 'Guess again, niece,' he said silkily.

Nell's brain worked at frantic speed. 'I see no other alternative.'

'No? And you so clever?' He stared at her with mocking eyes. 'Can it be that you have forgotten Hadleigh? Your mother's estate which will one day be your own? I cannot think how the solution has not occurred to me before. I am spared your insolence, the board cannot object to your playing house on your own property and when you outrun the bank, it will be your own inheritance you impoverish, not mine — I beg your pardon — your brother's. Margaret was saying only last night how much she would like to see Hertfordshire again. You shall accompany her there, Helena, and ponder the limited options open to ill-favoured disobedient hussies whilst proving whether you can live on nothing but the estate rents.'

The roaring was back in Nell's ears. 'Plus Mama's guaranteed income from Kydd,' she heard herself say in a voice which had become somehow cracked. 'Plus my own allowance.'

'Agreed. I will draw it out in cash and give it into your own hands on quarter day.' Her uncle laughed unpleasantly. 'I can't lose. It really will be too amusing.'

'And you are not to come with us and neither you nor anyone else is to meddle.'

'When would I find time? I have to be at Windown Park once the harvest is in here.'

'One more thing,' said Nell hastily. It would never do for him to think she had given in too easily. It might start him wondering why. 'If I make a profit this quarter and next, will you allow Kydd to frank me a London season?'

Jasper Kydd waved a careless hand and helped himself to cold meat. 'By all means. But you won't. A run-down manor with a household to feed and only your pin money to your name? You will be back before Christmas begging me to arrange a marriage for you.'

5

Annie stared. 'Hadleigh, miss? I grant it's smaller and easier to run than Kydd, but if you think Mr Jasper has any idea in half a year's time of honouring a promise made in anger now, you must have windmills in your head!'

Nell wriggled her arms into the newly-brushed pelisse. 'The season is a blind, Annie. Do you not see? Hadleigh is only *fifteen miles* from Half Moon Street!'

Annie's hand flew to her breast. 'Miss Nell! You're never telling me we're going to London without your uncle's consent?'

The joy Nell had been containing since the glory of the plan had burst upon her spiralled out. She danced gleefully about the room, seizing Annie's arms and spinning her round. 'He won't know! Once we are settled, we can leave Tom and Lizzie with Mama, and we will sneak away. We won't be there any length of time. Just enough to visit Mr Tweedie and find what is being done to locate my brother.' She cocked her head. 'Although we might also go to one of the warehouses for muslin and crape. I dare swear fabric is cheaper in

London than Northampton.'

'That's for sure. Oh, I'm fair flummoxed.' Annie knelt to button her mistress's feet into her boots. 'Fabric, you say? Which designs was you thinking of, then?'

A wide grin split Nell's face. 'Perhaps the Italian half-dress we admired from the *Belle Assemblée*? In an apricot or bronze?'

Annie sat back on her heels. 'With a russet spencer. You'll be needing a new wool pelisse too. The one you was wearing before the master died will never fit.'

Nell made a face. 'It may have to. I do not know what the Hadleigh income is. Enough to keep us snug, I hope.' She paused. 'And the horses. I *refuse* to leave Snowflake and Valiant, and we'll need the bays for the curricle. Will you look out my old clothes whilst I am visiting the Coppings? We must work fast to be ready by the quarter.'

★ ★ ★

Seth, predictably, was unworried by the coming removal. 'Got a nice little cob, they have,' he told Nell. 'Pulls the gig when Mrs Webb goes to village and Webb, he rides 'er into town for the mail when he's not doing the garden. Be nice for 'em to have a proper groom living there again. But who'll drive the

85

mistress's travelling carriage, Miss Nell, if I'm to bring Valiant and Snowflake? Tom's all right to sit along of you in the curricle, but he's no hand with anything larger.'

With the best will in the world, Nell couldn't see her way to feeding the four extra horses the carriage required. 'We can't take it, Seth. The horses are needed on the farm here. You shall go into town and hire a post-chaise for the journey.'

'What's mistress to go visiting in, then?'

Nell forbore to point out that the majority of her mother's morning calls these days took place in the convenience of her own head. 'I daresay there will be a landaulet in the stable.'

At Home Farm, Betsy Copping bid her daughter show how much her ankle was improved and then, without drawing breath, passed to Captain Derringer. With astonishment, Nell learnt Hugo had sought out Betsy's brother at Belmont and suggest he beg a lift on the perch with the groom when they came over.

'And fair grateful I am for he spoke real sensible to William, which he wouldn't listen to from his pa as I told you. Proper gentleman, the Captain is, as interested as can be in the work Jack does for Mr Belmont and how it's different from what he used to do here and said again how he'll do what he can for young Johnny. He asked was Johnny trained for groom work or did he just fall into it natural from being on the farm and did we have people we knew in the 28th that made him choose a line regiment instead of one with horses. And Jack told him it was Mr Jasper put young Johnny in the way of the North Gloucesters after the grief of the master's accident, and Johnny so taken up with shame he didn't care no ways whether he went for a foot soldier or an army groom at all.'

It made no sense. Why would Hugo be so interested? 'None of us blame Johnny,' said Nell hastily, staving off the threat of tears in Betsy's eyes. 'When Aristotle fell before, it was due to Johnny riding like the wind for the doctor that Papa's leg was set so quickly — and *entirely* due to Johnny and Seth that Aristotle himself survived.'

Betsy sniffed dolefully. 'Which if he hadn't done, master wouldn't have been riding him last autumn and wouldn't have died.'

'Fustian! As well say if it hadn't happened to be a fine morning, he wouldn't have gone out at all!'

The rest of the day passed without incident. Nell had hoped for the Hadleigh ledgers but her uncle shut himself into the study, saying disagreeably that Monday would be soon enough and she would be better served explaining to her mother how due to her own waywardness, they would both be removing to Hertfordshire at the end of the month.

'Hertfordshire?' said Mama, coming disconcertingly into the present. 'Are we going to Hadleigh, Nell? But how will Kit know to find us there?'

'The servants will tell him, of course,' said Nell.

Always assuming there were any left.

★ ★ ★

Sunday was a day when much could be accomplished, providing one went about it the right way. Even though Jasper Kydd accompanied them to church, curling his lip sardonically as all the servants hurried from their pews so as to be home before their masters, and standing by Nell's shoulder as she exchanged commonplaces with the vicar, she still managed to place one of their maids with that good man and a garden boy with the verger.

Captain Derringer was with Philip and a coterie of young bucks. Nell's pulse had quickened the moment she discerned him, but as he had afforded her the barest nod as they entered church and avoided her when she exited, she was now quite able to turn her back. To add to her sense of injury he was wearing that depressing black coat again. How could anyone care so little about clothes?

'You must come and drink tea with us this afternoon,' said Mrs Belmont. 'Just fancy, Philip would have me invite the Caldwells too! I suppose our discussion the other night put visiting Hadleigh into Margaret's head, did it? I hope it will help, that is all I can say.'

Nell smiled warmly. 'We all hope so, ma'am. She is a little brighter since you were so kind as to encourage her to talk of the old days. It must be a source of satisfaction to all Mama's friends to have her restored to health.'

Ha! Let her uncle now try to put it about that she was in disgrace. It would be established fact in the neighbourhood that the removal to Hadleigh was a scheme for Mama's well-being before Mrs Belmont had even reached the lych gate.

As Tom handed her into the barouche, Nell saw Hugo Derringer again. His head was up and he was staring directly at her, an expression of disquiet on his face. She turned away, refusing to admit that he unsettled her.

Jasper Kydd did not go with them to Belmont House. Nell could not conceive what he found to do shut away for such long hours in the study, but didn't let ignorance prevent her revelling in the sense of release. Obedient to Mrs Belmont's fluttering hints, she drew aside with Captain Derringer in order to let Emily and Philip talk together. It seemed Hugo was not avoiding her now.

'I like your friend,' he said. 'She is a good choice.'

'Why thank you. You must not forget to tell Philip you approve.'

'You think my opinion would weigh with him?'

'That does not appear a consideration with you, so busy as you are in other people's affairs.'

He looked at her for a moment, his brows straight and level. 'I collect you have been speaking with Mrs Copping.'

'I confess I find it puzzling that a gentleman so little connected with my family is being so very helpful to its employees.'

The transforming smile lit his face. 'Call me an active man with too little to occupy my time. On which head I am going to vex you further and tell you I do not like this latest venture of yours.'

Nell's chin came up. She was by no means ready to forgive him his cavalier treatment simply because he chose to smile at her all of a sudden. 'It is hardly a venture. Mama and I are removing to her own manor for a while.'

'Taking with you your footman, house-maid, groom and no doubt whatever other servant you cannot rehouse by the end of the month. On the battlefield, I would describe it as uncommonly similar to a retreat.'

She raised her eyebrows. 'From whom am I retreating? My uncle goes to Wiltshire at the same time.'

That had startled him. She saw his eyes flicker before he made a smooth recovery. 'Leaving no one at Kydd Court to supervise the estate? I am persuaded your brother would have you remain here.'

'Then my brother had best get himself back from India,' snapped Nell.

The arrival of the tea tray put an end to the exchange and gave her a chance to cool her heated cheeks. Why was Captain Derringer so concerned about her actions? There was nothing remotely lover-like in his bearing and he came close to giving her the cut direct whenever anyone of consequence was watching. As they drove back to Kydd a further thought intruded. It was an easy guess that Seth would be accompanying her to Hadleigh, but how had Hugo known so precisely about the rest of her household?

★ ★ ★

Hugo had never played billiards as badly in his life as he did that evening, but fortunately Philip was too engaged in marvelling over Emily Caldwell's diffident suggestion for dealing with a problem that had been plaguing him to notice.

Nell really was the most infuriating girl: if her uncle was returning to his own estate, then surely she had the perfect opportunity to put right some of his mistakes at Kydd Court. Instead she persisted in going ahead with this ridiculous Hadleigh escapade. In truth, he was disappointed. He hadn't thought she was the sort to tamely give up.

An unwilling smile tugged at his lips as he remembered how difficult he had found it not to physically shake some sense into her this afternoon. He had only been saved by the reflection that such an action would have given rise to all the speculation about him and his future prospects that he was anxious to avoid. There was no help for it: he must put forward his visit to Salisbury. A little distance would enable him to think of Nell Kydd more objectively.

The next morning Nell asked again if she might look over the Hadleigh ledgers. Her uncle replied curtly that he was going into town to authorize the change of business and she must perforce wait. As a steady rain precluded her driving out herself, she and Annie went through the contents of her trunks.

'This is nonsensical,' said Nell as gown after gown proved too short, too tight or simply unwearable. 'I cannot have grown this much in two winters!'

'I would say, miss,' answered Annie, 'that you've grown from a girl to a woman and that's all the change in the world.'

'Very profound,' muttered Nell, but as she stared at her unsatisfactory reflection, she admitted that her maid had a point. The sprigged muslin could easily be let out and its want of length made good with a second flounce, but it would still be the dress of a young girl trembling on the brink of adulthood and did not at all reflect the hard core of determination which Nell felt herself to possess these days. 'It is the materials and the cuts which are wrong,' she said aloud. 'Therefore it is a waste of time to alter anything but the riding habits and also the plain gowns that I can wear indoors whilst we are setting the house to rights. It is a shame, though, for I do need *something* unremarkable to wear during our visit to London.'

The weather cleared by midmorning so Nell, feeling responsible for Philip Belmont's precipitous courtship of Emily, took Mrs Kydd to call on the Caldwells to seek the lady's view of the matter. As they passed the head keeper's cottage, her eyes jerked sideways at the sight of a rangy brown gelding tethered outside. 'That is Captain Derringer's horse!' she said in surprise.

'Mrs Croft makes very good oatcakes,' said her mother placidly. 'Kit always contrives to find himself in the vicinity during rain.'

But unlike her opportunist brother, Hugo Derringer had not struck Nell as a man to seek shelter for anything less than a fully fledged thunderstorm. She drove on with a frown.

Conversation with Emily proved an impossibility since the first person Nell saw on entering the saloon was Philip himself, seated on the sofa next to her.

'Left her reticule behind yesterday,' he said, rising. 'Brought it over.' Beside him, a faint blush coloured Emily's cheeks.

'How thoughtful,' said Nell, her immediate question answered. 'Does your friend not accompany you?'

'Had to go into town,' said Philip.

Nell wondered by what feat of cartography her gamekeeper's cottage came to be on the route from Belmont House to town, but Mrs Kydd interrupted, regarding the room with strong disapproval and saying that she really felt people ought to be quiet when about to listen to a concert.

'We are not at a concert, Mama,' said Nell.

'Not?' repeated her mother in astonishment. 'Then we must make all haste and get there! I cannot abide latecomers! So ill-mannered!'

Nell met Emily's eyes helplessly. 'I do beg your pardon. I am afraid we had best — '

'Pray do not mention it,' said Emily. 'Enjoy the music, ma'am. You must tell us all about it when we see you next.'

Recalling Seth from the stables, they set off back for home. Nell glanced at her parent in fond exasperation. 'So, Mama, what is it we are to hear today?'

★　★　★

It was not the first time Mrs Kydd's foibles had caused an unexpectedly early return, so Nell was startled by the alarm in Tom's countenance when he opened the door to them. 'Tom? What is it?' She hurried past him into the hall.

Hugo Derringer stood by the table, one hand reaching for his hat, his face diplomat-smooth. 'How pleasant. Finding you out, I was about to depart.' He bowed to Mrs Kydd. 'I trust you are in good health, ma'am?'

'We are both well,' said Nell. 'I must confess to some surprise in seeing you. Were you not by when I told Miss Caldwell of our intention to call on her today?'

'I do not commonly listen to other people's conversations.'

'Then you are unique in the human race.' Nell tugged at her bonnet strings, frowning. Hugo was still wearing his gloves which should indicate that he had just arrived, yet they had not seen him as they drove up the sweep. She noticed that the study door was ajar. 'Is my uncle returned?' she asked Tom.

Sweat beaded her footman's forehead. He shifted from one leg to the other. 'No, Miss Nell. Will you be wanting refreshment?'

'Good gracious no,' said Mrs Kydd. 'I must get ready!' She disappeared up the staircase.

'Not for me either,' said Captain Derringer. 'I had not heeded the hour. I really should be — '

'What were you doing in my gamekeeper's cottage?'

He stopped in mid-sentence. Nell could

almost feel him shifting his ground. 'It came on to rain on my way over.'

'It was raining most of the morning. You must have been with Croft an unconscionably long time if you started off before it. What did you find to talk of?'

'Where game is concerned, Miss Kydd, men may talk forever.'

'That is not what I asked.'

He compressed his lips. 'We discussed the merits of small bore over large bore. Croft reckoned up the losses to poachers this season. I commiserated with him over the fires in your south coverts. I was also treated to a dissertation on the difficulties of protecting a large acreage without a full complement of staff. I must have a sympathetic countenance; I believe he aired every grievance you would expect from a man who does not have a bailiff to complain to.'

'He had one until nine months ago,' said Nell, firing up. 'My uncle dismissed him.'

'He appears to make a habit of such behaviour. Do you realize when you leave next week, the few retainers Kydd has left will have no one to turn to?'

Nell lifted her chin, furious with him for giving voice to her own qualms. 'Does your visit have any other purpose than to point out my failings?'

'Your obstinacy, you mean!' He took a hasty turn about the hall before facing her. 'I am aware of the awkwardness of your position. If you require advice, I can let you have the direction of a lawyer who — '

'What a well connected man you are, to be sure. One friend who is a lawyer, another in the 5th Division, still more around the country who have manors where you may stay whenever the whim takes you. Is this more of your diplomatic training? Never to cast anyone off who might one day be of use?'

His eyes blazed green fire, matching her own anger. 'Believe me, there are times when my upbringing is a severe handicap!' He gripped her hand, raised it to his lips and kissed it hard enough to bruise. 'Good day. I shall endeavour not to burden you with any further offers of aid.' So saying, he strode from the house.

★ ★ ★

After this disastrous exchange, the next few days were a blur of packing, rehoming servants, and duty calls. Nell was dismayed, when her uncle passed over the Hadleigh books, to find the Manor not as profitable as she had understood, but after working through the sums came to the conclusion that by marketing frugally and not using the 'retired cook from the village' above three times a week they would manage tolerably well.

Like a chafing shadow, Hugo Derringer's disapproval followed her wherever she went. He made a stiff apology when their paths crossed in town, disappearing before she could reciprocate. She glimpsed the skirt of his riding coat whisk into a shop when she accompanied her uncle to sign the Hadleigh agreement. He was in the smithy, grimly mute, when she left the bays to be shod. Nell felt all the injustice of this treatment after such a promising start to their acquaintance and after being merely nodded to the whole of one evening at the Graingers, she was within Ames ace of galloping in the opposite direction when she espied him on Conqueror's back next morning.

'Good day, Miss Kydd,' he said, touching his hat.

She started theatrically. 'Seth, did you hear someone speak?'

'Ah, I did offend you last night.'

She sent him a kindling look. 'Offend me? No, how could that be when you didn't come near me all evening?'

'Is your mistress generally out of sorts at this hour, Seth?'

'Been on the fidget all week, Annie says.'

'Thinking better of this harebrained Hertfordshire scheme, I hope.'

'I am not thinking better of it!' said Nell, furious. 'I wish I was at Hadleigh right now!' She glared at Seth. 'Nor have I been on the fidget. And I will thank you, sir, not to curry favour with my servants behind my back.'

'Behind your back?'

'It was not you who bought Seth a heavy wet at the Lion whilst I was in the circulating library, then? Next time you choose a confidante, Captain Derringer, let me recommend one whose tongue does not run on fiddlesticks.'

To his credit, Hugo did look slightly embarrassed. Nell's temper snapped. She remembered an old grievance which she had never yet brought up with him. 'And it may interest you to know that even if you *had* accosted me recently, I should not have spoken to you. Quite apart from making abominably plain your disapproval of me whenever we meet, how dared you carry the tale of the bull's escape to my uncle that time? A more ungentlemanly act I never met with!'

A look of deep offence overspread his face. 'I would not dream of doing such a thing!'

'Nay, that were Walter Harvey, Miss Nell.

Spilled it to Mr Jasper the very next day, he did.'

Nell whirled around in her saddle. 'Walter Harvey?' she said, stupefied. 'Why did you not tell me?'

Seth gazed back, his blue eyes wide. 'You never asked.'

Nell turned stiffly. Her mouth worked. 'It seems I owe you an apology.'

'Accepted,' said Hugo in a curt voice. They rode a little way in silence. 'I am going into Wiltshire tomorrow,' he said abruptly. 'I beg you will reconsider leaving Kydd Court.'

'Why? It can mean nothing to you.'

He looked away. 'I mistrust your uncle's motives in sanctioning your removal,' he said at last. 'I realize I have spent little time in this neighbourhood, but I would have expected by now to hear at least some small thing to his credit. I have not. It is all of a piece. Gathering bad crops before good is simple ill management, but what sort of man turns away experienced servants while keeping poor ones on?'

'He says he let go those who would find it easiest to get new positions.' Nell took a deep breath. 'And no, I will not back out. It is in the light of a wager. I prove myself able to manage Hadleigh and he will allow me a London season.'

Captain Derringer swung around. 'Your own uncle has made a wager with you? On those terms? Infamous!'

'Not so. It was my idea to show him that a manor can be run on a small budget. Also, if I am at Hadleigh I am free of his carping and his taunts, and he will no longer be fretting Mama or arranging unwelcome matches for me.'

'I never heard of anything so improper. The man is a monster! Giving a mere chit the authority to ruin herself!'

The tide of rage that had been simmering in Nell all week rose up. 'So you also think I will make a hash of it! Grant me strength! What is it about the male sex that makes them so obnoxiously superior?'

'You call it obnoxious to be concerned about a headstrong, half-grown girl alone, undefended and very likely starving? No doubt it would be the height of good manners to let you go to the sponging house without making the least push to deflect you?'

'Alone and undefended? At Hadleigh? When three maids accompany us and you know very well that both Seth and Tom go too?'

'And you know very well my opinion of Seth as a bodyguard! And you also know Tom's leg has not been strong since he broke

102

it falling out of the tree house!'

'That was *years* ago!' she said incredulously. 'It mended as good as ever after Kit spent his whole allowance on the very best doctor from Northampton. He hadn't a feather to fly with for the rest of the summer but didn't regard it one jot because Papa always taught us that our friends might take their own chances but we owe a duty to our servants to do the best we can by them. It is *killing* me to witness my uncle's callous disregard for them and that, sir, is the other reason I am going to Hadleigh and taking whom I can with me, for in spite of your empty assurances to Seth after my uncle turned them off, I know I can look after my people and they in turn will look after me!' Upon which she dug her heels into Snowflake's sides and galloped ahead, spending her sobbing anger in the thudding of the mare's hoofs and the flying tangle of her mane. She heard Conqueror's hoofbeats coming after her but did not slow until her rage had abated and the tears on her cheeks had dried.

They had left Seth behind. Kydd Court lay below them, handsome and serene in the morning light. Nell felt her breath catch in her throat as she gazed down on it. She *would* find Kit and save it from her uncle's maladministration.

Hugo halted next to her. 'Forgive me,' he said, reaching across and laying his gloved hand on hers. 'I had not realized your life to be so intolerable.'

'I manage well enough,' said Nell rigidly. 'Women have to, half-grown or not.'

His fingers tightened. 'I have said some unpardonable things during our past few meetings. I beg you will forget them.'

She would not let him get round her. 'Would *you* be able to if our cases were reversed?'

'I suppose not. Nell, I am truly concerned for you.'

She made the mistake of turning her head then and looking at him. There was no mask of politeness or reserve on his face. His dark hair was wind-blown, his eyes were worried, and she was unconscionably softened by the sound of her name on his lips. 'There is no need. Mama and I will be comfortable enough.' She nudged Snowflake to walk a few steps so that he had perforce to let go of her hand. 'When Kit returns, I know he will approve my actions.'

'Yes, very likely,' said Hugo with a rueful twist to his mouth. 'You are taking the horses, of course. Does Seth return for the curricle?'

'No, I am driving it myself. My uncle would likely sell it as soon as I am through the gates otherwise.'

He favoured her with an old-fashioned look. 'It would be useless, I collect, to mention that ladies do not generally drive across three counties in open carriages?'

'Uncle Jasper has already informed me of the fact. I do not see why. Gentlemen frequently do so.'

'Gentlemen have reserves of stamina. Also greatcoats to keep off the cold.'

'I plan to take Kit's old one. I am slightly more than seven, however much you seem to doubt it.' Her brow knitted. 'How did you know about Tom's leg?'

He bent to tease a burr out of his gelding's mane. 'I forget. Your brother must have told me when I twigged him at school for not having any blunt. Mayhap I should put off my departure and accompany you on the road?'

'My uncle would ask your intentions towards me if you did any such thing.'

He pursed his lips thoughtfully. 'I could wait for you at the turnpike.'

Well really! He need not be quite so blunt about showing his unwillingness as a suitor. 'We shall be quite safe,' she snapped. 'Tom and Seth are well able to hold their own and I daresay the post-boys will be likewise armed. I would not for the world put you to any inconvenience.'

'For an intelligent young woman, you frequently talk great nonsense.' He looked around as if gathering his bearings. 'I must go. Nell — you will take care?'

Thoroughly off-balance at his change in mood, she gave him her hand. 'I will.' It was on the tip of her tongue to confide her real reason for going to Hadleigh, but although they were not quite now parting brass rags, she was perplexed enough about his motives to keep silent. 'I bid you good day.'

And that was that. He departed next morning, so Philip told them, for his friends near Salisbury.

'Good,' muttered Nell. She put Hugo Derringer firmly out of her head, refused to dwell on his deep green eyes or his unexpected flashes of humour or the way his face lightened when he smiled, and concentrated instead on how many Kydd effects she could include in her packing without her uncle noticing.

The day before they were to go, Tom informed her that his parents would like a word. She braced herself for an unhappy parting. What she got was something else entirely.

'Olivant and I, Miss Nell, are coming with you and the mistress to Hadleigh!'

Nell stared at them, her knees buckling.

106

She rather thought her mouth might have come open. 'I — that is — ' She pulled herself together with a great effort. She could not possibly afford a full-time cook and butler. 'That will certainly be more comfortable for Mama, Mrs Olivant, but — '

'On account,' Cook continued inexorably, 'of Mr Jasper cutting back the staff again due to nobody in the house needing waiting on.'

This time Nell knew her mouth was hanging open. She looked incredulously at Olivant. 'My uncle has not turned you both off? I cannot believe it!'

Cook folded her arms. 'I never thought such a thing would come to pass and that's a fact. It won't be what we're used to, but Olivant and I are quite determined and I'll manage just fine with young Gwennie and a scullery maid or two from the village.'

The door opened. Jasper Kydd stood on the threshold, a thin smile playing about his mouth. 'Interviewing the new additions to your household, Helena? I am confident they will give satisfaction, though servants of this calibre are of course a trifle dear. I trust the expense will not distrain upon your purse too deeply?'

Anger poured into her, banishing weakness. He had *planned* this! He *wanted* her to fail. 'I do not regard the Olivants as servants. To me they are old and valued friends. Mama and I are delighted that we may count on the whole family's support at Hadleigh.'

Her uncle laughed softly. 'Bravo, niece. After such a speech I am almost tempted to pay your cook and butler's travelling expenses myself.'

'Thank you. That will be most acceptable for we shall certainly require a second post-chaise. Indeed, an honorarium from the estate would also be in order after their long service to the family.'

'Do not try your luck too far. I would hate to be standing in your shoes when it gave out.'

6

Shortly before nine in the morning on 30 September, a veritable procession was ranged on the sweep. The bays were harnessed to Nell's curricle. Next came two post-chaises piled high with luggage and each drawn by four horses. Finally Seth brought up the rear riding Valiant and leading Snowflake. The sad remnant of the Kydd staff clustered by the main door to wave them off.

Jasper Kydd strolled up to the curricle. 'Farewell, Helena,' he said. 'I wish you joy of your experiment. Pray do not hesitate to return as soon as you have run aground.'

He was so sure she would fail. Nell looked into his odious, mocking face and said, 'With no interference, I believe I shall get along prosperously.'

'A useful accomplishment to take into matrimony.'

'And even more useful if I remain unwed.' She turned. The post-boys were ready and the horses champing to be off. 'Ready, Seth?' she called, and at his answering yodel started the bays without a backward glance.

As it was a journey of some sixty-four

miles, it was fully seven o'clock and dusk was falling by the time they turned in at the gates to Hadleigh Manor. Stiff and cold after the longest day's driving she had ever done and on largely unfamiliar roads, Nell thought she had never seen so sweet a sight in her life as the lantern hanging ready in the porch and the welcoming glow from the front windows.

'Gently now, my beauties,' she whispered to the bays. 'You have done very well today, very well indeed. Bide just a few moments longer and Seth will take you to the stables.' Tom, no warmer than she, divested them both of rugs and helped Nell down before hurrying to Mrs Kydd's carriage. Nell's fingers were frozen to the bone inside her gloves, but no one could have told it as she shrugged off Kit's greatcoat and held out her hands to the elderly figures just emerging from the lit doorway. 'Mrs Webb,' she said. 'And Webb, too. How glad I am to see you both.'

'Oh, Miss Nell,' cried the old housekeeper. 'It's all grown up you are! You never drove this long way by yourself?'

Nell laughed. 'Tom spelled me but I own my hands are sadly chilled. It will be most agreeable to warm them by the fire.'

Mrs Webb looked along to the next carriage where Tom had the step down and was helping Annie alight. 'And have you really brought the mistress?'

'Indeed, I would not dare come else!'

The housekeeper took a few uncertain steps as Mrs Kydd descended on Tom's arm. 'Oh, Miss Margaret! Mrs Kydd, rather! Why would you not come before? So sad about the master! Webb and I both felt it — Oh, Miss Margaret!'

Nell held her breath as her mother blinked at the torrent of tearful words and then raised her head to take in the light issuing from the well-loved façade of the house. She almost felt like weeping herself as Mama smiled and said in a soft voice, 'Dear Mrs Webb. How glad I am to be home again.'

The occupants of the second carriage had also alighted. Olivant was already superintending the removal of the baggage from both vehicles into the hall. Webb, no fool for all his advancing years, appraised the mountain of trunks with his rheumy eyes and offered to lead the bays to the stables whither Seth had already gone with the riding horses.

'That would be kind indeed,' said Nell, 'and pray see to the postboys' comfort as well. They have been so very obliging towards us.'

Cook avoided the melee by directing her kitchen maid to bring 'that box there' along to the kitchen premises after her, with the result that Mrs Webb had barely finished drying her eyes, repeating how happy she was and apologizing for the scantily-cleaned state of the drawing room (funds not having been available for some time to employ anyone bar a woman from the village once a week to do the rough work) before a heavy tea tray with pot, cups and a plate of bread and butter was brought in for Nell and her mother. Recalled to a sense of her duties, the elderly housekeeper hurried out.

'Oh, how kind of Mrs Webb, Mama — this is the Derby service, is it not? She must have washed it just for you. I remember this flower design was your favourite from when we stayed before.' Suddenly nervous, Nell poured tea into both cups and took a comforting swallow. *Please, please let this work.*

Mrs Kydd sipped her tea, at one with the faded, chintz-hung room. 'We should have come before. Kit will find us here, won't he?'

Nell let out a breath she hadn't realized she was holding. Her cup rattled in the saucer. 'I may have to go to London to search for him. Will you mind being here without me?'

Her mother's smile was sweet and faraway. 'Goose! I shall be well looked after. And when you come back you will bring Kit.'

Daylight revealed the full extent of the manor's gentle decay. The shabbiness did not worry Nell, but room after room was discovered to be dusty and damp and in need of fires and thorough cleaning. Nor was there better news when she and Seth rode through the overgrown gardens to visit the tenants. All complained of the steep rents and lack of understanding shown by Jasper Kydd. As Nell made notes of each grievance, she could not help hearing Hugo Derringer's caustic remarks in her head. 'Go away,' she told his shade crossly. 'I can do this. Stop bothering me.'

But she frowned as she went through the ledgers. The books her uncle had handed over added up by themselves, but they did not tally with what the farmers said. She rode back to the least disobliging the next day and asked for all he could remember of the costs and yields of the past few years. Armed with these facts she attacked her accounts again.

Annie found her in the bookroom, surrounded by sums that made no sense and with a smudge of ink on her cheek. 'We've left the workbox at Kydd, miss, with all the patterns and trimmings and thread in it.'

Nell looked up. 'Oh we haven't! Are you

sure it has not become mixed up with the other luggage?'

'That was the first thing I checked. Mr Olivant hasn't seen it neither.'

'No, I remember now I had it in the small drawing room to mend a tear in my riding habit. It will still be there, I'll wager.' She considered the problem briefly. 'We cannot do without it, that's for sure. Seth will have to go back. If he ties the box securely and puts it in a sack, he can attach it to Valiant's pommel. At least we have plenty to do without needing to fill in our time mending!'

Determined to make as big a push as she could towards success, Nell stirred up her mother to attack the house the next day. They put on their oldest dresses, tied squares of linen around their hair and dusted, shook out books and curtains, and swept with a will. It was tedious in the extreme, but Mama seemed to enjoy the novelty. The work paid off when Tom showed the first of their morning callers (an elderly friend of the family who had heard via neighbourhood gossip of Mrs Kydd's return) into an airy saloon smelling of beeswax, whose clean curtains filtered the autumn sunshine and whose surfaces gleamed with polish.

The visit was successful, the dowager Lady Moncrief passing magnanimously over Mrs

Kydd's occasional conversational digressions, praising Cook's macaroons and certainly not disdaining the Madeira poured for her by Olivant (and where had that come from, wondered Nell). An invitation for them to take tea with her on the ensuing Sunday after church was accepted as graciously as it was tendered. Nell sighed with relief.

Seth returned a full day earlier than anyone expected. What had gone amiss? Nell hurried out to see him helping a small figure up from the ground where it appeared she had tumbled off Valiant's back. 'I got all your parcels, Miss Nell,' he announced, beaming. 'An' I brung Lily!'

'So I see,' said Nell a trifle blankly. Tom Olivant, arriving beside her, stifled a spurt of laughter.

'Found her, I did,' said Seth proudly. 'Outside the Cross Keys. An' she was crying, see, so I brung her along of me.'

Lily gulped. She was huddled into a threadbare cloak, clutched a bundle that clearly contained all her worldly possessions, and gazed with unadulterated adoration at Seth. 'Seth said as how I could stay, Miss Nell. Said there was a fair powerful lot of cleaning to do.'

Nell looked at the dust-streaked young housemaid she had last seen polishing the grand staircase at Kydd and passed a hand across her forehead. Another mouth to feed. 'So there is and of course we shall be very pleased to have your help, but will they not miss you at the Court?'

Seth interrupted in high dudgeon. 'No, for Mr Jasper turned her off!'

'That's right, Miss Nell,' said Lily. 'He said as how Kydd couldn't afford me no more and had I got any kin and when I said Cissy lives along of King's Lynn with her man and her baby he said that'll do and gives me five shillun for the stagecoach and my keep.'

'But Lily can't go to Lynn a'cos her Cissy's man hit her cruel the last time she was there an' told her she was stupid an' good for nothing. An' she didn't know what to do, an' she was crying, so — '

'And so you brought her here. Yes, I quite see. Thank you, Seth.'

'He was a hero, Miss Nell! Just like in them stories you used to read us. He hid me in the stable and brung me bread and cheese and ale and then put me on Master Kit's horse before it was even light this morning and told me to hold him close and not be afeared and I weren't!'

Lily was gazing worshipfully up at Seth again. Nell didn't know who she felt most irritated with: the little maid, Seth strutting like a cockerel, or Tom Olivant spluttering so hard with laughter he was likely to burst.

'Oh, for heaven's sake! Lily, go to the kitchen. Seth, see to Valiant. Tom, can you manage to bring in the items Seth was actually supposed to fetch?'

'That I can, Miss Nell,' said Tom, still grinning broadly. 'Seth, a hero! Oh my!'

★ ★ ★

Several things about Lily's story puzzled Nell, not least the intelligence that Jasper Kydd had not yet returned to Windown Park. While the girl tackled the bookroom hearth (spurning as wicked ingratitude the suggestion that she might need to rest after her long ride), Nell asked, 'Was anyone else turned off, Lily, or just you?'

'Just me, Miss Nell. Likely you'll need the sweep for this chimbly.'

'Yes, I daresay. I haven't had a fire in here yet. Do you know when Mr Jasper leaves Kydd?'

'No, Miss Nell. He's doing a list of the books in the library. This grate's near as bad as his study, so it is.'

A list of the books at Kydd? But she had helped Papa's secretary complete an inventory only two years back. Why would Uncle

Jasper need another one? Lily's second sentence penetrated her brain. 'The study fireplace? What's wrong with it?'

Lily raked energetically at the accumulation of years. 'Choked up with all the parchment Mr Jasper's been burning.'

Nell frowned. 'Parchment? How can you tell?'

'Real thick ash, not like logs. And a great lump of leaves fell through the bars just the other day and didn't burn.'

Letters, Nell supposed, which her uncle considered not worth preserving. But some of the people Papa had corresponded with were eminent figures. Surely their writings would be of interest and ought to be kept? 'I suppose you put them on the ash heap, did you?' she said aloud.

Lily looked shocked. 'Oh no. I give all the big bits to Clarrie for scraping down and re-using like Mrs Olivant has always taught us. All but the piece I dropped. Mr Jasper put that back on the fire.'

She continued with her cleaning, happily unaware of what she had said.

Lily had discovered a scrap of parchment which should have been burnt.

Lily had been dismissed.

Certain words of Hugo Derringer dinned in her ears. *I mistrust your uncle's motives*

. . . *What sort of man turns away experienced servants whilst keeping poor ones on?* But she had been cross with him, thinking herself slighted, and had given him back the same answer that Uncle Jasper had made her, that he had let go those people who would find it easiest to get new positions. Now she wished she had swallowed her pride and probed Hugo's thoughts further.

She headed for the kitchen. 'Lily gave Clarrie some pieces of parchment to be rubbed down and re-used,' she said without preamble. 'Where would Clarrie have put them?'

'Back of the dresser drawer,' replied Mrs Olivant. 'Where we always keep useful scraps.'

'Would she clean them straight away?'

'Lord love you, no. She'll have too much to do. Important, are they? Seth could have collected them with the other bits and pieces.'

'He didn't know about them. *I* didn't know until Lily told me just now.'

Cook tutted. 'That boy. Fancy doing something so bird-witted. Not but what I don't blame him, for he's powerful soft on helpless creatures and if ever there was a chit more helpless than Lily I wouldn't want to know her. And not but what Olivant isn't glad to have her here, neither, with all the work there is and her so willing, but I wouldn't want for her and Seth to get into trouble over it.'

'I don't doubt my uncle forgot her existence as soon as she was out of the door. Even so, if he *should* happen to call to see how we get on, it might be as well for her to be out of sight.'

Cook met her eyes for a long moment. 'I understand you, Miss Nell.'

★ ★ ★

By the end of the week, they had scoured the downstairs rooms, entertained callers, been invited out three times to drink tea and had dined one evening at the rectory. Nell had the satisfaction of knowing Mama to have been accepted and that in Mrs Webb she had a ready companion whenever Nell herself was not to hand. She was also mending matters with the tenants by employing two young hopefuls as garden boys and another under Seth as a stable lad. But nice as it was to see the rooms glowing, the walks being brought under control and the stonework emerging from a blanket of ivy, she was itching to be off. There was a very pressing item on her agenda.

Its attainment came much closer when Rose, who had been Mrs Kydd's personal maid for some forty years, confided a half-memory to Annie regarding a chest which used to reside in the attic. The chest, wrested from under a quarter-century of dust and lumber, was found to contain such treasures as oyster satin, Brussels lace, pale green gauze, ells of ribbon and a whole bolt of primrose silk.

Nell was thrilled on being shown this bounty. 'Rose, you have saved us pounds! The silk alone will easily make me a walking dress and pelisse that I may wear in London without attracting attention.' She fingered the glorious stuff. 'There is even bronze ribbon to trim it! Have we yellow thread enough, Annie? Can we make a start tonight? Once I am passable we can go to Half Moon Street.'

'That we can,' said Annie in satisfaction. 'And right pleased I'll be to get back to my proper work again instead of all this dratted cleaning!'

When Nell braced herself to tell the rest of the household what she was planning, she did not at all get the reaction she expected.

Cook chuckled. 'Bless me, Miss Nell. We knew you'd be off to the solicitor as soon as may be to find out about Master Kit. Stands to reason you would.'

Olivant handed Nell a ring of keys. 'Half Moon Street. I took the liberty of bringing them with us from Kydd.'

Nell sat down numbly. 'I thought I must have to go to the agent.'

'Easier this way, Miss Nell. Fewer explanations to reach your uncle's ears.' He cleared his throat. 'We all want to see Master Kit back again.'

* * *

The morning she had fixed on dawned wet, though it promised to clear later. Not for the first time Nell rued the lack of a covered vehicle in the Hadleigh stables. 'When we return, Seth, you can take the bays to Kydd and bring back the barouche. My uncle must have gone into Wiltshire by now. You can bring those pieces of parchment from the dresser too.'

'Told you as how we'd need a carriage,' said Seth, guilelessly pleased to have been proved right.

'It's an ill wind as blows nobody any good,' said Cook, up to her elbows in pastry. 'Now there'll be time to make a nice mutton pie, so as you won't have to go to a hotel for your supper.'

Nell didn't say she had had no intention of

dining out. Such a thing would have been awkward indeed for a lady alone and she was not perfectly sure how to go about it. What she had planned was to eat at a coaching inn on the way, then exist on bread and cheese until the following day and the journey back. However, she was solaced when the delay meant she received a letter from Mrs Belmont.

Nell had written to all their friends to tell them of their safe arrival at Hadleigh. Mrs Belmont's reply was just like herself, full of gossiping nonsense about servants and neighbours and the recent assembly at which Philip not only danced two sets with Miss Caldwell, but also took her into supper! Nell grinned, but her smile faded as she read the next sentence. Her uncle had only just departed! Mrs Belmont had quite thought he had left already since no one had seen anything of him, and she would never have known otherwise had their carriages not happened to cross in Oundle whither she had gone to visit an old servant and bespeak new table linen. She had had to rap hard on the glass to get his attention, she wrote, and he had looked quite startled to see her. Such a quantity of bundles and parcels in the chaise too! Mrs Belmont thought it must have been a most uncomfortable journey for him. But her dear Nell would be pleased to know that the new table linen would be in cream damask, with embroidered posies of . . .

Nell let the letter fall into her lap. Her uncle only just gone? And *a quantity of bundles and parcels* with him? She looked out of the window to see the weather clearing. She was strongly inclined to head for Kydd on the instant, but a moment's reflection told her it would then likely be another week before she could get to London. Kit must come first, he had to. 'Tom,' she called, 'tell Seth to ready the curricle. We're going now.'

It was cramped indeed with portmanteaux and baskets about the ladies' feet and Seth hanging on behind, but it would only be for fifteen miles and Nell was soon too concentrated on half-remembered roads and the increasingly busy traffic to pay heed to the discomfort.

'I have had the most horrible thought,' she said as she took the final corner into Half Moon Street and let go some of her pent-up breath. 'Suppose the house is let after all? There will be nothing for it but to find a hotel.'

'Doesn't look let to me, miss,' said Annie, scrutinizing the closed shutters and blank facade of the Kydds' unassuming town house. 'It'll likely be them damp kitchens and haunted attics that've set folk against it.'

Nell chuckled and jumped down. In a trice they had the baggage off and were effecting an entrance via the servants' door whilst Seth took the curricle to see what state the stables might be in.

The door opened into a silent, dust-layered kitchen. Light filtered down from the high windows at street-level, but when Nell investigated the stairs leading up to the rest of the house, she saw the space above was dark with drawn curtains and had a musty, unused smell. Good. All was well. Then, passing the fireplace, her heart nearly stopped — the kitchen grate held a faint suggestion of warmth. Very still now, Nell's eyes sharpened. There was a ring of wetness on one end of the table suggesting a pan of water had been set down at not too distant a time. Nell tiptoed once more to the door, all her senses heightened.

'Candle wax,' whispered Annie, pointing to tell-tale drips on floor and table.

Nell nodded. 'Heat, light and water,' she murmured. 'Eccentric requirements for a ghost. Hand me the poker.' She didn't stop to remove Kit's greatcoat, simply trod noise-lessly up the stairs and into the dark emptiness of the hall.

Half-way up the next staircase, she heard a sound that took her breath away — the barest click of a latch at the top of the house. The wild hope that had rooted in her heart from the very moment of sensing the grate's will-of-the-wisp warmth intensified. Incredible though the idea seemed, she could think of only one person who might have entered the house unnoticed and be hiding even now in the Kydd attics. It was starkly, madly impossible and yet . . .

Nell gained the landing and slipped into the open drawing room doorway from where she could just make out the next flight. Behind her a table gleamed dully, shrouded chairs loomed and paintings made dark rectangles on the walls. She had no attention to spare however, for further up again there was the merest suggestion of a shifting of the dimness. She slowed her breathing to an unaspirated thread, withdrew into the folds of the greatcoat, and waited.

The shadow on the stairs ghosted lower. Nell realized with a skip of her heart that it had avoided the betraying creak on the fourth tread without even needing to think about it. Then the clouds outside shifted and a pinpoint of dusty sunlight pierced the drawing room shutters to rest on moon-bright hair.

'Kit!' said Nell on a sobbing breath, letting the poker fall to the floor as she launched herself out of the doorway and into her brother's arms. '*Kit!*'

7

'Nell? Well, by all that's famous! What the deuce are you doing here?'

For a moment, Nell was overwhelmed by the sheer joy of knowing her brother to be alive and well. 'Looking for you, of course, numbskull!' She hugged him as if she would never let go, tears of relief and happiness coursing down her cheeks and soaking into his rough shirt. 'How could you do this to us, Kit? How could you let us think you were lost?'

He held her tight. 'Only for a very little while, brat. It was necessary, I promise you.'

'Necessary?' she gasped, pulling away. 'Papa has been in the ground these twelve months, Mama is out of her mind with grief, Uncle Jasper strides about Kydd as if he owns it, ruining all he touches and you say it was necessary for us to be desperately worried over you?' Relief turned to rage. She began to rain blows on his chest. 'Do you know how many servants are turned off? Do you know the privations the whole estate must bear? How *dare* you abandon us like that?'

'Ouch! Steady, Nell! No, stop it, you

spitfire!' Kit doubled up as a punch took him in the midriff. 'Enough,' he said, capturing her frenzied fists. 'I apologize. I am every kind of knave you care to mention. Just stop hitting me. Especially there.'

Nell shook off his hold, straining to see his face in the dimness. 'Why, Kit? Why are you hiding? I was never more frantic in my life than when the captain of the ship you booked passage on reported that you never set sail with him!'

There was a muffled thud from below. Kit's hand shot out to grip his sister's wrist. 'Nell, quickly, who is with you? Not my uncle?'

'Triple numbskull,' said Nell scathingly. 'Have you not been listening? Why would I have waited all these weeks to come without it being to avoid his having knowledge of it? That was Annie, unless Seth has been uncommonly fast settling the horses. I daresay she walked into the hall table. I hope she has not hurt herself.'

'Seth? Did you ride, then? Did you bring Valiant?'

'Truly, Kit, I begin to believe you have lost what little wit you once had! A young lady ride into London with a portmanteau strapped to her saddle? Nothing less likely to attract attention I dare say! And pray tell me why I would bring your horse when I did not even know you were here?'

'Then why did you come?'

'To see Mr Tweedie, of course!' said Nell, exasperated. 'To find what is being done to locate you!'

In the gloom, Nell saw an indefinable shade of concern cross his face. '*Is* something being done?'

'It certainly should be, but I don't know. That is why I came to London! Annie, it's all right! It's Master Kit, it really is!'

Her maid's voice came disapprovingly from below. 'Glad I am to hear it, but if it means we're to break our legs in the darkness, I'd as lief he was still missing.'

Kit's teeth flashed in a well-remembered grin that tore at Nell's heart. 'It should be safe with the blinds at the rear of the house open,' he said, moving into the dim drawing room to pull back the heavy brocade. 'I've been living in the garret. It's bright enough up there.' He turned. 'It's deuced good to see you again, Nell.'

'And you.' Then, as the late afternoon light illuminated the room, 'Gracious, Kit, you look terrible!'

His mouth twisted. 'You have not learnt tact then, whilst I have been away?'

'I should like to know who was to teach me. Papa died last autumn as I wrote, and

Mama . . . Mama has not been herself these many months.'

His hand tightened on a shrouded chair back. 'I know and I am sorry. Believe me, I would have come to you if I could.'

She stood quite still. 'You know about Mama? How? Those letters were returned unopened.'

His eyes glanced off hers. 'It is a long story, Nell.'

'Then we will need tea to wash it down. Cook put a packet in the basket. Shall we repair to the kitchen?' She slipped off the greatcoat and folded it over her arm as she spoke.

Her brother blinked. 'You have grown. Now I see what . . . Yes, let us have tea by all means.' As they crossed to the door he fingered the primrose silk of her sleeve. 'This is good quality. Where did you come by it? You must know I have become something of a connoisseur.'

'No one could tell it,' said Nell frankly. 'Those clothes you are wearing are shocking. You look like a discharged sailor down on his luck.'

'Excellent,' said Kit. 'Precisely the impression I was aiming for.'

'Trust me, you have succeeded. The reason, brother?'

'Why, so that when I slip out to the George & Dragon at night for soup and ale, or to a theatre gallery to remind myself of the world for a space, I may not be recognized as Mr Christopher Kydd of Northamptonshire, of course.'

'Oh, that explains it perfectly.'

Kit's face took on an unwontedly serious cast as they reached the bottom of the staircase. 'It will when you hear all. Nell, glad though I am to see you, I wish you had not come. I believe someone may be trying to kill me.'

Nell's heart skittered, but all she said was, 'Do you think I am grown chicken-hearted, to be frightened away by such a statement as that?'

'No, brat, but I would not have you involved.'

'You are out of luck then, for here I stay until you have told me the complete history.'

He gave a reluctant smile. 'In truth, now that you are here, I would welcome your company and your views. Sometimes the memory of my last weeks in India seems so fanciful I believe I imagined the whole.'

They descended to the kitchen, where Annie had coaxed a fire to life and set a kettle on to boil.

'That was well thought, Annie.' Nell

132

shivered as she glanced around the barren room. 'Kitchens are so lifeless when they are empty. They make the entire house seem dead. No wonder the agent could not let it.'

Kit's blue eyes danced. 'No, no, the poor man did his best, but really it would not have suited me at all to have a household in residence. Good day to you, Annie. I trust you are well.'

Nell's maid sniffed. 'Easy to see you've not changed, Master Kit. Ghosts in the attic indeed!' She looked him up and down. 'Lost your valet, have you?'

'I discharged him. Is that one of Mrs Olivant's pies? I have not tasted cooking like hers since I left home.'

Nell firmly moved the pie out of reach. 'One piece you may have with some bread and butter whilst you tell your tale. The rest is for supper. And you had best unbutton your story before Seth comes in or we'll never hear it to the end, the fuss he is bound to set up.'

Thus adjured, Kit bit into his slice of mutton pie, stretched out his legs in their deplorable trousers, and started to talk whilst Nell buttered bread and Annie made the tea. 'It started in Bombay,' he said. 'You know why I went — to sort out the muddle left to Papa by old Cousin Augustus.'

'Naturally I know,' said Nell. 'And I also

know that you would have gone even had the business been running smoothly and everything in apple-pie order. You were bored, brother of mine, and out-of-reason cross because Papa had a foolish prejudice about the heir to Kydd Court buying a pair of colours and playing soldiers against Napoleon.'

He grinned at her. 'Be that as it may, what I found was that however well the business may have been running when Cousin Augustus was in his prime, it was now not much more than a warehouse of silks, cottons and spices whose contents were being systematically plundered by the rascal who claimed to be our agent.'

'Whom you naturally dismissed. Is he the one who is trying to kill you?'

Her brother reached up a lazy hand to cuff her as she set plate and cup before him. 'If you want to hear, stop interrupting! Yes, I did dismiss him, and no, he was not overly pleased about it.' He frowned. 'I don't know if my letters accurately conveyed India to you, Nell. It is a place utterly unlike England. It attacks all the senses at once. It is beautiful and wild, rich with a thousand scents, colourful and noisy to the point of deafness. The wealthy live in undreamt-of luxury, yet it also houses some of the poorest people on earth.'

'I should like to see it,' said Nell wistfully.

Kit looked at her, his eyes sombre. 'I am not sure I do again. What I am trying to say is that after I had dismissed Jedpoor, taken an inventory, paid those people who had a claim on us and supplied those buyers who had been promised goods but not received them, I thought nothing of it when a heavy bolt of silk fell from the top of a stack, narrowly missing me. Likewise I put down as accidental a runaway cart that would have crushed me against the wall had I not leapt out of its way. Such incidents are part of the fabric of India.' He paused to drink his tea and eat another mouthful. 'I negotiated the sale of what remained of Cousin Augustus's business to a friend who is in trade out there. We were in a popular eating house, people coming and going all the time around us, when he suddenly told me to sit as still as if my life depended on it, then so fast I barely saw him move, flicked away a thin snake which had crawled on to my sleeve and killed it with one stroke of his dagger. A single bite, he told me, would have meant my death.'

Nell's hand had gone to her breast. 'Good God,' she whispered.

'The very next week I was thrown from my horse and we found a thorn under the saddle. That was the day your letter arrived telling me of Papa's death.' Kit's face became remote. 'I cannot tell you what I was feeling for you and Mama. It was impossible to think of Kydd without my father's benevolent presence. I headed straight for the shipping office and can only assume it was grief that made me so slow when a cut-purse took me by surprise and, not content with his booty, tried to make two of me.'

Nell jumped up in agitation. 'Kit, this is dreadful!'

His hand caught her. 'Peace, I am not dead yet. This last attack convinced me that I was, for some inexplicable reason, a marked man.'

'I am glad the heat had not quite addled your brains.'

He ignored this sally. 'Like you, I immediately suspected Jedpoor. My friend asked his local contacts to find out what they could. Word came back that there was a sum of gold available for the person who put a period to the life of Christopher Kydd. Indications were that Jedpoor was involved. Naturally, by the time we caught up with him he had abandoned his wretched family and was long gone. But — and this is when the shock really took hold of me — it seemed he was not the prime mover in the affair. His son, no doubt with an eye to a reward, confided to us that had any instructions arrived for his father, they *might* have had their origins in England.'

'But this is incredible,' cried Nell. 'Like some Gothic novel!'

Kit grinned ruefully. 'Sitting in the kitchen of our town house with a slice of Mrs Olivant's mutton pie inside me and my sister in a fetching primrose gown dispensing tea, it is incredible. Holed up in a stuffy office on the Bombay waterfront with knowledge of my father's death new in my mind, an ill-healed gash along my ribs and an aching head to boot it was rather more plausible, I assure you!'

'What did you do?'

'What anyone would have. I let it be known that I was returning to England, booked a passage on the most comfortable clipper in the docks, had my luggage taken on board, and then went for a last stroll.'

'You have an odd notion of *anyone*, brother,' said Nell acerbically. 'Pray what became of your unfortunate assailants?'

Kit chuckled. 'They ended the evening considerably the worse for wear in the harbour. My friend and I embarked the tramp steamer to Ceylon that night and took passage to Cairo from there. From Cairo we went overland to Alexandria — Nell, I promise you, you have never seen anything like the Nile and the great pyramids — and caught a ship through the Inland Sea to Lisbon. A tortuous journey that we hoped would sufficiently cover our tracks. As a further precaution, my friend persuaded an army officer he knew to smuggle us aboard a troop carrier bound for Portsmouth and thus I came safely home.'

'So safe that you are still in hiding.'

'It is the best way to gather information.'

'From whom? Your highly-placed companions in the George & Dragon?'

But Seth came in at this point. By the time his exclamations of joy (and lamentations over the sorry state of the Kydd stables) were over, Nell had had the opportunity to study her brother more closely and had come to certain decisions.

'How often does the agent bring people to view this house?' she asked, her voice cutting through Seth's painstaking recital of the current owners of Kit's former string of hunters.

'Rarely,' said Kit. 'There is no call to worry about me. London is fortunately thin of company during the Little Season and there are larger and better appointed houses than ours available to hire.'

'Good. Then we may take the Holland covers off the chairs in the drawing room,

138

which will be by far more comfortable to sit in than the kitchen, and ready one of the back bedrooms for me and Annie.'

Kit looked at her, dismayed. 'Nell, you are not staying?'

She patted his hand. 'Only for two or three days. I still have to call on our solicitor and, as I imagine you were too engaged in saving your own skin to think of adorning mine, Annie and I must needs make an urgent visit to Grafton House. This outfit you admire is the only passable one I possess.'

'But, Nell — '

'Furthermore, I believe Seth should set off at first light for Hadleigh, disclose your continued existence to Olivant and Cook and bring Tom back in the curricle to bear you company and be your deputy for when you cannot leave the house.'

'What, has the whole household come with you?' said Kit. He rubbed his head distractedly. 'Yes, Tom Olivant is a famous notion. A footman can go anywhere without attracting attention.'

'If we're to stay, miss, I'll air that back bedroom,' interrupted Annie. 'Seth, you come and set up one of the truckle beds.' She eyed her mistress. 'Strikes me he could bring Lily as well as Tom. She might not have much up aloft, but she lays a good fire and stirs a stew as well as any other and if I'm gadding about to solicitors and warehouses and suchlike with you, she'll serve to keep the place in order.'

Nell cut across Kit's protestations to applaud this as an excellent suggestion.

'I still do not see why you must needs go to Tweedie,' he said once they were alone. 'I do not want to be found. You must realize that.'

'What I could bear to know is how hard they are looking for you,' said Nell. 'Kit, I don't know if I can explain how *wrong* things have been at Kydd this last year. Not just Papa's death and Mama retreating into her own world. I could cope with that if I had a free hand with the estate. But my uncle has mismanaged since the day of Papa's accident and yet all Mr Tweedie says when I remonstrate is that the board have every faith in him. They cannot know the true state of affairs. If Uncle Jasper is gammoning them that all is well when he says to us that we must needs sell your horses and turn away all the servants if Kydd is not to go under, then I would like to find out why!'

Kit was listening to her intently. 'I had not thought of it like that,' he said. 'Yes, it would indeed be valuable to know how the board think Kydd is faring.' He made an impatient gesture. 'I wish I could go with you.'

'Impossible. Even wearing Tom's livery, Mr

Tweedie would only have to take one look at you to know you were no footman.'

Kit's eyes lit up in mischievous glee. 'What if I were veiled?'

'You have been too long in India, brother. In this country, footmen do not commonly wear veils.'

'I was not thinking of going as your footman, my dear, but as your maid.' He jumped up and roved the stone-flagged kitchen. 'It would be easy. Everyone says I make an excellent female whenever we do charades. With a print gown, drab cloak and veiled bonnet, Tweedie will never recognize me! I can sit at the back of his office and listen to all he tells you, for you know you will forget the half of it as soon as you are on the street again.'

Nell was stung by the injustice of this. 'I will not! And pray where are you to find such a costume? I have nothing with me but my nightclothes and my green velvet, and if you think you can fit Annie's dress, your eye for size has sadly deteriorated!'

'I suppose you are right. But it would have been fun.'

'I see your trouble. You are restless, stuck here all day. You must come back to Hadleigh when I have completed my business. We have already settled that Seth is to fetch the barouche from Kydd. No one would see you inside.'

Her brother's face eloquently expressed what he thought of an eighty-minute ride behind a mere two horses in a closed, under-sprung carriage.

Nell chuckled. 'Yes, but Kit it would do Mama so much good! I may tell her I have seen you, at least?'

He took her hand. 'Of course. Nell, I am truly sorry how much you have had to bear this year. Had I been at home — '

'Had you been at home there would have been nothing to bear! You would have sent my uncle back to Windown Park in a brace of shakes and we would have rubbed along very tolerably.' She stifled a yawn. 'Is it dark enough yet for you to buy some ale to go with this pie? Excesses of emotion are extremely tiring. If I do not sup soon and go to bed, I shall in no way be fit to make sense to Mr Tweedie tomorrow.'

He brother flicked her cheek as he glanced at the high window and stood up. 'I shall be safe enough. You will not mind going to Tweedie's alone?'

'I will have Annie with me — and even in the most far-fetched novels that have come my way, no one has ever come to grief in a solicitor's office!'

It had not escaped Nell's notice that for a man in hiding (one moreover who's last received letter from her had been sent a full year previously), her brother was uncommonly well informed about her recent life. She refrained from probing that evening, being both too emotionally worn and too engaged in answering all his questions about Kydd, but was determined to find out his sources the following day.

Before information however, before even a visit to Mr Tweedie, came something of far more importance: a descent on Grafton House to purchase desperately needed materials for her depleted wardrobe. Woken betimes by the unaccustomed city noise, Nell pooh-poohed Annie's suggestion that she should stay where she was until washing water was brought up to her.

'Why should you do all the work when there are only the two of us here?' she said reasonably. 'I am very well able to heat some water on the fire and it is far more sensible for us to wash downstairs. That way I can make a pot of tea whilst you go to the baker and we will be in good time for the warehouse. From all that I have heard, even during the Little Season it will have as many people as it can hold by ten o'clock.'

Thus it was that Nell was alone in the basement kitchen, having washed and set the tea on to draw, when a clatter of boots on the steps announced a surprise caller. A shop-boy almost certainly, carrying purchases for Annie, and as Nell was clad only in a nightgown, with her hair tumbled down her back, she retired in haste to the pantry.

She was utterly confounded when instead of a knock, the visitor shouldered the door open, dropped something heavy and soft onto the flagstones and shouted cheerfully, 'What, up already? Burn me, but hot water's a welcome sight. Mind if I use it? Just got off the night mail — been travelling in my own dirt for hours!'

She knew that voice and could hardly credit her own ears!

Hugo Derringer!

Hugo Derringer, from whom she had last parted on the rise above Kydd Court with tears of rage and helplessness streaked on her cheeks! Hugo Derringer, who had been fully cognizant of her concern over her brother! Hugo Derringer, who had known Kit was in Half Moon Street all the time and had not made the least push to reassure her! It was evident now where Kit's information on her doings had come from: Hugo had been spying on her!

Furious, Nell erupted from the pantry — just as her quarry stripped off coat and shirt and plunged his head and a good proportion of his upper body into the wash water. Nell stood transfixed as with his eyes screwed shut, Hugo lathered soap all over his torso and then proceeded to rinse himself off using her facecloth.

She must have made some small, stunned sound for he tilted his head towards her, water dripping from his dark hair. 'Soap in my eyes. Toss me the towel can you, Kit? Sorry I didn't warn you of my arrival, but I had word that your unlovely uncle returned to Windown Park yesterday, so thought it best to be off. Have you been to the livery stables? Is Conqueror's lame fore better? If so, I'll ride over to see what sort of ham-fisted job your sister is making of living at Hadleigh. Can you believe that chit? Sheer folly! She has got to be the stubbornest, most wilful — Hey!'

The towel caught him squarely across the face. Trying not to even think about his disturbingly well muscled chest, Nell had the satisfaction of seeing his jaw drop as he blinked stinging eyes open and assimilated her presence.

'I congratulate you,' she said in a shaking voice. 'Your powers of recuperation must be something quite out of the ordinary. No one would think to look at it, that that sabre wound was less than a year old.'

Bemused, Hugo glanced at the curving, faded, clearly old scar on his left arm.

'Although as I recall,' she continued (flaying herself for not having realized until that moment that on several occasions he had ridden without the slightest trace of stiffness), 'the discomfort it gave you varied. Next time you must take care to pierce it afresh to remind you of your part. I would be more than happy to help, if you are squeamish about doing the deed yourself.'

'Miss Kydd — ' He put a hand on her arm to interrupt her.

'*How dare you!*' The shock of physical contact — the damp warmth of his palm striking through the thin cotton of her sleeve, the nearness of him, the nakedness of his chest adorned with whorls of fine black hairs and tiny drops of water — gave her voice a hysterical edge. 'I do not know what manners are like in India,' she said, quivering with the effort of not turning tail and fleeing from his overwhelming presence, 'assuming you are Kit's merchant friend and not an invalided-out soldier at all, but I assure you that in England it is not at all the done thing to manhandle ladies, no matter how *stubborn and wilful* they may be!'

That got to him. She saw fire leap into his eyes. 'I was not manhandling you! What the devil are you doing here?'

'Shopping,' she said. 'Which prompts me that I must don raiment more suitable for visiting linen-drapers.' With a certain retaliatory pleasure she noticed his face turn crimson as his eyes took in her unbrushed hair, the broderie anglaise nightgown and her bare toes peeping out from under its hem. 'Although compared to some, I feel positively overdressed,' she said, following up her advantage and just wishing that that same hem was not quite so frivolous. 'I should warn you, Captain Derringer, that my maid will be back shortly. If you do not wish to lacerate any more female sensibilities, I suggest you get a clean shirt out of your valise and put it on.' Upon which note, she poured herself a cup of tea with unsteady hands and retired upstairs to hurl herself in mortification on to the bed she regretted ever leaving.

The 'cup that cheers' cooled her heated body, but did little to soothe the chaos of her thoughts. The image of Hugo's naked, damp skin persisted in coming between her and any rational reflection. 'For heaven's sake! You have seen boys' forms before!' she chided herself. 'Think of all the times you spied from the bushes when Kit and his friends were

147

splashing around in the bathing pool!'

The difficulty was that Hugo was far from a youthful stripling and her rapidly maturing sensibilities knew it! How she was going to meet him again without the heat of anger to sustain her, she had no idea. Nell blushed over and over to think of herself facing him so furiously, clad in only her nightgown and without a stitch on underneath. Outside her door, thunderous steps raced towards Kit's attic. Opening it a crack she heard raised voices and a shout of laughter from her brother. There was an answering growl from his friend. Nell closed the door, finished her tea and dressed with as much speed as her nerveless fingers could muster.

8

Nell was still trembling with reaction when the hackney reached Grafton House. She shook herself and turned to the jarvey with an apologetic smile. 'I beg your pardon. I foolishly neglected to enquire of my footman how much extra to give in addition to your fare. Will you tell me what is appropriate, please?'

Taken aback (being, as he confided, more used to passengers who argued every penny and were convinced he might have taken a cheaper route), the driver named a modest sum and promised to wait until she had transacted her business.

Grafton House was astonishing to country-bred Nell. Northampton certainly had nothing to compare to it. Even her schoolgirl excursions spending pin money in the Pantheon bazaar had not prepared her for the confusion of quite so many bolts of material, quite such long tables piled with bargains, quite so many *people*. 'How are we ever to find what we want?' she said to Annie. 'And how are we to be served when we do?'

'Patience, I reckon,' replied Annie. She

surveyed the most popular tables. 'Push and shove might not go amiss, neither. What's your fancy to start with? Muslin, cambric or poplin?'

'Goodness, I don't know. Stay, what is that amber bolt? Italian crape? At only five shillings the yard? The very thing for a second walking dress. And can you tell what that pale green material is? It is the prettiest colour.'

Rather later, having decided that none of the silks matched the quality she had on, and agreeing with Annie that the two-shilling-a-yard muslins were false economy for they would part company as soon as ever a stitch was set in them, Nell was the thrifty possessor of amber crape, apple-green cambric, cream-checked muslin and Indian cotton spotted with tiny fawn flowers.

'Will there be anything else, ma'am?' asked the assistant.

'I was wanting woollen cloth for a winter pelisse,' remembered Nell. 'In brown or green.' She grimaced at the crowds between her and the wool bales. 'Another day, I think.'

'There's the end of a piece here as might suit you,' said the assistant, rummaging under the counter. 'It's not enough for a pelisse, but it'd make a spencer.' She drew forth just such a fine soft russet wool as Nell had been hoping to find.

Four shillings was duly added to the tally, the parcels stowed in the hack and the jarvey directed to Lincoln's Inn. Before many more minutes had passed, Nell was having her hand wrung by an astonished Mr Tweedie.

'Bless my soul, Miss Kydd, I had no notion you were in town. I understood from your uncle that you and Mrs Kydd were still in mourning and now fixed at Hadleigh. Not but what you do not look delightful,' he added hastily. 'I have always thought it unfortunate that young ladies should be forced by custom to wear such colours as are so unsuited to their looks.'

Nell smiled and rescued her hand. 'Thank you, we are at one in that opinion. Mr Tweedie, I am come on rather a delicate matter. I wish to ask how much you know of what is passing at Kydd Court?'

The solicitor blinked, bewildered. 'What is passing? Why, what should be passing? The last account from Mr Jasper Kydd reported the harvest in and all in readiness for the spring.'

Nell regarded him straightly. 'He did not mention, then, that funds are so low as to preclude my having a season in London next year?'

'What's that?' Mr Tweedie's spectacles fell off his nose in surprise. 'My dear Miss Kydd, there has been a sum set aside for that very purpose these past three years!'

Nell exhaled sharply. 'I knew it! My uncle denies its existence. I collect he has also not apprised you that the estate is in such poor standing as to necessitate the turning away of most of the staff?'

'Poor standing? No such thing, I assure you. No, he has explained it most carefully. He is merely shutting up the Court so that you, and particularly your mother, may enjoy the comfort of having your familiar household staff around you in Hertfordshire. He has already drawn the next quarter's wages for them.'

He had done what? 'Then how does it come about that I am to pay each and every servant at Hadleigh out of the rents, my allowance and Mama's income?'

Mr Tweedie's mouth opened and shut. He sank into a chair for support. 'Such an arrangement would be infamous. Are you sure you have not misunderstood? I know you have not always seen eye to eye with your uncle. He makes no secret of his opposition to your, shall we say radical, upbringing. Perhaps this is his idea of a little joke, a May-game?'

'My uncle would not know a May-game if it were woven in coloured ribbons and dangled in front of his eyes. I have a document signed and witnessed by the notary in Northampton in which I am given complete control at Hadleigh — including the collection of rents and the payment of all household expenses.' She waited for the information to settle. 'I am likewise in earnest about Kydd Court. I believe my uncle to have bungled the management of the estate and falsified his report to the board so that he may not be brought to account.'

The solicitor wrung his hands. 'These are contradictory stories for sure. It must be a misunderstanding. I shall consult with the other board members as to the best course to follow.'

'Dear sir, can you not look into it yourself first? I have had experience of my uncle's uncertain temper. I would prefer not to have him apprised of my actions until you, at least, are convinced.'

'Oh dear. Yes, I do see. I daresay I can find how the finances stand without arousing suspicion.'

'Can you tell me if the search for my brother continues? I know the estate was funding one, for the expense of it was the reason my uncle gave when he insisted on the sale of Kit's horses.'

'I — yes, I was not altogether in favour of . . . Especially when they did not fetch as much as was . . . And since then there have been more demands. Dear me!' Mr Tweedie took his spectacles off and polished them in some agitation. 'I will not conceal from you that after your father's excellent understanding and punctilious address, I find Mr Jasper Kydd rather trying.'

'You mean he is uncivil and rude and rides roughshod over anything not to his liking? Yes, I know it.'

The solicitor looked distressed at her plain enumeration of these failings. 'It would,' he said, 'be unprofessional of me to let personal prejudice affect my work. What you have revealed, however, begs the possibility that I may sometimes have accepted as fact what ought to have been more thoroughly checked. Before I raise anything with my colleagues, I will go very carefully through those papers I possess and will also contact the East Indies Company who were originally entrusted with the search. When are you in London again?'

'I am putting up in Half Moon Street for the present. I have a great deal of shopping to do now that I am out of mourning.'

'Bless my soul, I had not realized your mother was well enough to be in town. I must pay her a call.'

'No!' said Nell hastily. 'I mean, she is at Hadleigh still.'

'Then who resides with you?'

The artless question caught Nell completely unprepared. Clearly it would shock Mr Tweedie beyond measure to know that not only was Nell companionless, she had slept the previous night in a barely-aired chamber and eaten her supper off an earthenware plate at the kitchen table. 'A distant cousin of Mama's,' she invented. 'She is something of an eccentric, but happy to oblige whilst Mama is indisposed.'

'I see.' He paused delicately. 'It occurs to me that you may not have enough funds for your present needs. If I may be of assistance . . . ?'

Nell smiled and rose. 'You are kindness itself, but I am going on very well for the moment. I will not trespass longer on your time. Good day.'

'Your servant, Miss Kydd.'

Nell's last view as he saw her and Annie to the door, was of him polishing his glasses and peering worriedly after her. 'Half Moon Street, if you please,' she said as they settled into the hack. 'Oh, if I have not forgot Mama's pearls! Can we make a short halt at Bridge's in Bond Street? I have to leave something to be cleaned.'

At the jeweller's, Nell told Annie to stay in the vehicle as she would not be above a moment. She deposited her mother's necklace and earrings with an assistant and was just about to step back into the carriage when a piercing call attracted her attention.

'Miss Kydd! Do pray stop! It is you, is it not? I declare we have not seen you these last two years or more!'

Nell stiffened in horror. Surely her ears had deceived her? She turned slowly. Bearing down on her with every evidence of delight were the formidable forms of Lady Norland, Miss Sophia Norland and Miss Euphemia Norland. 'Good day,' she said faintly, 'how, er, unexpected.'

'Miss Kydd! I was sure it must be you, though I declare you are quite grown up! You look surprised! You are thinking that at this season we are generally in Kent. Well, and so we are, my dear, but Sir Thomas had urgent business in the City and the girls and I were determined that whatever he professed, he could not *truly* wish to spend his leisure time in some comfortless hotel, so we have opened the town house for a couple or three weeks as a treat for him and followed him up. He was very much affected to see us, was he not, girls, thinking us still at Deal.'

Nell was obliged to turn her reaction at the thought of the hapless Sir Thomas's face when apprised of his 'treat' into a cough.

Lady Norland was instantly solicitous. 'There, if we are not keeping you out in this horrid wind and without a cloak too. I declare you girls are all the same. Don a fetching costume and all thought of covering it up flies out of your heads.'

Miss Sophia and Miss Euphemia laughed heartily and abused their mama as shockingly old-fashioned.

'I was distressed beyond expression to hear of your papa's sad accident! I wrote to poor Margaret at the time — I daresay she told you of it. In the prime of life too. His neck was broken, was it not? Such a very accomplished and distinguished man that one quite forgave his absent-mindedness, you know. I remember him once not turning up to a rout-party of mine at which I had *told* him he was to be the guest of honour, giving as his excuse next day that he had recently acquired some famous portfolio or other and had become so engrossed in it that he failed to mark the passage of time!'

Nell made a further strangled noise to which Lady Norland fortunately paid not the slightest attention.

'I had not thought it could possibly be a twelve-month yet, but I perceive from your attire that it must be so?' She paused inquiringly.

'The year is just up,' said Nell, hurrying into speech before the flow restarted. 'Which is why I am very briefly in town, my wardrobe being sadly lacking after so long in mourning.'

'Yes indeed. You girls grow at such a pace these days. I am sure *I* never did. Why, Sophia was only presented a year last spring and already we are having to make over her gowns for Euphemia for she has quite burst out of them.'

'Mama, you put me to the blush,' giggled Sophia, nevertheless thrusting forward the bosom of her walking dress to prove her parent's point. 'As though I would not have new costumes this year!' She met Nell's eyes archly. 'And how is Mr Christopher Kydd, may I ask? Is he in town too?'

Nell noticed with fascination two rows of cherry-red flounces peeping out from the skirts of Miss Norland's blue pelisse. Mama had become prophetic! Pinning a social smile on her face, she said, 'My brother is in India still. Forgive me, I really cannot keep this driver's poor horse standing much longer. It was very pleasant to see you again. Pray give my regards to Sir Thomas.'

'Certainly, my dear. I suppose you are being presented in the spring? I must call in Half Moon Street to see if your Mama and I cannot arrange a little something between us. Euphemia is to make her comeout too, you know. It is by far more agreeable to make first appearances amongst friends.'

'Mama is at Hadleigh at present. She is indisposed.' Too late, she saw the same question surfacing on Lady Norland's lips that Mr Tweedie had uttered. 'Her cousin kindly bears me company.'

'You will like the season enormously,' said Sophia, uninterested in this rapid fabrication. 'I have been telling Effy that with two of us out we will have prodigious fun this year. Poor Gussy is quite green with envy.'

'She is sulking at home with Edmund and our governess,' crowed Euphemia, a brash-looking girl as generously proportioned as her sister and suffering from as few inhibitions. 'I go about with Mama and Sophy as I am sixteen now.'

'Which cousin stays with you, my dear? I am giving an informal party on Saturday. Quite small, you know. Just to accustom Euphemia to company. Nothing to be in a quake about. I will send you both cards for it.'

Nell's mind went a terrifying blank. 'Cousin — Cousin Jane,' she said, praying that since this meek spinster never left her elder brother's household in Chester, she would be safe in borrowing her name. 'But we depart for Hadleigh soon, so . . . '

Lady Norland was frowning. 'She would be a Rawdon, then? I am not familiar with all of your dear mama's relations.'

'Yes,' said the harassed Nell, 'Miss Jane Rawdon. But as I say, I am afraid it will not be in our power to — '

'My, look at the time,' cried Lady Norland. 'Come, girls, we must not stand around chatting all morning, you know, enjoyable though it is to renew old acquaintances like this. Your father will wonder what is become of us! Good day, my dear. Remember me to poor Margaret.'

'Good day, Miss Kydd. We will call on you soon,' promised Sophia.

'Soon,' echoed Euphemia, not looking in the least as if she needed to become accustomed to company.

'Over my dead body,' muttered Nell collapsing into the hackney. 'Annie, as soon as Tom Olivant arrives, remind me to warn him that should any of that dreadful family call, I am permanently not at home!'

★　★　★

As it happened, Tom had not only arrived, but was already engaged in setting the

160

knocker back on the front door when the hackney drew up in Half Moon Street. Nell was perturbed. Suppose the agent came to show someone else the house? He would be bound to notice. On the other hand, if Lady Norland did call to leave cards, she would think it strange that there was no sign of occupation. Before Nell could decide what to do for the best, Tom ran down the steps to carry their packages, wreathed in such smiles it was clear he had met Kit and had the evidence of his own eyes of his master's survival.

In the hall, Lily was on her hands and knees, vigorously scrubbing the tiled floor. 'I'll get on to the stairs soon as may be, Miss Nell,' said the little maid, beaming up at her. 'We'll be spick and span in no time, you'll see. Fancy me being in Lunnon! You could have knocked me down with a feather when Seth said as how you'd sent for me! And Mrs Olivant says to tell you the mistress is well, so there's no call to fret over her or to hurry back.'

'Thank you, Lily.' Nell began to feel dizzy in the face of all this activity. She untied her bonnet strings and laid the primrose-trimmed confection on the dusty side-table, from which unsuitable resting place Annie immediately bore it upstairs. 'Tom, where is my brother?'

The footman grinned. 'In the stables. Seth was set he'd want to look over the bays, seeing as how he never got the chance yesterday.'

'Then I shall go to the kitchen and make some tea. No, don't tell me it's not my place or we shall fall out. I have just had the appalling misfortune to meet Lady Norland and her daughters and need to get over the shock and think what is to be done next. By the by, if she ever calls, I am *not* at home.'

Setting the water on to boil in the empty basement, the events of the past twenty-four hours suddenly overtook Nell. The fire blurred and swam in front of her eyes. She sat abruptly at the table, knuckling her temples. Kit, Hugo Derringer, Mr Tweedie, Lady Norland . . . and now Tom and Lily arriving and shaking the house up. She badly needed a period of quiet reflection to sort her thoughts into order.

The kettle boiled. Nell roused herself with difficulty, and had to admit to relief when Tom came in and firmly took over.

'Your parcels are in the drawing room,' he said, spooning tea into a newly-washed Sèvres pot and setting a matching cup, saucer and milk jug on a tray, 'and Lily's put a match to the fire. Ma sent a nice plum cake, but she says you're not to go letting Master Kit eat it all and leaving you with just the crumbs.'

'That sounds lovely,' said Nell. 'I cannot think why I feel so feeble and nonsensical.'

'That's easy to answer, Miss Nell. You're the one as is holding us all together. I wouldn't be in your shoes, not anyhow.'

Nell smiled weakly as she climbed the two flights of stairs to the drawing room. It was nice of Tom to bolster her confidence, but she rather thought there was a simpler cause. She waited until he had set the tray down on a table next to the sofa before saying, 'Is Captain Derringer still with Master Kit?'

'Aye.' To her surprise, Tom flushed and fidgeted with his hands. 'I'm sorry, Miss Nell,' he burst out. 'I should never have kept it from you that I recognized the captain from the time he stayed at the Court when we were lads.'

Sheer surprise kept Nell silent. Hugo had mentioned more than once that it was his first visit to Northamptonshire. But then, he had lied about everything else, why not that too? And if he had been at Kydd before, any number of discrepancies and odd occurrences fell into place. 'The tree house,' she said with certainty. 'He stayed the year you all built the tree house and you broke your leg.'

'Aye, that's how I remembered him so well. He knew what to do to keep me still and comfortable while Master Kit rode for the doctor. I knew I should have told you, Miss Nell, especially when he showed up in the Cross Keys for a yarn and then wanted a sight of Mr Jasper's study, but he said as how he was looking into things at Kydd on the quiet.' Tom took a deep breath. 'And we all know nothing's been right since the master died.'

Nell reached for the teapot, feeling oddly divorced from reality. 'I can forgive you for that, Tom — Captain Derringer is very persuasive — but please, *please* tell me you did not know my brother was here?'

'No, Miss Nell! On my honour, no! I *couldn't* have not told you that!'

She took a sip of tea and felt better. 'On reflection, if you *had* known, you would have saddled the first horse you could steal from under Seth's nose and come hotfoot to find him. Has he told you why he is living here in secret?'

'Aye. Doesn't seem possible, does it?'

'No.' She heard voices on the stair. 'The inspection of the bays would seem to be over. You had best bring two more cups. Or more likely a jug of ale from the George & Dragon.'

Tom grinned. 'That'd find better favour. I'll see to it.'

Nell moved to the table as he left and was

absorbed in measuring the amber crape when the gentlemen entered the room. There was a moment when she felt Hugo Derringer's eyes on her and just *knew* she was going to freeze with embarrassment, but Kit strolled over to join her and made everything easy.

'Back so soon?' he said. 'Are you rolled up then?'

'No indeed,' she replied. 'Those who recommended Grafton House to me had quite the right of it. See for yourself the bargains Annie and I fought the crowds for. We failed only to find woollen cloth for a winter pelisse. So knowledgeable as you are these days, you will tell at a glance how much we ought to have spent.'

'A challenge, is it?' He began to undo the other parcels. 'Do you help me, Hugo?'

After a moment's hesitation, his friend also crossed the room. 'Your ignorance may remain unexposed a while longer. I have an apology which it is imperative I make before I am a single minute older. Miss Kydd, I deeply regret having to deceive you whilst I was in Northamptonshire.'

Nell met his eyes coolly, by no means ready to forgive him. 'I accept the apology, but not the necessity.'

'I didn't know how far I might rely on your discretion.'

'You thought me a gabster. I see.'

'No!' Then less forcefully, 'You must see that it was not my life I was putting in danger.'

She felt a tiny spark in her breast. 'If it had been, you would have told me all?'

He hesitated. 'I might,' he said. 'God knows it was on the tip of my tongue on more than one occasion. Your mother very nearly undid me.'

'Oh. Yes, she recognized you, of course.' Nell bent her head to hide a smile. 'You must have wondered what she would say.'

'I was in terror of it until — '

'Until you realized her utterances are in general so disjointed that few people pay them any heed.'

Hugo put his hand on her arm. 'Please. The deception gave me no pleasure. Will you not listen to our whole account? I believe when your story is added to ours, you will understand why I had to be so careful.'

His clasp was warm and vital. Nell couldn't help comparing it to this morning's touch and remembering her proximity to his bare chest. She took a steadying breath. 'Am I to be allowed a part in this affair after all?'

'Not by my choice. I would have you away and safe. Your brother, however, is of the opinion that you would become enmeshed wherever you were.'

'He is correct.'

'Then as the lesser of two evils, you had best be under our eyes where we can protect you.'

Nell's lips quivered. 'It cannot have been *all* a hum,' she declared. 'You must have once been an officer.'

Kit laughed aloud. 'He was. Bought a pair of colours as soon as he left Eton.'

The dark green eyes flashed sideways to him. 'And sold out as quick when I realized the reality of warfare was a far cry from my romantic imaginings.'

Romantic imaginings? Hugo Derringer? Nell gave a disbelieving snort.

Tom and Annie entered with ale, cold meat, pickles and bread and butter. 'I'll thank you not to finger that muslin dirty, Master Kit,' said Annie. 'Which will I get on with, miss? The crape or the cambric?'

'The cambric I think, though I won't have a pelisse to wear with it. My merino shawl will have to suffice. But cut the pieces in here where it is warm and light. Tom will help you extend the table.'

Kit poured himself a tankard of ale and squeezed Nell's shoulder fondly. 'This is what I have missed,' he said. 'The everyday business of people about me. I approve your purchases, sister. What was the sum?' When she told him, he whistled. 'Grafton House would never do as an outlet for you then, Hugo. They would bankrupt you in short order.'

Nell sat back down on the sofa. 'You really are in trade, Captain Derringer?'

'I am.' Her brother's friend helped himself to bread and meat and ate one-handed. 'I am too impatient for diplomatic life, so as soon as my guardian saw he had correctly predicted my distaste for senseless slaughter, he found me a position with a merchant friend of his.' He gave Nell his sudden, swift smile. 'The life suited me: bargaining, juggling transport and payloads, spotting openings and opportunities. You see now why I was so alarmed to think you cosy with the Duke of Wellington. His aides would have known very well that there had not been a Captain Derringer of the Dragoons these few years.' He took a draught of ale. 'On which head I have to say, Kit, that with the exception of a few interludes, I did not enjoy my sojourn in Northamptonshire. I have never before appreciated the difficulties faced by a professional spy. It is a life fraught with inconvenience. Not in the least the sinecure you would have had me believe.'

Grinning, Kit seated himself next to Nell.

'Inconvenience? How so?'

Hugo leaned one elbow on the mantel-piece. 'Many things of which you, my friend, hatching the misbegotten scheme from the rosy glow of your garret had no idea. Quite apart from remembering to favour his injured limb at all times to give credence to being recently wounded,' he glanced slyly at Nell, 'it was speedily borne in on me that a spy's greatest difficulty lies in preventing an examination of his antecedents. The most idle of questioners would have cut *my* story to ribbons. A spy must therefore stick to dull sporting conversation in order to be thought a bore and not worth bothering about, and dare not exchange pleasantries with pretty girls for fear their mamas will grow interested in his prospects.' His eyes met Nell's — was that a message for her? He continued. 'To which end I might add the indignity of being obliged to wear the same coat for days together and foregoing the services of a valet to give the impression of appearing impecunious.'

'You have forgot that spies must also make a practice of suborning servants behind their mistress's backs,' said Nell.

He smiled at her over the rim of his tankard. 'Does that still rankle? Ah, I perceive Tom Olivant has confessed. Forgive me.'

169

It did not seem to Nell that Hugo had any real expectation of not being forgiven. And he *did* use that smile. 'It is not so much what you did, as that you made me out a fool that I particularly object to,' she said with some asperity.

'It was not my intention, I assure you.'

Nell set her cup down with deliberation. 'Then suppose you tell me what exactly was your intent?'

9

Hugo gestured towards Kit. 'It is your brother's tale.'

Kit sipped his ale as if pondering where to begin. Seen in profile, the crease on his brow gave him a maturity which his open countenance had lacked two years ago. 'I told you of the attempts on my life and the indications that the orders had come from England,' he said at last. 'To begin with, my sole intent was to get out of India by a route unknown to my assailants. En route to Cairo however, and with leisure to think, it occurred to Hugo and me that there was very little to stop my enemy returning to the attack once I was back in this country.'

Nell half rose. 'In England? At Kydd? Ridiculous!'

Kit's blue eyes met Hugo's dark green ones for an enigmatic moment. 'I will not always be at Kydd. And although one can look constantly over one's shoulder, it might become a little wearing, even for me. But if I were not to return, my enemy would imagine his scheme carried. He would think himself safe and be more likely to give himself away. Thus by concealing myself, watching and waiting, it should be a simple matter to isolate him.'

'It seems to me impossible. How would you know whom to watch for?'

Kit's mouth twisted. 'It is not so very difficult, Nell.'

'I do not see it.'

'What your brother is saying is that once the shock of discovering someone disliked him enough to relieve the earth of his presence wore off, it was plain who the prime suspect must be.'

'You were not wont to be so slow, Nell. Who stands to gain by my death?'

Dryness invaded Nell's mouth as she tumbled to their drift. 'My uncle!'

'Exactly so. He stands next after me in the entail.'

'But he hates Kydd Court. He is forever comparing it unfavourably with Windown Park.'

'Land is land. After Jedpoor's son implied the assassination orders came from England, we realized whoever it was would have to know who to contact. Also, they would have had to have sent those orders considerably in advance of the attacks from the mere fact of letters taking several months on the journey.'

'So, if it *was* my uncle — which it could have been because didn't one of his sons go out there to curry favour the year before Cousin Augustus died? — he sent word to Jedpoor before Papa's accident even?'

'According to our reckoning, yes,' said Kit.

'But why? What would he gain by removing you from the succession *then*? Papa might live for years. Mama might have a late-born son as the Graingers did. And if he wants to inherit, he has the most misguided schemes ever for increasing the estate's profitability!'

'I confess that is a puzzle. When we arrived back and Hugo found a missive from Philip Belmont relating that Jasper Kydd was selling all my hunters and turning away the farm hands, I wondered if our ideas about him were wrong and he was simply making the most of my absence to spite me. I know he bore me a grudge from Cousin Augustus leaving the Indian concern to our branch of the family rather than his.'

'So I think also. If you had seen the odious look on his face when he said you might re-hire the servants when you returned, knowing perfectly well that there would not be the means to do it . . . '

'As to that,' said Hugo grimly, 'in his original communication to your brother, the solicitor estimated the Kydd estate as bringing in some four thousand pounds per annum.'

'Four thousand? But the way Uncle Jasper talks, you would think us lucky to clear four hundred!'

Hugo nodded. 'Too many puzzles altogether. Which is why Kit persuaded me to foist myself on Belmont to see the lie of the land.'

'What did Tweedie have to say this morning, Nell?'

'That the accounts show nothing wrong, that my London money was laid by three years ago, that . . . ' Nell raked her fingers through her hair. 'Oh, none of it makes sense! Not but what my uncle must be planning *something* questionable, with his drawing wages out for servants whom I am now paying, staying overlong at Kydd after Mama and I departed and dismissing poor Lily like he did. Plus there is Mrs Belmont's account of his crowded chaise at Oundle.'

Confusion creased Hugo's brow. 'Who the devil is Lily? And what has a crowded chaise to do with anything?'

Kit grinned. 'Lily is the maid who chivied us out of this room earlier in order to polish the furniture into submission. Beyond that I am as much in the dark as you.'

Nell blushed. 'I am telling the tale sideways. What I meant was — '

But Tom interrupted, entering the room

with a tray on which an ostentatious gilt-edged card rested. 'It's all bobbin, Miss Nell,' he said cheerfully. 'She sent a footman. I didn't have to tell anyone you weren't at home.'

'*Sir Thomas and Lady Norland request the pleasure of Miss Jane Rawdon and Miss Helena Kydd at . . . .*' Nell read aloud. 'Oh dear, she really has invited us. How very awkward. I must write a note from Hadleigh giving my apologies.'

'The Norlands?' said Kit with lively horror. 'How do *they* know you are here?'

And from Hugo, severely, 'Miss Kydd, I cannot think it wise to advertise your presence in this house. Your situation is too irregular.'

'I didn't!' said Nell indignantly. 'I am not quite a fool! Lady Norland observed me in Bond Street and if you know of a civil way of escaping someone who used to have a tendre for Papa and who never listens to a word anyone says because she is too busy talking, I wish you would tell me!'

'True, Hugo, the woman is a veritable harpy. She fancies herself literary and was forever haunting my father's set when in town. Face like a horse, I promise you, and her daughters as bad.'

'Which reminds me — Sophia particularly

175

asked after you, Kit.'

'Good God, what did you tell her?'

'That you were still in India. Even Sophia cannot pursue you across two oceans. Oh, and Euphemia was with them and grown just as bold as her sister. Lady Norland had the happy thought that the two of us might like to come out together in the spring.'

'No!'

'I had to invent Mama an indisposition which necessitated my going back to Hadleigh immediately. But then I wished I hadn't, for of course she wanted to know who chaperoned me and I could hardly say it was you, could I?'

'Hence Cousin Jane. I was wondering where she had sprung from.'

'But Tom is going to say that we are neither of us at home to anyone who calls, so that is all right.'

Hugo evidently did not share her confidence. 'I could wish,' he said heavily, 'that you had stayed in Northamptonshire and left this business to us.'

Nell narrowed her eyes at him. 'I might, had anyone thought fit to tell me they were dealing with it!'

'Pax,' said Kit. 'If it isn't like you, Nell, to never let a grudge lie.'

'Excuse me, brother of mine, it is Captain

Derringer who is forever dinning in my ears that I should have stayed at Kydd! And another thing,' said Nell, suddenly struck. 'If you have had these terrible suspicions about my uncle all this time, why did neither of you put me on my guard? What if he had attempted something against *me*?'

Her brother and his friend exchanged glances. 'Oh no,' said Hugo, folding his arms. 'She's ripped up at me already. You tell her.'

'We didn't think he'd bother,' said Kit apologetically. 'You know how he is — never thinks girls are of any account.'

'He tried marrying me to Philip,' said Nell, much offended.

This was too much for her companions' gravity. Kit burst out laughing. 'Hugo told me of Philip's proposal. Lord, I wish I'd been there to hear it!'

'Really, I had no notion my doings were so amusing!' Nell crossed the room in a swish of primrose silk. 'If you'll excuse me, *gentlemen*, Annie and I have a gown to assemble.'

'Ah, Nell, don't poker up,' said Kit penitently. 'Tell us of Lily and the chaise at Oundle.'

Nell sat down at the table next to Annie. Her maid had cut the cambric with dispatch. There was already a seam to sew. Nell

threaded her needle, eyed her brother tren-
chantly and recounted what she knew.' . . . And
I have racked my brains and still cannot think
why Uncle Jasper should be making another
catalogue of the library,' she finished.

'I cannot think why he should be in
Oundle,' said Kit, frowning. 'It is not on his
road to Wiltshire.'

Hugo stood up. 'We need to secure those
pieces of parchment without delay.'

Tom entered again. 'More cards, Miss
Nell.'

'More?' exclaimed Hugo wrathfully. 'Burn
it, I knew how it must be as soon as you set
foot in the metropolis! Who else did you meet
on this ill-advised outing?'

'No one! Lady Norland has evidently
distributed the news. Yes, you see, *Mrs Arthur
Gibbs and Lady Sowerby*, both cronies of
hers. Now what do I do? I can hardly leave
cards in return.'

'Neither can you produce Cousin Jane for a
morning call,' said Kit.

'You can return to Hadleigh and make an
end to this folly!' snapped Hugo.

Nell's lips twitched. 'Poor Cousin Jane,' she
murmured to her needle. 'She was so looking
forward to a sojourn in London.'

Captain Derringer looked as if he was only
not replying with great effort.

Nell sighed. 'Alas, much as it distresses me to gratify you, it would be sensible for me to go back tomorrow and send Seth on to Kydd for the barouche and the parchment. There is reason enough, for there is no covered carriage at the Manor that Mama may use. I will, of course, be uncommonly dull after the excitement of the last two days, but shall amuse myself by exercising the horses, since we left only a stable boy with them.'

'I would as lief you did not have to go,' said Kit, crossing to the fire and stirring it with his toe.

'You differ from your friend then,' said Nell tartly. 'He can hardly keep the joy from his face.'

Hugo shot her an amused look.

She glanced at her brother's averted head. 'Tom and Lily will be here. If you want business around you, sit in the kitchen with them. Tom says the silver needs a deal of polishing. I will come back for you as soon as Seth returns.'

Kit walked to the window. 'Which stable boy did you bring?'

'None. I have hired the son of one of the Hadleigh tenants, though it was more to smooth over the damage my uncle has done there than for any other reason. I must pay conciliatory calls on them all again when I get

179

back. Do you think I might ride around alone, or should Webb come with me?'

'Deuce take it, Nell, they are *your* tenants!' Kit took a restless turn about the room and picked up a book she had left on the side table. '*Marmion*! Of all the romantic piffle! Did you bring nothing decent to read?'

Nell was exasperated. 'If I had *known* you were here, I would have put in *Gulliver's Travels* or a nice body-strewn play of Mr Shakespeare! I will take out a subscription at the circulating library before I go. What is your fancy? Have you read *Waverley* yet?'

'No, will you indeed?' said Kit, brightening. 'That would be first rate.'

'Devil a bit, Kit, where are your wits?' expostulated Hugo. 'Miss Kydd go to Hookham's? Based on this morning's showing, she will meet three acquaintances who will then pass on her being settled in Half Moon Street to a half-dozen more!'

'You talk as if London were swarming with my friends. It is no such thing, I assure you. Meeting the Norlands was the veriest mischance.'

'Nevertheless, if you will oblige me by remaining within these walls until the curricle is at the door, I will go myself to a bookseller to find your brother some reading matter.'

'For pity's sake, Hugo, you cannot keep

laying out your blunt on me!'

'I have so little to spare after all,' retorted Hugo. 'It will be slight enough. I need not buy new. There are plenty of shops in these times selling goods others are compelled to dispose of.'

Nell wrinkled her nose. 'Pawnbrokers.'

'You're very nice all of a sudden. Where do you think Hugo got these duds of mine from?'

Nell shuddered and reapplied herself to her seam. 'I have been trying not to think of them.'

Kit laughed and beguiled her with a wicked description of the soldier's uniform, complete with resident wildlife, with which he had disguised himself in Portugal. From there, the conversation turned to the men's travels. Nell sewed and listened and if she thought Kit and Hugo made light of their experiences, she kept her own counsel. She was just so glad to have her brother safe. When Tom came in with candles and the information that he had taken a can of hot water to her room that she might change for dinner, she was honestly surprised at the passage of time and how much of the new dress she and Annie had completed.

'Though it is only a meat pie with buttered mushrooms and plum cake and fruit and a cheese to finish,' the footman said apologetically.

'A feast,' said Nell with a smile. 'I expected nothing more.'

Hugo needed no pressing to dine with them instead of repairing to his solitary lodgings. There was a smile in his eyes when Nell re-entered in her velvet gown. It recalled to her their first ride and his comment that green suited her. It gave her a mortifying check to realize that what she had then taken for admiration had been simply a cover for asking questions about the Kydd estate, but she hid her discomfort by roasting her brother on his lack of sartorial attire. At the end of the evening, Hugo promised to be back early enough the next day to set Nell, Annie and Seth on their way to Hadleigh.

'Though I am sure it is only to make certain of my really having left London,' said Nell to her brother as they parted for the night.

Kitt chuckled. 'Hugo will never believe females are not all lovely, fluttering creatures whom one has a duty to protect and cherish.'

'I had not discerned an abundance of cherishing,' said Nell, thinking of the forthright language that had issued from Captain Derringer's lips the day she had saved Jenny Copping from the bull.

182

'He does not know you as I do.' Kit squeezed her shoulders fondly. 'Deuce take it, Nell, I wish you were not going. I had forgotten how complete you make a place. Hugo remarked on the change here straight away.'

He had? 'It will be for but a few days, and you may visit Mama yourself as soon as we can smuggle you there in the barouche.'

'That will be something. I have wronged her indeed. Is she very much changed?'

Nell paused before she answered. 'She has been better since we came to Hadleigh. I believe she will be more improved still once she sets eyes on you.'

'Nell, you do understand it was not my wish to deceive you? It was simply that I could not see how to let you know I was alive without my uncle getting wind of it.'

Nell raised her eyebrows. 'I believe that once in my *presence* you had no such desire, but in my absence it was easier by far to let yourself be persuaded into caution by your friend.'

Kit reddened. 'Hugo is a good sort.'

'Just a little inflexible in his opinions, I know. Good night, Kit. Sleep well.'

'And you, Nell.'

★　★　★

The next morning they had finished breakfast, and Nell had pulled on her gloves and
was adjusting her primrose-trimmed bonnet
in the looking glass ready for the journey,
when Hugo's knock was heard at the door.

He tossed a parcel to Kit and eyed Nell's
elegant figure with disapproval. 'Have you no
cloak? I cannot like you driving across
Finchley Common looking so modish.'

'Well, if that is not the least handsome
compliment I ever received!' said Nell
indignantly. 'There is simply no pleasing you.
First you are all afire for me to leave London,
now you wish me to stay for lack of a
concealing garment.'

'I did not say that. I would as lief my
friend's sister were not held up by highwaymen is all.'

Nell gaped at him. 'Highwaymen? In broad
daylight? Goodness, I would never have taken
you for a reader of romances. I had been
certain Pope was more to your taste.'

Hugo eyed her frostily. 'There is a great
deal of sense and fine irony in Pope's
writings. Indifferent imitators alone have
caused his fall from fashion. Why do you not
wear your grey pelisse?'

'Because it was the most depressing
garment ever and I have given it to the
poorhouse with the rest of my mourning. I

have only the pale grey silk and black taffeta cloak left and *they* are going to the Poor Clares at the earliest opportunity!'

'I agree nothing could have shown you to less advantage, but would it not have been prudent to — '

'Where did you get these?'

Nell and Hugo broke off their argument to stare. The words were Kit's, but the cracked, shaken voice was a far cry from his normal insouciance. His hands grasped three books. Discarded paper and string lay unheeded at his feet.

'A small bookshop near my lodgings,' said the captain. '*Not* a pawnbrokers,' he added pointedly to Nell. 'I know how you admire Cowper. Was I wrong?'

'These are from Kydd! This is my own copy of *The Task*. The flyleaf has been removed, but see, here is the very inkblot I made when Papa would have me copy out my favourite passage for Dr Porter on purpose to show that not all small boys were savages.'

Nell flew to her brother's side. '*John Donne — Songs and Sonnets*. Oh Kit, surely this is ours also? Of the Shakespeare there can be no doubt. I know every crease in the pages. What does it mean?' She looked in bewilderment from her brother to his friend

185

and caught the spark of realization that flew between them. 'My uncle!' she said. 'It must be my uncle! *A quantity of bundles and parcels*! Good God, what else has he disposed of?'

'Proof at last!' said Kit, his eyes hard with triumph. 'He is selling off the Kydd library to make good the deficit in the accounts and has invented a new catalogue to show nothing amiss. That must also be why he drew the extra wages! Out with one hand and in with the other. Nell, you must see Mr Tweedie at once.'

Nell was in such a rage that it was a few moments before she could control her voice. 'The effrontery! He must imagine me an imbecile to think I will not notice that these books are missing from the library the moment I return! How dare he sell what Papa spent a lifetime collecting! Captain Derringer, will you conduct me to this bookshop straight away that I may see what else is there?'

'But you are going to Hadleigh . . . '

'With our possessions even now being spread across half of London? I thank you, no! Let Seth go straight to Kydd with the bays to fetch those parchment scraps. It may be they are the missing flyleaves.'

'Surely they would be vellum.'

Nell seared him with a look.

'The horses,' he said, not giving way. 'Who is to exercise them if you do not?'

Nell felt she would scream if he voiced one more objection. 'We will bring them here!' she said through gritted teeth. 'First we shall go to the bookshop, then you can accompany me to Hadleigh in the curricle, appeasing your qualms about my attire by shooting dead any stray highwaymen we may meet. Seth will then take the bays on to Kydd whilst you and I ride Snowflake and Valiant back!'

'Famous!' cried Kit. 'By Jove, it will be something to see Valiant again.'

'To be tended by whom?' said Hugo, exasperated. 'You seem to have forgotten your groom will not be here. Do you think to turn stable-hand yourself?'

'Livery,' declared Kit in high good humour.

'Oh, you do not mind laying out my blunt on your horses then?'

Nell stamped her foot. 'You must see that I cannot return tamely to Hadleigh while this perfidy goes unchecked! Do you mean to help me or not?'

Hugo began to itemize exactly why he had never liked a scheme less. Kit interrupted, serious again. 'Save your breath, Hugo. You need someone at the bookshop who will recognize our editions, and much as I wish otherwise I cannot do it. The bookseller must be questioned on where he had them. If my uncle brings in more volumes another time, the man might in all innocence report our interest. The moment I am described, my uncle will know the game is up and we will never bring him to justice.'

'He may describe Miss Kydd as easily.' But Hugo's tone was weakening.

Nell exchanged a triumphant look with her brother. 'That is of no account. It would not even enter my uncle's head that having once ordered me to Hadleigh, I am not still obediently there.' Seeing him yet dubious she said soothingly, 'Come, we shall be a newly-engaged couple setting up our library on a budget, and make such a good play of it that your bookseller will never think us anything else.'

Hugo Derringer, if anything, looked less charmed than ever.

★   ★   ★

If the proprietor of the bookshop was surprised to see his customer back so soon, he hid it admirably. In one blink of an eye he took in Nell, hanging lovingly on the gentleman's somewhat stiff arm and hurried forward eager to be of service.

Nell blushed and dimpled as Hugo

explained stiltedly that his betrothed had been so enraptured by the three volumes he had brought her that she had insisted on accompanying him to choose more of her favourites for their embryonic library. 'For I do feel,' she said, fixing large, soulful eyes on him, 'that there is nothing quite so cosy as a shelf of old friends in one's first home.'

The bookseller beamed, assuring her that she was quite in the right of it. And whilst she flitted from rack to rack uttering small cries of '*Robinson Crusoe* — the very thing for a winter's evening, I do declare!' and '*Waverley*! Why, this is almost new!', she heard him make bold to wish Captain Derringer joy.

'It is not often a man is fortunate enough to attract a prize combining both beauty and brains, sir. You must be a happy man indeed.'

'Oh, I am,' said Hugo stoically.

'What a splendid establishment this is,' trilled Nell, getting into her role and dancing back to the counter with an armload of volumes. She tapped Hugo's gloved hand playfully. 'You see now how clever I was to dissuade you from going to Hatchet's? I will make you a famous, thrifty wife indeed! I daresay our library will cost but a fraction of the price by purchasing it here and there is something so comfortable, you know, about housing books that have been someone else's treasures. Do you not think these works are happy to be going to a good home to be cherished and read over again?'

As she skipped off again, Hugo said to the proprietor, 'I am glad you have so many of my betrothed's favourites. When I suggested we set up a small library, I had not fully comprehended her range of taste.'

The bookseller beamed over the growing pile of books. 'A delightfully well read young lady,' he said. 'You are indeed fortunate. Doubly so, for most of these were brought in only the other day by a gentleman who had suffered financial reverses and was forced to find immediate relief.'

'I am sorry to hear it,' said Hugo. 'There are many such cases these days. I hope he did not think it long before he might be brought about?'

'As to that I couldn't say,' said the bookseller. 'I know I owned myself surprised that he would not pawn the volumes, so as not to be irretrievably parted from them, but he said if he did, the temptation would always be there to redeem them instead of using the money for the better good of his family.'

'Sound judgement indeed. I wish him well. Was his appearance still quite gentlemanly? Some people can let themselves go when they find themselves in such straits.'

'No, no, a very dapper dresser indeed. A smart blue coat with a grey waistcoat and matching pantaloons. And he spoke in a very genteel way. I am sure if he had not said the money would do his family more good than ever printed words could, no one would take him as being in need.'

Nell had added more books to the counter whilst listening to this exchange and now said, her eyes wide. 'How very singular. I am convinced one could live on poetry for weeks on end without experiencing hunger! Do you not think so, my love?'

Captain Derringer's lips betrayed a faint tremor. 'I believe most people would compound for bread and cheese once in a while rather than a steady diet of ambrosia.'

She giggled at the apt rejoinder. 'You are ungallant. Oh, *Paradise Lost*! May we buy that as well?'

'Ambrosia, indeed,' said the proprietor, taking the edition from her. 'Will there be anything else?'

Nell tucked her hand into Hugo's arm and peeped up at him from under the brim of her bonnet. 'I think not, or I shall never be brought shopping again. Have I quite ruined you?'

Just for a moment, his deep green eyes met hers with unusual warmth. Under her gloved hand, the muscles concealed by a fashionable coat of Bath cloth tightened. 'I have a few shillings left,' he said, then with his other hand deliberately pinched her chin. 'And I can always extract my payment later.'

Nell gasped with shock and tried to pull away before remembering her part. 'So you can,' she said, her cheeks hot.

The bookseller smiled indulgently as he made up their parcel. 'Where shall I have the boy deliver it, sir?'

A reprehensible smile creased Captain Derringer's mouth. 'We will take it with us,' he said, releasing Nell to feel for his pocket book. His eyes met hers again. 'And perhaps try the effect of milk and honey instead of a light nuncheon. I wonder, my dear, if we should rather look to employ Lord Byron than a cook? Our dinners will then be something quite out of the ordinary.'

Nell's foot in its serviceable half-boot accidentally came into contact with his toe. She didn't think it had made the slightest impact through the gleaming Hessian, but it relieved her feelings wonderfully. 'You are teasing me,' she said with what the proprietor considered to be delightful good humour. 'You know very well that it would hurt poor Bessie's feelings dreadfully if we do not engage her sister.'

To her consternation, he drew her hand

back inside his arm. 'True. We shall have to remain conventional. I wonder, sir, could your boy summon us a hack?'

He retained her arm outside the shop with enough firmness that Nell felt she had definitely provoked him too far. Then, as he casually addressed the shop boy, she realized he was doing it to leave himself no way of holding the parcel. Clever, she applauded, and listened appreciatively to the way he drew the lad out.

'At least this is one package you will not have to carry through the streets.' He patted his pocket with his free hand as if in search of something.

The boy's sharp features noted the gesture. 'Don't worry me, sir,' and as a gleam of silver appeared in the captain's glove added in a burst of loquaciousness, 'That were all bunkum what the cove as sold them books said about pop-shops.'

'Really?' murmured Hugo. He tossed the shilling idly.

The boy's eyes followed the gleaming arc. 'I reckon as how he was stringing *him* a line.' He jerked his head at the shop. 'When I opened the door, he had a chaise waiting with more stuff in and the first thing he said to the driver was to take him to old Levy's in Kettle Street.'

The shilling passed into the lad's hand. 'Levy being a pawnbroker, I take it?'

'That's the dandy, sir.' The boy waved energetically at a hackney carriage that had just turned the corner.

Hugo's hand went back to his pocket. 'What day would that have been, I wonder?'

The boy opened the door of the hack for Nell. 'Saturday, sir, not a doubt. Thank you, sir.' He passed Hugo the parcel of books and shut the door with a gratified flourish. 'He was close-fisted an' all,' he yelled as the jarvey signalled his horse to walk on.

Hugo gave the direction. He had disengaged Nell's arm, for which she was profoundly thankful. The moment of intimacy in the book-shop had been most disturbing. She lifted her chin resolutely. 'It is proved then,' she said. 'Such a costume as the bookseller described I have often seen my uncle wear. Why do we go to Half Moon Street and not to this Mr Levy?'

He looked at her with a measuring gaze. 'Is there nothing you are not equal to?'

She blushed, sensing a reproof. 'I am afraid I embarrassed you. I thought it best to act as unlike ourselves as we might.'

'You succeeded. I do not know whether the proprietor most envied me or sympathized for allying myself to such a rattlepate.'

'At least if he describes the purchasers, my uncle will never suspect us. But you have not answered me. Do we not investigate what he has pawned?'

'A pawnbroker's establishment is really not a place to which a gentleman would conduct a young lady.'

'Oh.' Nell digested this. 'Then how are we to know what is there?'

'I will take your brother this evening under the pretext of getting more clothes. That will give him sufficient excuse to poke about. The pledges are not likely to be in plain sight; a broker is not permitted to sell unredeemed items until the loan-period is up. Indeed, it is to be hoped that there is nothing Kit prizes too highly on view. A show of anger on his part would be fatal. The slightest suspicion that any articles are stolen would have Mr Levy disposing of them as soon as may be.'

Nell bit her lip. She saw her companion glance at her.

'Be easy,' he said. 'After dark, it is safe enough for Kit to be abroad. His face will be shadowed and he is a competent actor, you know.'

'I do not fear for him,' said Nell in a constrained voice. 'At least, not overly so. It is me. Will you despise me if I say I am glad I am not to go? So lately as I have known privation, I own I cannot feel anything but distress at the thought of people being obliged to pawn their property in order to live. I know I should feel oppressed surrounded by the evidence.'

To her surprise, Hugo pressed her hand gently. 'Such delicate feelings do you credit.'

She gave a rueful smile. 'You must be amazed to find I have any.'

'Believe me, you are constantly surprising me.'

10

The journey to Hadleigh had not started propitiously. Hugo had been adamant that though a lady driving her groom through London might not occasion comment, a lady driving a *gentleman* would attract the very attention they were trying to avoid. Nell had perforce to sit rigidly next to him whilst *he* drove *her* curricle. To be fair, he was no mean whipster, but there certainly did not seem to be as much room on the seat as when she shared it with Tom or Seth. Concentrating on the horses would have taken her mind off the uncomfortably narrow gap between his hip and hers.

Behind them, Seth was telling over the route to Kydd in a semi-audible rumble which did nothing to distract her. For want of any other occupation, Nell checked the contents of her reticule for the fourth time: a letter from Kit to Mama; scraps of fabric to match against thread and trimmings for the new gowns; the list of items Annie wished Mama's maid to pack.

The road dipped then rose again. A bend caused the capes of Hugo's greatcoat to brush against her pelisse. Highgate came into view. Nell pulled the strings of her reticule tight and gave herself a mental shake. This was ridiculous, there was still a full hour's journey ahead of them. 'A lady may drive a gentleman around Hyde Park,' she commented brightly. '*The Lady's Monthly Museum* says it is quite de rigeur, provided one does it with distinction.'

'Miss Kydd, in a weak moment I may have agreed to help bring your horses to London, but I give you fair warning that if you ride within a mile of Rotten Row before you are legitimately chaperoned, I will book the first passage back to Bombay and leave you and Kit to your own devices.'

That was better. Nell felt an immediate sense of release at his astringent words. She grinned. 'If it is not an impertinent question, why have you not done so already? By my reckoning, you have been away from your business well over half a year. Surely it must suffer?'

'Bombay is not my only base,' he said. 'I also have an office in Alexandria where we stopped to allow me to catch up with certain of my affairs, and another one in Brussels. I thank you for your concern, but my agents are accustomed to doing without me for considerable periods. In truth, it is only my own vanity which insists on burdening them with my presence from time to time.'

This Nell did not believe for a second. 'Kit told me you did all the buying.'

He looked fleetingly gratified at her knowledge. 'It is true that I have had the good fortune to find quality products, but once contracts have been agreed and enough money has changed hands to ensure the weavers do not take their next lengths elsewhere, nor the farmers their crops, the rest runs itself.'

'Oh well, if you do not wish to puff off your consequence . . . '

'I assure you my industry is mostly restlessness. I enjoy being up and doing.'

Nell glanced at him sceptically. 'Which is why you interested yourself in my brother's predicament and buried yourself in the country without even a change of coat, I suppose?'

The ancient Berlin they were following up the hill suddenly took it into its head to stop in order that its occupant might hail an acquaintance. Muttering a restrained oath, Hugo negotiated the obstacle. Nell assumed his confidences were over. She was once more trying not to fix her mind on the proximity of his broad shoulders and close-fitting breeches when he said in a rather different tone, 'Twelve years ago I arrived at Eton bereft of parents, friendless, wary, and stiff with

199

diplomatic manners. Within the space of a single day, I had lost half a term's allowance to your brother at whist, won a quarter of it back playing Speculation, suffered a black eye alongside him when he disputed the right of some senior boys to set us to their chores, dosed myself liberally with the best gingerbread I had ever tasted from his provisions and been reduced to tears when he recited Shakespeare to us after lights out.'

His cheeks reddened under Nell's astonished gaze. He looked straight ahead, his attention on the horses.

'I expect that would have been the Agincourt speech,' she said, pulling herself together. 'Kit always used it on tutors when he wanted a half-day holiday.'

There was a stiff pause. 'Minx,' he said without rancour. His hands in their tan leather gloves relaxed on the reins. 'Throughout our schooldays, Kit supplied the vivacity and easy generosity of companionship missing from my life and I repaid him by pulling him out of God knows how many scrapes. I could no more not help him now than I could fly. He would do the same for me without thinking twice.'

'No doubt about that. Thinking twice has never been Kit's forte. But he would not have your business suffer because of our troubles.'

Again she got the quick smile that made him appear so much less stiff. 'You may be easy on that head. My parents left provision for my sister and myself. My guardian has ever been at pains to ensure my portion unconnected to any rise and fall in my profession.'

Nell felt a prickle of interest. 'You have a sister?'

'Yes, Isabelle. You would like her, I think. She has been married these last three years to a diplomat attached to my guardian's service in Vienna.'

Hugo talked of life abroad so well and entertainingly that they passed through several hamlets without Nell being aware of them. Then she heard Seth stir and say, 'Finchley Common. Keep 'em steady, Captain. I'm a-watching out.'

'Really, Seth,' she scolded with a laugh. 'You said as much coming down and never a sinister stranger did we see nor are we likely to! Not only is it broad daylight but we are in an open carriage. What brigand in his right mind would be likely to attack us?'

'None, I trust,' said Hugo. But it was noticeable that he drove the bays at a rather smarter pace across the wide stretch of open ground.

★　★　★

Mrs Kydd was embroidering new chair backs when they arrived. 'Nell,' she said, giving her daughter a kiss without evincing the least surprise. Her eyes went to the tall figure whom Olivant was divesting of his greatcoat. 'Hugo, my dear, how delightful to see you again.'

Nell dropped to the footstool by her mother's feet and warmed herself at the fire. 'You did recognize him, Mama! I wish you had let me know, but it was clever of you not to tell Uncle Jasper.'

'Jasper?' Her mother's face looked vexed. 'Now, don't say he is here!'

'He is not,' said Hugo, coming forward and saluting Mrs Kydd's hand. 'Last heard of in Wiltshire, I promise you. May I second your daughter's admiration. I was in a quake lest you gave me away.'

'But why ever would I?' said Mrs Kydd, bewildered. 'I rarely speak to Jasper at all if I can help it. I cannot imagine why he is so much with us when it must be plain he is not wanted.'

'Kit thinks he is trying to steal Kydd,' said Nell casually. She heard Hugo's sharp intake of breath, but kept her eyes on her mother. She was not deceiving herself: Mama was more alive to the world even than she had been three days ago. 'I have a letter from Kit for you, Mama. He sends you all his affection, but cannot come himself until Seth fetches the barouche.' She took her mother's hands. 'He believes his life to be in danger. It is important no one suspects him to be in England until we have sent my uncle packing for good.'

Margaret Kydd gave no sign of having heard these last words. 'I knew you would find him.' She turned a glowing face on Hugo. 'She always could, you know.'

'I remember,' said Hugo. 'Roosting in the tree house, swimming in the bathing pool, potting rabbits on the heath . . . '

'You should not have tried to lose me so often,' said Nell. 'Mama, you do understand? No one is to know Kit is in London?'

'I do not *comprehend*,' said her mother, 'but I understand perfectly. I will tell nobody outside the household. You shall give me the whole history at dinner.'

Nell bit her lip. 'I'm sorry, Mama, we cannot stay. I promised Kit we would ride back today. Seth is to go on to Kydd for the barouche. Is there anything he can fetch for you?'

Her mother smiled. 'No, my love, I have everything I need here.'

Nell left her reading Kit's letter, directed Hugo to the stables and herself escaped to the kitchen for a conference. She found Cook incensed that Tom had seen fit to conceal Hugo's identity from them.

Olivant, polishing glassware, let his wife have her grumble out, but took the professional view. 'Discretion,' he said, a note of approval in his voice. 'Say what you will, Mrs Olivant, discretion is what a gentleman wants in his footman.'

Nell gave a wry smile. She had always known Tom was Kit's man rather than her own. But there were more pressing matters to discuss than her footman's loyalties. She acquainted the staff with the discoveries of the morning and asked if they had any ideas on how to ascertain what else was missing from Kydd.

Olivant spoke. 'Hannah was taken on at Belmont House, Miss Nell. She's dusted the Court effects every day these past seven years. If any are gone astray, she'll know it. Could you write a note to Mrs Belmont asking if she may be excused for an hour to pack something up for you? Seth could deliver it, drive Hannah back and tell her what you really want her to do.' He pursed his lips. 'Providential, bringing all the Madeira with us. I'll wager not many of the master's bottles are still in the cellar. But *they* won't have been sold, they'll be on Mr Kydd's own table.'

'I hope their contents were so shaken by the journey as to render them undrinkable,' said Nell. 'I cannot understand how he thought to escape detection. We would be bound to notice the depredations when we return.'

She was aware of a wave of embarrassed pity from her household. 'It's as plain as the nose on your face,' said Cook. 'He don't think to see any of us back there again. First he kicks us out, then makes *you* as mad as fire and so set on proving yourself, you'd die rather than crawl home.'

Nell swayed. Her uncle had planned this rape of the Court? For how long?

Cook tutted. 'Where are my wits? It's tea you need, Miss Nell. Go back to the drawing room and I'll send something in directly.'

'No, or at least yes, but not yet. I must first tell Seth about Hannah.' She forced her whirling thoughts to still themselves. 'I had hoped to ride around the tenants also, but I don't believe there will be time.'

She said much the same to Hugo, encountering him outside, and was surprised and touched when after a small hesitation he said, 'I am at your disposal another day, if you should wish it.'

'I would be very grateful. But why should you take so much trouble?'

He gazed out over the railed paddocks. 'I have no land myself, so cannot pretend to any vast knowledge,' he said, 'but looking about me, it seems clear that this would be a tidy manor had it not run so sadly to waste. So little time as you have been in residence, yet it is already evident that you are setting improvements in motion. Such endeavours are deserving of help.'

Nell eyed him suspiciously. 'It is not that you think to persuade me to stay, then, and finish what I have started?'

His look of pained affront was almost convincing. 'What do you do with your stableboy when his charges are gone?' he said, changing the subject.

In the corner of the yard, young Dick Farmer swept industriously.

'I had thought to set him to the gardens for the nonce,' said Nell, and had to hide a smile at the boy's dismayed expression. 'What else can I do?' she murmured to Hugo. 'The cob will hardly occupy all his time and it would undo my good work with his father if I lay him off again.'

'Valiant is strong enough for two,' suggested Hugo. 'If the lad would like a trip to London . . .'

Seth's voice issued approvingly from inside the stable. 'That's a rare good notion,

Captain. Master Kit'll like it better'n letting strangers have the care of his mount.'

Nell's mouth fell open. 'You cannot mean it? Balance a squirming boy before you for fifteen miles?'

'Lunnon? Oh, Miss Nell, can I?' Dick had dropped both his broom and all pretence of not listening in on the conversation. 'I'll be right as a trivet, I'll be. I won't get me 'ead turned by all the sights and the finery, nor I won't get led astray, I promise you!'

'What about squirming?' said Hugo.

'Strike me dead if I do!'

The scheme had merit, but Nell was not about to let Hugo win so tamely. 'I see what it is,' she said, recovering her wits. 'You wish to save yourself the expense of keeping my horses at livery.'

'What else?' said Hugo with a grin. His eyes danced. 'And Dick can tend Conqueror and his tack as easily and I shall save on that expense too.'

'He can an' all,' agreed Seth, taking this statement seriously. 'Like that, he will. Good horse, your Conqueror.'

Dick fervently promised to polish as much leather, fill as many nosebags and shine whatever number of bits and stirrups as he was required to, just so long as he might see the fabled capital.

So Nell and Hugo visited one of the tenants after all to acquaint them with their youngest son's absence. Nell reflected later that she could scarcely have done a better day's work. The Farmers were flushed with pride at the compliment to Dick's abilities: the mother would sing Nell's praises to any neighbour rash enough to call within the next few weeks, and the father would now be on her side at all future tenant meetings.

Back at the Manor, Nell and Hugo found they were not to be allowed to leave without a meal inside them. When Nell protested that she could not possibly do justice to the array set out in the dining parlour, Cook said in a no-nonsense voice that what wasn't eaten would be packed up to take back to Half Moon Street. From previous experience, Nell knew it would be impossible to convince Mrs Olivant that the horses were overloaded until her cook actually saw them sunk up to the fetlocks in mud with her own eyes, so she merely cast an apologetic glance at Hugo and ate as quickly as good manners permitted.

The hour was considerably advanced by the time they were ready to set out. Nell bit her lip at the way Hugo was eyeing the position of the sun. 'I am sorry,' she said. 'I should have foreseen that Cook would bring dinner forward. That is the disadvantage of servants who have been acquainted with one for ever. They are apt to insist they know best. But we should still complete the journey in daylight, should we not? The horses are fresh and we will not have the weight of the curricle to hold us back.'

He looked down at her, his deep green eyes wry. 'I own I would prefer to leave you here for the night and come back for you tomorrow, but as I see your lips even now framing a protest, I will keep my reflections to myself.'

She dimpled at him. 'Very noble of you.'

The first part of their route was accomplished speedily enough, but at Ware they were held up due to a carriage ahead of them having been put into a ditch by another, and the horses and grooms from both trampling about the road in a decidedly perilous fashion.

'The poor people,' said Nell, seeing a dazed lady in a lilac-striped gown with a purple turban askew on her head sitting by the roadside being revived by a younger girl and her maid. A boy stood on the fallen coach shouting encouragement to the grooms. Nell reined in and called down impetuously, 'Shall we stop at the next posting house and ask them to send assistance?'

The girl looked up. 'That would be kind

indeed. We passed a hostelry not long since which our groom said he would go back to, but I fear it is taking all his skill to steady the horses.'

Nell immediately gave the girl her assurance, and by speaking softly and calmly to Snowflake, got her mare past the trampling hoofs and nervous whinnies of the carriage horses without mishap. She looked up to find Hugo's eyes on her. 'Well, what else could I do?' she demanded. 'You and I can hardly right the coach by ourselves.'

There was a lurking smile in his eyes. 'You disappoint me. I was beginning to think nothing beyond you.'

'That is mere foolishness.' She trotted beside him stiffly. 'What is it? Why do you look at me so?'

'I beg your pardon. It is simply that most people would have passed by such an accident with no other thought in their head than to be glad it was not they who had been overturned.'

'The less credit to them.' She looked at him challengingly. 'What would you have done, had you been alone?'

He smiled. 'Exactly what you did. Except — '

'Except what?'

'Except I would most likely have asked Dick or that youngster to hold Valiant whilst I lent the grooms a hand.'

Nell's grip on the reins faltered. She glanced back involuntarily. 'Oh! Should we — ?'

He reached across and laid one gloved hand on hers. 'No, Nell, we should not. We will deliver the message as promised, leave our goodwill for their journey and continue with ours. I mislike the look of this sky.'

Nell glanced up, startled. Clouds were starting to build and there was a cold edge to the wind which had been absent earlier. 'Mayhap the wind will blow them away,' she said, but having lived in the country all her life, she did not believe her optimistic words and could tell that Hugo did not either.

They did not linger at the posting house. Nell saw Hugo eye the lowering sky and matched her pace to his. The first fat drops of rain fell just as they gained Finchley Common. Hugo slowed from a canter to a trot.

'It will do us no good here to let the horses stumble,' he said brusquely. 'Have you a cloak you may put on?'

Nell shook her head. 'There was not room in the boxes. Do not fear, it will not be the first wetting I have received.'

'Even so, you had best wrap the horse blanket Seth tied to the saddle around you. I would not have you catch a chill whilst in my charge.'

As they penetrated further across the heath, the gloom deepened and the rain increased. All the lurid romances Nell had ever read unfurled their pages in her head. She was not laughing at the idea of highwaymen now — there were no other travellers on this stretch but themselves, and every bush seemed to hold twice its complement of shadows.

'Nell,' said Hugo's low voice after perhaps ten minutes of her seeing ghosts behind every tree. 'I do not wish to alarm you, but I believe there to be a horseman in that copse ahead of us to our right.'

Terror sheeted through her. She lifted her chin. 'What must I do?' she said, amazed to hear her voice so calm.

'If it is only one man, we are safe. He cannot hope to cover both our horses. Indeed if it were not for the weather I believe we would be safe anyway, but we unfortunately present a picture of a young family carrying all our possessions with us and on an evening like this, two or more men might think to cut their losses and take what they may get before laying up in the dry for the night.'

'You could run one of them through with your sword, Captain,' came Dick's thrilled whisper.

'I could of course,' agreed Hugo, a shake of amusement in his voice. 'But what would become of Miss Kydd whilst I was doing so?'

'Give her one of your pops?'

'The very thought, Dick, strikes terror into the breast. I think subterfuge is our best answer. Miss Kydd, could you contrive to slump somewhat in your saddle?'

'As if we have been riding a long time and are weary?' said Nell, catching his drift. She did so on the instant and even managed to sway convincingly.

She heard his low chuckle. 'Capital. And now, Dick, curl up against me and feign sleep.'

'Ain't we to shoot 'em, then?'

'Curb your disappointment. We shall gammon them finely instead. They will think us bone-tired and easy prey and will relax their guard. And when I give the word, we will up and gallop past them faster than this year's Two Thousand Guineas winner at Newmarket.'

Dick curled obediently against Hugo's chest, clutching his bundle. Nell slowed Snowflake even more and swayed again. Hugo bent towards her solicitously. 'They are coming,' he said on a thread of breath. 'Two only, thank God. Break when I tell you, 'ware rabbit holes, and do not stop for anything until you reach the end of the common.'

Nell nodded to show she understood and jerked herself upright. Hugo's eyes must be honed indeed to pick out the shadows even now slipping from between the trees. She supposed it must come from having been a soldier and wondered with a shiver what he had *not* told her about life in Sir Arthur Wellesley's army.

The two men brought their horses down the rise and stood squarely in their path. They were big men, dressed in old, greasy greatcoats and had coloured neckerchiefs masking the lower halves of their faces. What light there was scudded across long-nosed pistols, trained unswervingly on their victims' hearts. Nell found she didn't at all have to fake her cry of alarm, nor the way her right hand went instinctively to Hugo.

'What is it?' said Hugo to their aggressors. 'What's amiss?'

'Nothing at all, my hearty,' said one of the men, nudging his horse forward. 'Leastways, not if you and your good lady sees things our way.'

'What-what does he mean?' said Nell in a high, quavering voice. She pressed gently on Snowflake's flank to make her mare skitter nervously to the left. To her satisfaction, the second man moved to cover her, opening up the road ahead.

On Hugo's lap, Dick yawned. Hugo put an arm around him protectively. Nell could almost see the first man's sneering smile under the neckerchief as he relaxed his guard.

'Rough evening,' said the man. 'You'll be wanting to finish your day's journey. And so you shall, just as soon as my partner and me have taken a memento or two of our meeting.'

Nell gave a faint moan and shrank in on herself. Watching her, her captor grinned nastily. She saw the tension go out of his thigh muscles and his hand slacken on his mount's bridle.

'Don't touch her! You may have my money! All of it!' said Hugo, transferring both reins to his left hand and feeling desperately inside his coat with his right.

'Now, now,' said the first man, lowering his pistol slightly and reaching forward to halt Hugo's arm. 'I'll do all the fetching out that's necessary. Very sensible of you, if I might say so. My partner and I appreciate it. You'd be surprised the number of — '

'*Now!*' yelled Hugo, and toppled the man with a hard sweep of his right fist even as Nell gave Snowflake the off and surged forward, bent low over her mare's neck.

For several seconds she was aware of nothing except the twin thudding of her heart and Snowflake's hoofs as they flew over the ground. Then she heard other hoofbeats coming up hard and fast behind.

She tangled her hands in the mare's mane, urging her on, not daring to look round, not daring to check that it was indeed Hugo and not their adversaries. It wasn't until the edge of Finchley Common was gained and she saw signs of habitation ahead that the blood pounding in her veins and head cleared enough for her to hear her companion say, 'Easy, Nell. We have left them far behind. You have done very well. Very well indeed. Oh, my poor girl — quick, Dick, down and take the reins. Whoa, there. Whoa.'

11

Dry and warm again in her velvet gown and merino shawl and sipping a restorative cup of tea before the drawing room fire in Half Moon Street, Nell felt her face blaze anew at the culmination to the Finchley Common adventure. That her weakness had done her no disservice in Hugo's eyes was immaterial. The feelings he had engendered when he'd caught her as she'd slid from Snowflake's saddle were beyond her power to describe. They had taken her completely by surprise. No one had any right to be so strong and yet so delicate of touch. No one had any right to laugh so softly in her ear and call her a poor, brave girl in such bone-melting tones. And no one, no one at all, had the right to cradle her against their immensely comforting chest as if she were the most precious thing in the world.

The faintness had been only momentary. No sooner had Hugo felt her move than he'd released his hold and set her gently on her feet. 'Are you all right?' he had asked. 'Do you wish to rest before we proceed? There is an inn nearby.'

'No, no,' Nell had said, her eyes anywhere but on him, her face radiating more heat than the fire in the Great Hall at Kydd when the wind was from the east. 'I should like to be home and dry as soon as may be.'

And he had lifted her back into the saddle as if she weighed *nothing*, hauled Dick up before him and they had continued without mishap.

The drawing room door opened. Nell's heart instantly set up a faster beat. For a moment she hardly saw Kit, all her attention was on Hugo coming in behind him. Their eyes met. Nell felt the deep green of his scrutiny arrow straight into her soul. 'Are you recovered?' he enquired in a voice which seemed to bring angel choirs and trumpet voluntaries along with it.

'Thank you, yes.' Embarrassed, she turned her gaze aside and focused on her brother. In preparation for his foray to the pawnbroker, he looked more disreputable than ever. In addition to his distressing clothes, he had crammed a perfectly dreadful seaman's hat over his bright hair, he was unshaven, and the unmistakable aroma of the stables showed that he had renewed his acquaintance with Valiant prior to appearing before her.

He grinned. 'Well? Shall I be recognized?'

'Oh, I do hope not,' she said.

Kit crowed with laughter and bid her a careless farewell. 'Don't wait up, my dear. We may drop into the George & Dragon for a heavy wet on the way back.'

Nell wished them good hunting and turned resolutely to threading an emerald ribbon around the neck of the cambric dress. She would be glad to get it finished; she was becoming tired of wearing the primrose silk every day.

Tom came in to remove the tea tray. Nell asked him whether Dick Farmer had settled in all right.

Tom chuckled. 'Tucked up happy as a grig in the stall next to Valiant. Said Seth would have his hide if he didn't bed down in the straw with the horses. The captain's going to take him to the livery stables in the morning to show him where to fetch hay and oats and suchlike.'

'Captain Derringer is?' said Nell, surprised. 'That is very good of him when it is hardly his concern.'

'Said as how he was going to fetch Conqueror anyroad, so young Dick might as well come along and make himself useful.' Tom grinned. 'Lad's powerful struck on him. It was 'the captain' this and 'the captain' that all the time he was eating his supper. Diddling them highpads has made him a

219

right hero in Dick's eyes. Those cronies of his at home are going to be sick of the sound of his name.'

Nell smiled too. 'Yes, he will be in high fettle to return with such a tale, though for my part I would as lief the journey had *not* proved so eventful. How has my brother been today?'

Tom grimaced. 'In a rare old hobble. He don't like not to be doing when other folk are. That's why he was so full of bounce tonight. We shan't see them back early.'

Nell laid the dress aside with a sigh. 'It is no use, I feel by far too stupid to sew tonight. Will you tell Annie I should like to retire early, please?'

'She's been making your room ready this last half-hour. Never you fret, Miss Nell. I'll wait up for Master Kit.'

Nell ascended the stairs trying not to feel disgruntled that she was surrounded by people who knew her better than she did herself. It didn't help that she was perfectly well aware of what was at the root of her fidgets: she had exhibited a maddening, feminine weakness in front of Hugo Derringer and he had honoured her for it. He *liked* frail, delicate creatures who sat in drawing rooms and sewed and fainted when held up by highwaymen. He was comfortable with them.

And just for a moment, in his arms on the edge of Finchley Common, Nell had known an earth-shattering longing to be exactly what he desired. She shook her head. It would never do. She was a stubborn, self-willed hoyden and everything he disapproved of. They would be back on their normal footing by midday tomorrow.

The next morning Nell awoke betimes to find Annie searching the contents of the bandboxes brought from Hadleigh.

'Stockings,' said her maid without preamble. 'Did Rose not put them in?'

'I didn't look. It was so late by the time Cook had insisted on us eating that I simply checked the straps were secure and set off. Have I none left? We could go to Grafton House if you wish. They were cheap enough there.'

'Likely we'll have to. We forgot linen for underskirts last time.'

Nell chuckled. 'It must have been the sight of so many bargains. Quite blinded us to the necessities of life. We will go directly after breakfast.'

The expedition was successful. Nell returned to Half Moon Street having also expended a judicious sum on figured muslin, a pair of ivory satin slippers and emerald green kid gloves which would go very nicely with the cambric gown. 'Still no wool for a pelisse though,' she said as Tom paid off the driver and gathered up the packages to take them indoors. 'Is my brother with the world yet, Tom?'

'The captain knocked him up before fetching young Dick along to the livery stables,' said Tom cheerfully. He broke off, looking up the street. 'Here he is now.'

Nell turned. She had no time to control the glad skip her heart gave at the sight of Hugo striding towards her with his Bath cloth coat buttoned up against the cold, his buckskin breeches well brushed and his Hessians gleaming. Warmth blossomed inside her and she felt a smile curve her lips.

'Miss Kydd, Tom Olivant tells me you have been out this morning. Is this wise? Have you forgot what happened the last time?'

Nell's smile faded. Chagrin made her voice sharper than she intended. 'No, I have not, which is why I went so early. And yes, it was wise, unless you would have me sit around barefoot.'

'Better barefoot than discovered to be living here unchaperoned! Your fictitious relative will hold up near as well in London society as my exploits in the Peninsula would have done against a real soldier.'

'Stuff and nonsense,' said Nell hotly. 'As I

do not intend to visit, 'Cousin Jane' will do very well.'

'I cannot like it.'

'No one is asking you to. Do you stay on the doorstep all day to argue or will you come in?'

'I am not arguing. I am giving my opinion. It is madness for you to — '

They were interrupted by an eye-smarting town coach which pulled up with much rattling of traces and stamping of hoofs. Until the footman descended and opened the door, Nell assumed the coachman was simply resetting his horses. She was horrified to see the statuesque bulk of Lady Norland, resplendent in taupe satin with puce stripes, squeeze herself out of the aperture.

'I was sure you would not yet have gone to Hadleigh. Sophia! Euphemia! It is as I predicted. Miss Kydd is still in town and will be able to come to our party.'

'Lady Norland, how do you do? I fear I — '

But Lady Norland's attention was rivetted on Hugo Derringer. 'You have a visitor, I see. Will you not introduce us?'

It was only by averting her eyes from Hugo's thunderstruck face that Nell was able to keep her countenance enough to say, 'I beg your pardon. May I present Captain Derringer, a friend of my brother. Captain

Derringer, Lady Norland, the wife of Sir Thomas Norland.'

In the blink of an eye, Lady Norland assessed Hugo's looks, his crisply tied neckcloth and the cost of his attire and came up with a possible marriage prospect for her daughters, both of whom were also now out of the coach. 'It occurred to me,' said the matron majestically, 'that as I am unknown to Miss Rawdon, she might feel awkward about attending our little gathering, so I have come on purpose to introduce myself and set her mind at rest.'

Nell swallowed. 'You are kindness itself, but I am afraid it is not in my power to reward your thoughtfulness. My cousin was not feeling at all the thing this morning and I doubt very much of her receiving visitors today.'

At which Hugo bowed with what Nell considered to be remarkably indecent speed and said, 'You will wish to sit with her. I shall call another time.'

'No, no,' cried Lady Norland, not to be baulked of her prey. 'No need to run away on that account. Even should Miss Rawdon be indisposed, I can be reckoned no mean chaperone, you know.'

Nell was left with very little option. Avoiding Hugo's fulminating eye, she invited the company inside. Lady Norland accepted in high good humour, subjecting the hall furnishings to a thorough scrutiny as she sailed past, making Nell glad of Lily's obsession with polish for the first time since the little maid had come to London.

Sophia and Euphemia were not so restrained. 'I have never been in Half Moon Street before,' said Euphemia, looking about her. 'Are all the houses so small inside?'

'Pretty much, I believe,' said Nell, leading the way upstairs to the drawing room. 'Could you bring refreshments, Tom, for Lady Norland and her daughters? I take it my cousin keeps to her room still?'

'She does, miss,' said Tom, an impassive London footman to the life.

'Inform her maid I will come to her later.'

'Perhaps, Mama,' said Sophia Norland archly, settling herself in the drawing room, 'Miss Kydd and Captain Derringer would rather we did not stay.'

'Naughty puss!' said Lady Norland, tapping her daughter's hand. 'As you see, Captain, I have not raised my girls to be mealy-mouthed.'

Sophia looked complacent, thrusting her bosom forward to advantage as she un-buttoned her swansdown-trimmed pelisse and fussed with the arrangement of her flounced skirts.

Hugo's countenance was more polite and distant than ever. 'I assure you my errand hardly requires the presence of a chaperone. It is merely to inform Miss Kydd that I have lately returned from Wiltshire where I met one of her uncles. A Mr Jasper Kydd. He is quite well and sends his compliments.'

Nell opened her mouth to reply to this piece of fiction, but once again was forestalled by Lady Norland.

'Wiltshire! Well I declare! A business acquaintance of Sir Thomas's is just up from Wiltshire. I daresay he also knows of your uncle, Miss Kydd. You will be able to ask him tomorrow.'

Sophia fluttered her eyelashes. 'I hope you are able to come to our party, Captain Derringer.'

Nell stiffened. She saw Hugo note her reaction with an infinitesimal glance. The corner of his mouth twitched. 'Thank you, but my man of business is due in town and I am likely to be engaged with him for the next two or three days.'

Sophia pouted, but Euphemia stared. 'You would rather talk business than come to a party?' she said in astonishment.

'When my agent travels from Brussels on purpose to see me, yes.'

'As would any man of sense,' said Nell

tartly. 'And especially so lately as the region has known conflict. Captain Derringer takes his commitments seriously.'

'It is to his credit then that he makes the time to tell you your uncle is well,' flashed back Sophia. She fluttered her lashes again and leaned forward artfully to brush a stray cotton thread from her skirt.

To Nell's fury she saw that Hugo had ceased to look frosty and was observing Sophia Norland's manoeuvres with appreciation. Tom Olivant, however, entering with a tray of Madeira, ratafia and lemon biscuits, was unprepared for the full glory of the low flounced neckline and had to pause for a moment on the threshold to regain his aplomb.

Lady Norland accepted a glass of ratafia and said comfortably, 'Well, and if he comes so far, I daresay he will not object to an early close to business. I depend on seeing you, Captain Derringer. It will be quite informal, you know. And if you have not any evening gowns as yet, Miss Kydd, and are troubled about dressing up, what you have on will do very nicely.'

Nell kept her tongue behind her teeth with difficulty, merely murmuring, 'You are very kind,' and waiting for the interminable half-hour to finish. There really was a great deal to be said for Mama's practice of conducting morning visits internally. One was so much more in control.

At length Lady Norland cast a regretful glance at the last two biscuits on the plate and rose from the sofa. 'May we drop you somewhere, Captain Derringer? The carriage will easily hold one more if you do not object to a slight squeeze.'

'I am sure Effy and I do not mind a crush,' said Sophia with a coquettish glance and a wriggle of her bosom.

'Oh no, the more the merrier,' agreed Euphemia, aping her sister's stance.

But this was too rich even for Hugo. 'Thank you, but I have left my horse in livery and must retrieve him.'

'Oh,' gushed Sophia. 'You rode here this morning! For my part, I think there can be no finer sight than a gentleman on horseback.'

Unless it is the sight of a gentleman in regimentals, thought Nell waspishly. Or a gentleman in evening dress. Or a gentleman at the altar.

Her unwelcome visitors departed, bearing Hugo with them. Observing them from the front window, Nell saw him bow and set off up the street, to be out of sight before the ladies had crammed themselves back into their equipage.

'Lord, I thought they would never go,' said Kit coming up behind her and peering likewise around the curtain. 'They talk even more than I remembered and to just as little purpose. What the deuce possessed you to invite them in?'

'I invite them?' said Nell bitterly. 'What sort of ninnyhammer do you take me for? Lady Norland invited herself. That woman is a *leech*.'

In the street, the footman finally got the carriage door shut and swung himself up as the coachman gave the showy chestnuts the off. Kit grinned. 'I'd have given a monkey to see Hugo's face when they suggested he squeezed in with them. Fancy staring at those two articles all the way to Lamb's Conduit Street!'

'Kit! Were you listening at the door for the entire visit?'

'I didn't see why you should have all the fun.'

'If that is your idea of fun, brother, I can only suggest you make haste to find a fitting costume for their 'informal gathering' tomorrow night. You will likely laugh yourself into stitches.' She let the curtain fall and moved back towards the drawing room.

Kit followed more thoughtfully. 'I would if it could be done. I should like to meet this gentleman from Wiltshire and find out how my uncle comports himself at Windown Park.'

Hurried footsteps sounded on the treads. Nell glanced down the stairwell to see Hugo on his way up. He had evidently ducked along the first practicable alley and come in via the rear entrance.

'Craven fellow!' cried Kit. 'Why would you not go with them when you were asked so particularly? It is my belief Sophia Norland's heart is quite broken.'

Hugo awarded his friend a lifted eyebrow. 'That would be a feat indeed.'

'Can it be that you did not succumb to the young ladies' charms?'

'In general I prefer such charms to be less obvious. Miss Kydd, because of Henri's visit, I fear I cannot ride with you tomorrow as I promised. I have arranged for a groom from the livery stables to attend you on Valiant instead.'

Nell was inclined to be resentful of such high-handedness, but Kit said with a frown. 'You really expect Henri? I thought that a hum to put off Lady Norland.'

'No, I received word this morning that he expects to be in London later today.'

'And did he say whether he had any news of — ?'

'It was only a brief note.' Hugo turned to Nell. 'We must also put off scouring bookshops and the like, but as you cannot expect Seth's return until Tuesday with information on what else is missing from Kydd, I hope it makes little odds.'

'No indeed,' said Nell. 'How shocking if I should complain of neglect after my homily on good business practice to Miss Norland. Dear me, what it is to be hoist with my own petard.'

Hugo gave her the smile which had such a peculiar effect on her insides. 'At least promise me that you will not go searching for Kydd effects on your own?'

'No need to worry on that score,' said Kit. 'She will have me to entertain her. When do you expect to be finished with Henri?'

'I cannot tell. I may call in tonight if it is not too late.'

★   ★   ★

'Why is it that men imagine women to be such poor creatures?' Nell asked Annie later as she tried on the new gown in front of her glass. The soft green became her well, the emerald trimming around neckline and sleeves at once lifting it out of the ordinary and enhancing the sparkle in her hazel eyes.

231

'So they can feel superior, miss,' said Annie through a mouthful of pins. 'Else they could hardly live with themselves if all they had on their side was brawn. That's the hem finished. Just the underskirt to fix.'

Nell rotated thoughtfully as Annie crawled and pinned. 'Did you never wish to marry, Annie?' she asked.

'Aye, when I was younger. But he went off to be a soldier and I misliked the thought of such a life so I bided where I was.'

'I should not let the hardship stop me.'

'No, I daresay. But if you was to wed a soldier, he'd likely be an officer with money of his own for quarters. The common army in wartime, which is all my suitor could offer me, is no place for a respectable female.'

'Captain Derringer said fighting did not come up to his romantic imaginings. That is why he sold out.'

'Then he is a sensible man. Why folk must think cutting each other down heroic, I don't know. I've no patience with it.'

Nell looked affectionately at her maid's bent head. 'Did he never come back, your sweetheart?'

'It would have made no difference if he had. What's done is done.'

★ ★ ★

Nell and her brother spent a peaceful evening, talking over old times at Kydd, and discussing the improvements they would make once he was out of hiding. By morning, however, Kit was restless with inactivity. When Nell and the livery groom got back from their ride (a very boring one since the man had evidently received orders from Captain Derringer not to go above a trot and to keep away from fashionable haunts), he set to work rubbing Valiant down saying, 'What an age you have been. I've a good mind to get my hands on some groom's togs and come out with you myself another day.'

'No reason you shouldn't at Hadleigh. But too many people know you in town. The penalty of having been the most handsome buck on the circuit in previous years. How did you amuse yourself before I got here? You were quite alone then.'

'Slept during the day and went out at night. Galleries are only a shilling, though you don't see much of the stage. I gave up on all the opera at Drury Lane but I've got the farce at Astley's pretty much by heart now.'

'Splendid. You shall perform it for us this evening. Lily will never have seen anything like it. I do understand, Kit. You feel trapped inside this house. I too, but for different reasons. You are fettered by caution, I by conventions. Women have far less freedom than men.'

'Poor Nell. When I am at liberty again, you can keep house for me. That will be more comfortable for you.'

'Why thank you, brother,' said Nell. 'You are all thoughtfulness.' She went back to the house to change out of her habit resolving that as soon as Seth returned, she would get Kit to Hadleigh if she had to render him senseless herself.

She came down fully prepared to turn the drawing room into a makeshift theatre, but instead found Kit waiting, his eyes sparkling with incipient mischief.

'What are you hatching?' she said with foreboding. She looked at the wrecked bundle on the table. 'Why have you undone my dress? Tom was to have taken it to the Poor Clares today.'

'How would you like,' said Kit, 'to go to the Norland party tonight?'

'To view the ostentation on Lady Norland's table and watch Sophia Norland thrusting her bosom at every eligible male who comes within her orbit? Not at all.'

'No, to meet this gentleman from Wiltshire who may know of our uncle.' He shook out Nell's pale grey silk and held it up against himself. 'Do you not think I would make a splendid duenna, my dear?'

Nell's mouth fell open in shock. 'Kit, you cannot! Indeed you must not even dream of such a thing! No, really, you *cannot* dress up as Cousin Jane. Not in a roomful of people. Think of the scandal! You will never get away with it.'

A devil-may-care smile played about her brother's mouth as he tugged off his coloured neckcloth and unfastened his waistcoat. 'You think not? With rouge, paint, your shawl and Annie's veil? Shall we see? You were never wont to refuse a challenge, Nell.'

'This is madness,' said Nell, watching him helplessly. 'Act the farce for us instead. I have not been to a play these eighteen months. Oh for heaven's sake, Kit, that is not the way. You will tear it clambering in like that. See, hold the gown so . . . ' and before she knew it, she found herself easing the loosely-fitting sleeves over her brother's arms.

'What do you think?' Kit viewed his reflection in the glass with satisfaction. He prodded the limp bodice. 'We will have to pad it. Does this truly fit you?'

Nell blushed scarlet. 'Yes it does! Although the colour never became me as well as it does you. But it will not do, Kit, you know it will not. Private theatricals are all very well, but even if Tom shaved you afresh and we hid

235

your face behind quantities of veils, the gown is quite six inches too short and you do not talk like anyone's maiden aunt.'

'Now that, my love,' said Kit, simpering behind his spread fingers and lisping in an unnerving imitation of Charlotte Grainger, 'is untrue as you very well know. Have you forgotten the way I fooled Philip Belmont when I dressed up in Mama's gown one Christmas?'

Nell remembered the occasion with a jolt. Kit had been a quarter sprung and quite appallingly convincing. She stared at her brother in consternation. He was looking in the glass again and trying the effect of a remnant of linen she had left on the table as a cap. Daring shimmered all over him. Nell clutched at her hair. She knew this mood. If she made too much demur, he was entirely likely to go to the Norland party on his own. 'I cannot think it healthy, this passion you have for donning women's clothing,' she said, hoping to joke him out of it.

'You could put a taffeta flounce on the gown,' Kit coaxed. 'You could, Nell, you know you could. And we could crimp my hair at the front. And we need not stay so very long . . . '

★   ★   ★

Jolting on the uneven paving in a hackney carriage several hours later, with Kit, powdered, painted and unrecognizable in silk and taffeta on the seat beside her, Nell decided she must have run mad. 'Your friend is going to wash his hands of us once and for all this time. And I cannot say I blame him.'

Kit rapped her knuckles in the selfsame gesture that Lady Norland had used the day before. 'He will never know, my love.'

'How can you be sure? Suppose he calls on us this evening?'

'He is engaged. His man brought round a note.'

'Kit, *please* reconsider. This is not a festive-season charade. Think of the scandal should you be discovered. And although I have no great love for Lady Norland, she would be mortified to know she had been made a fool of.'

'Hush dear, you are beginning to sound like Hugo himself.'

Nell ground her teeth. Her brother seemed to have donned a new personality along with the grey dress. He wasn't stepping out of it even to argue with her.

They had arrived too late to be announced. This was the single agreeable circumstance of the evening. For as Nell stood on the threshold of a sumptuous crimson-and-gold saloon with fifty chandeliers blazing a testimony to Sir Thomas' business prowess and Kit murmuring, 'Isn't this nice, dear? I am so glad we came,' in her ear, she realized three appalling things in swift succession.

The first was that 'informal' was a misnomer. Her primrose walking dress would never have done. Even the green cambric, suitable though it was for the sort of cards-and-light-supper-and-very-young-ladies party she had imagined, positively shrieked 'country nobody' in this gathering.

The second was that Kit was going to behave outrageously. He already had an amiable simper on his veiled face, had waggled his gloved fingers at an imaginary acquaintance and had accepted a glass of ratafia with a tittering laugh.

The third thing, though, was worse. The third thing was so much worse that Nell almost turned tail there and then and fled for the safety of the departing hackney. Hugo Derringer, as fine as she had ever seen him in a dark green tail-coat, light green brocade waistcoat with silver embroidery, and cream-coloured skin-tight pantaloons, was even now swivelling his head from Sophia Norland's garnet-bedecked décolletage and elaborately curled coiffure to stare straight into Nell's eyes.

12

Hugo looked at her for a full second before transferring his gaze to Kit. Then he returned his attention to Sophia Norland's blatantly inviting costume and gushing conversation. Like water dousing flame, Nell's desire to flee vanished.

'Should we pay our respects to our hostess?' said Kit, placidly sipping his ratafia. 'It would be shockingly remiss not to.'

Nell lifted her chin and turned her back on Hugo. 'By all means.' She slid her gloved hand under her brother's arm to make their way through the glittering knots of people.

Lady Norland professed herself in transports to see them and was delighted to make the acquaintance of 'Cousin Jane'. To judge by her stressing what old friends the families were, confiding her determination to help launch dear Helena into society and sighing soulfully over dear Christopher's continuing sojourn in India, she had by no means given up on the idea of Kit (and his acres) as suitable husband material for one or other of her girls.

Nell could wish the case otherwise. 'Cousin

Jane' agreeing earnestly that all young men with the temptation of a recent inheritance needed the steadying influence of a good wife was almost more than her stretched nerves could bear. She wished again that they had not come when Lady Norland extricated a useful fondness for whist from Nell's supposed chaperone and declared her intention of introducing Nell herself to a poet whom she had on good authority would soon become all the rage.

'I hope the play is not too high,' said Kit with a titter on the way to the card tables. 'People are apt to get so cross when more than penny points are at stake.' He sat down, dropped his fan, beamed guilelessly at his fellow players and fussed with his reticule. Nell left him with profound misgivings.

The poet was a young man who had a great deal to say about himself and whose style was as artificial as his golden locks, starched shirt points and elaborate cravat. Nell murmured platitudes, fanned herself, and wished the clock would move faster and that the candles were less plenteous.

'Miss Kydd,' said a voice of ice behind her shoulder. 'May I fetch you a lemonade?'

It wasn't so much a request as an order. Nell's legs buckled treacherously. The poet sniffed and stalked off to deliver his

240

pretentious nonsense to someone more appreciative. Nell laid her hand on Hugo's arm. 'Thank you,' she said. 'It is a trifle warm, is it not?'

The sinews under his close fitting sleeves of dark green superfine were taut with anger. The tension transferred itself to her and shivered up her arm. 'What are you doing here?' he said between clenched teeth.

Nell decided on an airy tone. 'We thought we would try whether this Wiltshire gentleman knew of my uncle.'

She could almost feel the effort Hugo made to keep the snarl out of his voice. 'Did you indeed? Then it will doubtless delight you to learn that Mr Stapleton not only knows of your uncle, he is currently negotiating the sale of some land to him. If your name is mentioned anywhere in his hearing, the news that Jasper Kydd's insubordinate niece is in London will get back to Wiltshire before the week is out!'

Nell's hand flew to her breast. She had *known* this was a foolhardy outing. Not that she was going to give Hugo the satisfaction of admitting it. Besides, she had feelings of her own to relieve. 'Really? When we arrived you seemed too preoccupied in enjoying certain *obvious charms* to be doing any investigation.'

'Such was my intent,' he snapped. 'Had you observed more closely you would have seen I was using the conversation with Miss Norland as a cover to listen to Mr Stapleton's dialogue with Sir Thomas.'

'You are becoming a proficient dissembler then,' she said, keeping a social smile on her face to mislead any watchers, 'for I should have sworn there was nothing on your mind than what was in front of you.'

'Let us hope Sir Thomas is of the same opinion and does not make the connection between us. You must go home at once. It is madness your being here. Where is your misbegotten brother?'

'Fleecing the dowagers of their penny points. You are being ridiculous, we cannot possibly leave this soon without giving offence.' As she spoke she smiled and bowed to two ladies who had left cards in Half Moon Street.

Hugo thinned his lips, barely containing his temper. 'Kit has gone beyond the bounds this time. Do not deny this mischief was his idea. It is intolerable of him to have embroiled you in it. Whatever possessed you to agree?'

'He would have done it alone else. You know how he is. He hates it that others are expending effort on his behalf, while he chafes at home. He will be piqued that you saw through his disguise. Did you recognize him immediately?'

'No.' Hugo's voice held unwilling admiration. 'I have frequently remarked that your brother is a consummate actor. I should not have known except that seeing you and remembering that grey gown, I deduced who your companion must be. Just pray no one else has reason to suspect. I suppose your servants are all aware of this caper? Did Tom Olivant at least not try to make him see sense?'

'Tom? It was Tom who shaved him and who went to the pawnbroker for shoes and gloves that would fit!'

Nell was not aware of any bitterness in her tone, but Hugo's next words were less censoriously spoken. 'I will talk to Kit. Persuade him that he feels faint, so lately has 'Cousin Jane' been unwell.'

Nell glanced across the room to the card tables. 'I doubt you will meet with any great success whilst he is winning.'

'Then I will cut into the game and take a hand against him!' It was Hugo's turn to force an amiable smile onto his face as he bowed across the room to an acquaintance. 'Your brother may be the better able to sustain a part, but I can generally make my cards count for more. Offence or not, you must go. I will do all that is necessary here.'

Nell drew breath to protest that he took altogether too much on himself but they were interrupted, first by Lady Norland who had noticed the poet's defection and came to introduce the stammering second son of one of her oldest friends to Nell and then by Euphemia Norland who was pursuing her mama to remind her she had promised dancing.

'Well, and so we shall have dancing, my love. I daresay the musicians can play Scottish and Irish airs as well as these fine orchestrations of theirs.'

'Famous!' said Euphemia, clapping her hands. 'I'll warrant you are a prodigious dancer, Captain Derringer.'

'I am a better card player, Miss Norland.'

Lady Norland chuckled and rapped his knuckles familiarly with her fan. 'All you gentlemen are the same. I declare Sir Thomas would play whist all evening if he was allowed. But I fancy I have the upper hand tonight! After all, it is not every day you get the opportunity to dance a reel with a pretty girl, now is it?'

Nell had to bite her cheek in order to keep a straight face. It was perfectly obvious which *pretty girl* was under discussion here. Good manners made it impossible for Hugo to do ought else but request the pleasure of leading his hostess' daughter into the first set. She herself accepted Mrs Gibbs's stammering son's invitation for much the same reason.

Euphemia was exultant. 'Sophy will be mad as fire that I have secured you and she not. I must tell her at once!' She sped off on her mother's heels.

'A delightful girl,' murmured Hugo. 'So untrammelled by any delicacy of mind. I shall make my bow to your cousin whilst I am yet at liberty, Miss Kydd. Your servant, Gibbs.'

Nell persevered with Mr Gibbs, subtly manoeuvring until she could see past his shoulder to watch Hugo engage 'Cousin Jane' in conversation between rubbers. She wondered if Mr Stapleton was amongst the gentlemen playing whist, but bethought herself that even if he was, he would never connect a Miss Jane Rawdon, spinster of uncertain age and peculiarly fortunate card-player, with Jasper Kydd Esquire, landowner.

Lady Norland's voice was heard at the far end of the saloon, announcing that she knew the company would not object to an impromptu hop for the amusement of the younger guests before supper. As Sir Thomas's idea of suitable refreshment for his visitors was as generous as his candles, not a voice was raised in demur, one merry gentleman protesting that surely

Lady Norland would not be so disobliging as to exclude the less-than-young guests from dancing also!

Nell finished her lemonade, reflecting that until Kit could be persuaded to leave, dancing was as safe a pastime as any. She was not so graceful or light on her feet that she would be in any way remarkable, so it was in the highest degree unlikely that anyone should feel constrained to point her out to Mr Stapleton.

This comfortable thought lasted no longer than the moment when she and Mr Gibbs joined the set to discover all the other females wearing fortunes in jewellery and lace. How was she not to stand out in simple green cambric with no other adornment than a pearl necklet and earrings? (Highly suitable for young ladies according to the *Ladies' Monthly Museum* — it was a pity none of the other young ladies in the room appeared to have read the article.) Looking across to the next set it was plain the Norland girls would rather find themselves in a debtor's prison than be seen wearing mere pearls. Nell had already had occasion to notice that Sophia's low-cut rose-pink gauze over deep pink satin was complemented by thoroughly ostentatious garnets, but even Euphemia at only sixteen years of age had sapphires to go with white muslin over cerulean silk. Nell resolved that on her next visit to Hadleigh, she would introduce the subject of the topaz set that had belonged to Grandmama and did not suit Mama's fair colouring at all. Looking at the gowns on show, she also had some pertinent thoughts regarding lengths of oyster satin and sea-green gauze. How low, she wondered, could Annie be induced to cut a neckline?

In revolving these designs, Nell neglected to pay attention to the dance. To her mortification she felt her foot come into contact with that of a neighbouring gentleman.

'I beg your pardon,' the gentleman said instantly.

'No, no, sir, the fault was mine. I was not attending.'

'Who can blame you? There is so much brightness and sparkle here it would catch the interest of the most jaded party goer.'

Nell felt her colour rise. The gentleman took her for a schoolroom miss and no wonder, given her costume. He was approaching middle age, but dressed younger than his years in a natty blue-and-cream frogged waistcoat, and was as nimble on his feet as the young bucks around them.

'I dearly love a hop,' he confided now, his

eyes twinkling. 'If more of the men I spend so much time soberly sitting and talking with would exercise their minds and limbs in this fashion, I feel sure business would go altogether better.'

Nell smiled and at the next turn of the dance asked, 'And your wife, sir? Does she enjoy dancing too?'

She had been correct in surmising him to be married. 'Very much,' he said readily. 'Alas she is at home with our children at this season and must make do with the monthly assemblies, but we will all remove to London in the spring and then we shall be merry until dawn every night.'

Another turn separated them and Nell was reclaimed by Mr Gibbs. Through a gap in the set she caught a glimpse of Hugo, his heavy brows drawn together as he glanced in her direction. She wondered what she had done to incur his displeasure this time.

When the music ended, she noticed the gentleman in the blue-and-cream waistcoat move towards her. Her spirits lifted wondrously. Nothing does a person's self-esteem more good than to know that someone whose foot has been trodden on is prepared to overlook the fault enough to request the next dance.

Before the gentleman had covered half the

distance, however, Hugo was at her side and had his hand on her arm. 'Your cousin is asking for you,' he said in a voice which brooked no disagreement.

Nell glared at him. He begrudged her one more dance?

'You should go to her,' he said. 'I do not think she is well.'

'The old lady looks p-pretty s-sound to me,' Mr Gibbs objected.

Hugo seared him with barely concealed irritation. 'Appearances are deceptive at this distance.'

'Yes, but there are tabbies enough at hand to f-flutter around her. I don't s-see why Miss K-Kydd should have to — '

Just beyond Mr Gibbs, the nimble-footed gentleman paused, an arrested expression on his face.

Hugo's fingers closed on Nell's arm. The iron pressure through her elbow-length gloves was unmistakable. 'I beg your pardon, Mr Gibbs,' she said hastily. 'Thank you so much for our dance. I enjoyed it tremendously.' And to Hugo, in a lowered tone, 'There is no need to be quite so rough, nor in such a hurry. We will be remarked. I had settled with myself to come after the next dance.'

'There is every need,' he growled, not letting up his pace. 'The gentleman in the frogged waistcoat is Mr Stapleton!'

Nell gasped. 'Lady Norland said Mr Stapleton was one of Sir Thomas's business acquaintances! I expected him to be older.'

Hugo made an exasperated sound. 'I am in business myself yet you will allow that I am not yet in my dotage?' he snapped. 'Though I often have cause to feel it when confronted by your brother's idiotic pranks! Tell me at once, what did you speak of to Stapleton?'

'Nothing. The merest commonplaces, I assure you. We were not even introduced. He cannot know who I am.'

'Unless he heard that gapseed Gibbs announce it to the whole room!'

They slowed to an agonizingly decorous stroll as they neared the card tables. Under cover of her gown, Nell aimed a kick at her brother's leg. Kit immediately doubled up.

'Miss Rawdon, are you ill?' Two of Kit's fellow whist players started from their seats.

'Cousin Jane,' cried out Nell at the same instant, 'what is the matter? Oh, I knew we should not have come out tonight!'

Kit pressed a fluttering hand to his chest. 'I believe I must make my cards over. I do not feel at all well. I wonder if it was the fish at dinner?'

'Very likely,' said Nell. 'Let me get your vinaigrette. Captain Derringer, would you be good enough to ask the footman to procure us a hackney carriage? I must give our apologies to Lady Norland immediately.'

'Certainly. I think you are very wise. I daresay once at home your cousin will be quite herself again.' His eyes met hers with just a flicker of clandestine humour.

For a pulse beat, Nell's heart quickened at the shared jest. Then the moment was gone as Hugo turned away on his errand. For the benefit of any interested observers, he behaved with the slightly bored politeness expected of a gentleman towards a friend's relations as he gathered up belongings and delivered the ladies to the footman. Nell however, could not suppress the thought that after bidding them adieu, he walked back into the overheated saloon with an air which in any other man might well have been described as smug.

Far from being abashed, Kit was in high fettle. He pulled off his lawn cap and veils when they got back to Half Moon Street and told Tom to bring brandy. 'Nuisance about supper,' he said. 'I was looking forward to Lady Norland's table.'

'For shame!' said Nell, intercepting the brandy bottle. 'You have just fooled that poor woman to the top of your bent and should be grateful to have come out with a whole skin.

You look thoroughly disreputable. Not a single drop of this do you have until you are wearing your own clothes again.'

Her brother's eyes danced. 'But you hate my clothes.'

'I had rather see you in them than in skirts! You were positively dangerous tonight, Kit!'

'One of my better performances,' said Kit complacently. 'Quite as good as my impoverished seaman. Perhaps I shall give Mr Kean a run for his money.'

'It is Kydd Court you should be aiming at, not Drury Lane. Oh Kit, Hugo said Mr Stapleton is selling Uncle Jasper some land to swell his estate! Why then should he be so determined on *ours*?'

Kit's gaiety fell away. All at once he looked taller, older, the grey silk gown a grotesque anomaly. 'I don't know, Nell, but by God I'm going to find out. Monday morning you and I will both see Mr Tweedie. I want a conclusion to this charade.'

★   ★   ★

Sunday, as might have been expected, brought an early visitor to Half Moon Street in the shape of Hugo Derringer. Nell, fixing her ruffled silk bonnet with its frivolous primrose and bronze ribbons ready for

252

church and eyeing him sideways in the glass, felt an unmaidenly stab of regret that he was back in his riding coat. Her colour soared as she realized he was watching her. 'I suppose you do not object to my going to church?' she said in a challenging voice, to cover her confusion.

Hugo removed his hat and gloves and laid them on the table. 'Since I cannot see that my approval or otherwise carries the slightest weight with you, I shall refrain from making the obvious comment.'

Her eyebrows rose. 'The consideration has never prevented you before.'

'I am concerned merely for your reputation. Is your brother up?'

Nell seethed at this off-hand dismissal. 'He is breakfasting in the drawing room. If you wait a moment before ascending, I shall be out of earshot and you may abuse him as much as you choose.'

He gave a faint smile. 'Perhaps that would be as well. You look very picturesque this morning.'

'I look the same as I did on Thursday when you told me I was too modish to drive to Hadleigh.'

'But today is Sunday and your costume therefore unexceptional. Which church? Somewhere out of the way, I hope?'

Nell was sorely tempted to say the Chapel Royal just to see his reaction. 'St Mary's. We always attend services there when in London. Come Annie, we do not wish to be late. Where is Lily? Or will she go with Tom and Dick this evening?'

There was an odd look on Hugo's face. 'You take good care of your retainers' moral welfare.'

'Of course,' said Nell. Her eyes caught on his. 'It would do you no harm to accompany us.'

'I would with alacrity,' said Hugo, 'except that I have engaged to conduct Henri Dessin to the Catholic service later this morning.'

Nell did not believe this assurance for one moment. She had never yet met a man who took church-going as seriously as females did. Even Papa had derived more benefit from debating the sermon with the rector afterwards than relieving his soul with worship at the time. 'A fine excuse,' she scoffed.

He looked at her enigmatically. 'I assure you, it would give me great pleasure to stand next to you in church.'

Nell stared at him, parted her lips to speak, doubted, and fell silent. He could not mean what his words seemed to imply. Why, he never opened his mouth except to disapprove of her. Annie reappeared to say that Lily

254

would attend the evening service. Nell barely heard her. She left with the memory of Hugo's deep green eyes boring into her, her mind in a turmoil most unfitting for devotional activities.

He had gone by the time she and Annie returned. Kit was in the drawing room alone, leafing through Cowper. One look at his mutinous face was enough to inform Nell that Hugo had not pulled his punches.

'Of all the curst flat days, Sunday is the worst,' he grumbled, throwing the book aside.

Nell took off her bonnet and calmly began to unfold the figured muslin on the table. 'Be thankful you have not been at Kydd this year, with Uncle Jasper frowning if you so much as smiled at a jest in a book on a Sunday or set a stitch in anything less worthy than a sheet which needed darning.'

Kit's expression became thoughtful. 'Aye, that is something which I cannot understand, the length of time he thought necessary to spend with you. From what Hugo gathered last evening, he has been after this parcel of land from Stapleton for years but would never stump up the asking price until now. Windown Park, you know, was split at the time Jasper purchased it — I doubt he could have afforded it else, being the younger son — and he has been trying ever since to reunite it. Indeed, the one time we were there I remember he gave Papa and me a tour, pointing out where the boundaries once were and what he had already done to restore them. It is something of an obsession.'

Nell listened as she laid out the pieces for a simple round gown. 'You are saying you would expect such a man to remain with his own lands and leave Kydd to fend for itself?'

'Yes. Would not you?'

Nell grimaced. 'I assumed he stayed overlong in order to be disagreeable. Did Mr Stapleton say anything about my uncle?'

'Apparently the gentleman was so taken with you Hugo did not dare approach for fear of being asked who you were.' Kit's blue eyes danced. 'He was not at all impressed by our meddling.'

'*Our* meddling! I like that. It was your idea, brother. I only went to prevent you from being hung. Did he stay long after we left?'

'He would remain to eat, I suppose. Why do you ask?'

Nell coloured. 'No reason.' She hoped very much that he had not stayed. The thought of Sophia and Euphemia vying with each other to be the one taken in to supper on his arm was insupportable. She eyed the figured muslin balefully. She could see exactly the gown she wished to make. It was low cut, would drape temptingly over her curves, accentuate her figure perfectly and would drive the beholder wild with desire. Unfortunately it would almost certainly get her barred from Almack's and other ton gatherings if it were ever seen in public and would likely be impossible to dance in. Nell sighed and picked up her shears. 'Do read to me, Kit,' she begged. 'Have you started *Waverley* yet? If I must make insipid white dresses for the spring, I should so much prefer not to die of boredom whilst I do it.'

Kit grinned and picked up Scott's novel. 'Courage, sister,' he said. 'Sew bravely now and as a reward I will teach you a card game I learnt from the soldiers in Lisbon. If all else fails, I intend using it as a means to regain our fortunes. Then later we can rehearse breaking the news of my continued existence to Tweedie.'

★ ★ ★

The morning did not bring any alteration of her brother's resolve to talk to their solicitor. What it brought was Kit himself, in grey silk and Nell's paisley shawl, to the breakfast table.

'What are you doing?' shrieked Nell, doubting the evidence of her own eyes.

257

Her brother gazed at her in simpering surprise. 'I thought to have some sustenance before we visited Mr Tweedie, dear.'

'Don't do that,' begged Nell. 'Don't turn into Cousin Jane as if you only have to don a cap to become her. It's unnatural, Kit.'

'He does it very fine, Miss Nell,' said Tom, handing her the toast.

'That is what worries me!'

Kit reached for coffee. 'You used not to be such a gudgeon, Nell,' he said in his normal voice. 'Why should I not get into the part before we go out?'

Nell pressed her fingers to her temples, too distressed to be tactful. 'Because it reminds me of Mama talking to non-existent visitors as an escape from reality! Because I want the brother who taught me cricket, took me riding and gutted my fish sitting here beside me, not some eccentric stranger! Why cannot Mr Tweedie come to us? That is what I thought you meant.'

'Gudgeon,' repeated Kit fondly and continued to eat a hearty meal. 'It's only acting, Nell.'

Nell could not dissuade him. She pointed out that daylight was a lot harsher on painted imposters than candlelight. She said she would go herself with Annie to Mr Tweedie and acquaint him with what had passed. She suggested sending a note by Tom asking him to wait on them at home. All in vain. Her last hope was that Hugo would put in an appearance to intercede with his friend, but when ten o'clock came with no sign of him she was obliged to abandon even this idea. Instead she took her place in a hack next to Kit, resolving to burn the grey silk on the kitchen fire as soon as ever her brother took it off!

Mr Tweedie was, to put it mildly, horrified when the pair of them appeared in his chambers. 'Mr Christopher!' he said in appalled tones, his shocked, elderly eyes taking in every detail of Kit's fabulous appearance.

'Morning, Tweedie,' said Kit cheerfully. 'Don't set up such a screech, man, you'll have everybody in here. Send your clerk for refreshments and I'll explain why I'm dressed like this and why I don't want it known I'm back.'

But when the whole tale was unfolded, it was not that Christopher Kydd of Kydd Court, Northamptonshire was strolling around the metropolis in a gown that upset Mr Tweedie most (causing Nell to speculate on what some of his other clients got up to), but that if the story ever came to light, she would be known to have been living in Half Moon Street unchaperoned.

'But I am not,' she said patiently. 'I am with Kit.'

To which Mr Tweedie replied repressively that she was as yet very young. London society was unlikely to view such a scapegrace as her unmarried brother sufficient protection.

'Never mind that,' said Kit. 'What we want to know is what you have found out regarding my uncle?' He went on to relate more exactly all that had befallen him in India and the conclusions he had drawn.

'And now Uncle Jasper is actively buying up land to expand his Wiltshire estate,' said Nell. 'That does not sound as if he is planning to make any great stay at Kydd, does it?'

Mr Tweedie hemmed and hawed and mumbled about good landlords always being on the lookout to increase their holdings for future generations.

Nell shook her head decidedly. 'That will not do for my uncle. I do not know how he appears to his tenants at Windown Park, but at Kydd and Hadleigh he is viewed as a very bad landlord. He must have wasted hundreds of pounds if the discrepancies between the Hadleigh accounts and what my tenants say is to be believed. I still do not see where the money has gone. It is one of the things I mean to inquire into as soon as Kit's affairs are resolved.'

Mr Tweedie wrung his hands. 'Finances are not at all a suitable business for a young lady to — that is, I should be happy to recommend — '

Nell met his look candidly. 'I do not have the funds to employ a professional,' she said. 'Besides, it is no longer an issue. My uncle has made over the Hadleigh dealings to me and Mama. I know I can bring the Manor about and wish to learn what has previously transpired for my own satisfaction only. I would rather you concentrated on investigating the mishandling of Kydd. Your fee will then come out of the estate.'

Kit had been watching the interchange, his blue eyes bright with amusement. 'My sister has the right of it. There has been some serious maladministration over the past year for which the board is responsible. In addition to his deceit over the servants' wages this quarter, we have also discovered my uncle to be selling Kydd effects which I cannot believe has been condoned by — '

'Selling Kydd effects? My dear Christopher!' The solicitor jumped up from his chair, far more agitated than at any point in the interview thus far.

'Books from the library,' said Kit. 'My

sister and my friend will testify where and when they were found. Also several items at a pawnbrokers which I saw with my own eyes and had the greatest difficulty preventing myself from reclaiming on the spot. Naturally I did not think it wise to ask the pawnbroker for a description of his client, but the bookseller and his shop-boy described their vendor enough that there is no doubt of his being my uncle. I believe they would identify him in the flesh as easily. When our groom returns from Kydd tomorrow, we expect to hear what else has disappeared from the Court.'

Mr Tweedie moaned and twisted his pen in his hands. 'This is terrible. Your father's library! And doubtless all in cash. No trace. No trace at all. Christopher, you must see that I cannot possibly bring this up with Mr Jasper Kydd's lawyer. I should be served with a writ for slander before I was back in my own rooms!'

What Kit had said about the shop assistant had brought the glimmering of an idea into Nell's head. 'Did I see an office boy in the outer room? The one at the bookseller's appeared uncommonly au fait with his master's business. Could your boy perhaps fall into conversation with the lad from my uncle's man of affairs?'

A look of startled respect came into the elderly solicitor's countenance. 'Yes,' he said. 'Yes, now there is a thought indeed. Alfred would be delighted to be given licence to jaw to a rival firm.'

Nell rose. 'We shall leave the matter with you. You will call on us in Half Moon Street when you have any information?'

Mr Tweedie followed her pointed glance at Kit in his 'Cousin Jane' regalia and said hurriedly, 'Oh yes, dear me, yes. Christopher's public appearances should certainly be kept to a minimum.' He took off his spectacles, polished them distractedly and then replaced them. 'I may not have shown it in the first surprise of your arrival, Christopher, but I am very glad you are back. I will be even more so when you are able to take up your rightful place.'

'Not to mention in his rightful clothes,' muttered Nell.

13

Nell was unsurprised when Hugo was shown into the drawing room later. She *was* surprised to see that he had a companion.

'Miss Kydd, may I present my Brussels agent and good friend Henri Dessin? I have brought him to bear your brother company whilst you and I ride. He has some documents for Kit to look over regarding the Bombay enterprise.'

Kit had already jumped up, an expectant light in his blue eyes which did not seem to Nell to betoken business. Nor did she miss the unspoken communication between the three men, but not liking to appear a managing harridan before a stranger said, 'You do us a great kindness, Monsieur Dessin. Even the best of sisters fret their brother's nerves. I daresay Kit is longing for the chance not to have to mind his language at every second sentence.'

'I cannot believe you would fret anybody's nerves, Mademoiselle,' the agent said gallantly.

Nell cast an arch look at Hugo. 'Then Captain Derringer has not acquainted you with our exchanges. I may yet pass myself off with credit.'

Outside the room, she directed Tom to take in refreshment, enquiring without much hope of a favourable answer whether the larder would stretch to providing dinner for their guests.

'Not properly it won't, Miss Nell. I could get something in from one of the hotels.'

'Then we had better do so. I pray Seth arrives tomorrow with Mrs Olivant's new supplies. I had no notion eating in town would prove such an expense.'

'He'll be here,' said Tom. 'He'll have been that fidgety with it being Sunday yesterday, he'll have set off at first light this morning. A night's rest at Hadleigh and we'll likely see him before breakfast.'

Nell chuckled and hurried to her bedchamber to change into her apricot riding habit. It was the newest one she possessed, having been made just before Papa's accident. Not that she particularly wanted to show herself to advantage, of course.

They turned north, away from the fashionable promenades. She sighed, wondering when the day would come that she could ride through London without checking every face, and sought for something unremarkable to say. 'I hope being in Brussels did not cause

Monsieur Dessin undue suffering during the Waterloo action?'

Hugo smiled at her. 'It would take more than a full-scale battle raging a few miles away to cramp Henri's business transactions. Indeed, as things turned out, his familiarity with the various regiments proved fortuitous.'

'How so?'

There was a tiny pause. 'Oh, armies are always after supplies, you know. The horses are lively. Are you averse to giving them their heads on Hampstead Heath? It is not more than five miles distant.'

Nell turned to him in surprise. 'I should like it above all things,' she said. 'But does such an expedition suit your notions of propriety?'

'I see little risk. Your London acquaintances will be showing off their finery in Hyde Park at this time of day.'

She raised an eyebrow. 'You do not consider female fashions of any account? That is sad talk for a silk and muslin merchant.'

He directed an exasperated glance at her. 'I implied no such thing and well you know it. May we not have just one conversation without arguing?'

'We can try,' said Nell with a laugh. 'We can always fall back on what Papa used to describe as 'active discussion' if we get bored.'

'I fail to see how anyone blessed with you for a companion could possibly have leisure enough to be bored,' said Hugo with feeling.

'Tell that to Kit. After losing fabulous sums to him at cards yesterday, I was forced to interest him in emergency procedures for restoring the house to an unused-looking state to pass the hours. We had got it down to eighteen minutes before it was time for dinner.'

They paused to negotiate a crossroads. Nell was gratified to see laughter on Hugo's face. 'An excellent distraction! Is there anything you cannot do?'

Nell grinned. 'Many things. I am no hand in the kitchen at all. Dishes take too long to cook and I forget them, or they require constant attention so the moment I turn away to do something else they spoil. I can shoot game, though. Our keeper taught me when he found me dismantling his favourite shotgun at the age of seven. If I cannot persuade Kit to Hadleigh any other way, I shall challenge him to a coney contest.'

Hugo smiled. 'You are a pearl amongst sisters and Kit is an ungrateful blackguard if he cannot see it.' His eyebrows drew together. 'What is it? What have I said?'

Nell shook her head, vexed with herself. 'Nothing. The word 'pearl' reminded me of the Norland party. All those jewels! I was never more jealous of unlimited wealth in my life.'

Her mare jibed as she tightened the reins. Hugo reached across to steady her. 'Jealous?' he said, flatly incredulous. 'You? Of those empty-headed ninnies? I cannot believe it.'

Empty-headed ninnies? Confusion hit Nell's heart. She fixed her eyes on the rise of Highgate Hill. 'I felt plain, countrified and out of place,' she said. 'And you were as fine as fivepence and moved amongst those people as though you went to gatherings like that every day.'

'A trick. A diplomat's stock-in-trade which I ingested at my guardian's knee. Such occasions are all front and no heart; I sickened of them years ago.'

'Then — you did not enjoy it on Saturday?'

His eyes met hers. 'My one thought the whole time you were there was to get you away.'

This was not as reassuring as it might have been. 'And after we had gone?'

A faint wash of colour appeared under Hugo's tan. 'To wish you back again,' he admitted. 'Whatever else you may be, you are *not* insipid.'

The road grew more crowded. Nell was glad of the excuse to concentrate on her horse. She felt all the force of Captain Derringer's compliment. 'I daresay it was not the most intellectual of gatherings,' she said after a while. 'But I should have liked to dance more all the same. I haven't since Papa died.'

'No,' said Hugo slowly. 'I was forgetting.' He cleared his throat. 'Perhaps when you are back at Hadleigh, there might be an assembly I could escort you to?'

Nell felt a tingling quiver run through her. She met his eyes again. 'That would be' — she hunted for the right words — 'very nice.'

Hugo opened his mouth to speak again, but they had reached the Heath and both horses were whickering enthusiastically at the swathes of grassland. Nell grinned as Snowflake made plain her thoughts on days of confinement. 'I am afraid if you tell my mare she may not canter, she will never forgive you.'

Hugo smiled back. 'Nor would this beast of your brother's. Shall we make for that spinney?'

Snowflake needed no second urging. She skimmed past couples strolling, youths exercising dogs, other equestrians and small knots of children with their nursemaids. One such group caught Nell's eye. They were gesticulating at a nearby tree. 'Oh Hugo, the children's kite has become tangled,' she called, pulling up. 'If you will hold Snowflake, I believe I might — '

Captain Derringer had already turned Valiant to head for the group. 'And rob me of my chance to be a hero?' he said, a martial glint in his eye. 'Oh no, I have your measure now. As soon as I espied that rag of blue and yellow, I knew you would insist on rescuing it and was determined to be before you.' He beckoned to the oldest boy in the party, a sporting lad who was telling the nurse it would be no great matter to climb the tree, good clothes or no. 'Now then, young sir. Do you suppose you can hold my horse whilst I go after your treasure?'

The boy's jaw dropped as he took in Valiant's gleaming black magnificence. 'I should say so,' he said with enthusiasm.

Under Nell's amazed and wholly disbelieving gaze, Hugo divested himself of coat, waistcoat, hat and gloves, balanced competently on Valiant's back and then swung via a sturdy branch to clasp the trunk of the tree. She had to crane her neck as a few athletic stretches took him into the leafy crown, only an agitation in the branches marking his progress thereafter.

'It is very kind of the gentleman, miss,'

ventured the nursemaid.

'It is astonishing,' returned Nell.

An ominous, ripping sound made them both wince. 'He's got it!' shrieked the smallest girl, letting go of her sister's hand in her excitement and jumping up and down with delight, and indeed the blue and yellow kite fell to the ground on her words, its long tail fluttering behind it.

Hugo followed more circumspectly, flushed and panting a little from the exertion, with his linen shirt torn and stained green from the tree, but looking very well pleased with himself nevertheless. The children clamoured to thank him. He shook his head cheerfully. 'I should rather thank you. It is not every day a grown man has licence to climb such a fine tree. If I were you though, I would choose more open ground the next time you fly your prize.'

The children assured him that they would, brushed leaves and twigs off him enthusiastically and helped him back into his waistcoat and coat.

'A hero indeed,' said Nell as they started back. 'I am impressed, Captain Derringer.'

He cocked an eye at her. 'You called me Hugo a moment ago.'

Nell blushed. 'I — was concerned for the children. It was quicker to say.' For some reason she found it hard to look at him. It was as if the kite's rescue had enabled him to strip off more than his coat. He was positively bursting with vitality and maleness. Nell found it enormously disturbing.

He smiled at her now in a way which set her legs trembling and reminded her too clearly for comfort of his strength and gentleness after Finchley Common. 'I liked it,' he said.

Nell swallowed and quickened Snowflake's pace. 'You are being very amiable today. Is there some reason?'

'Does there have to be?'

'I had expected you to disown us entirely after Saturday.' Even as the words left her lips she berated herself. Fool that she was! Why had she said something so *stupid*? Had her wits gone begging? Did she want him to be angry with her again?

His mouth twitched. 'I considered it, but on reflection decided life would become uncommonly dull were I to do so.'

'Ah yes. I remember now, you do not like to be inactive. You and Kit have that quality in common. May we gallop back to the road, do you suppose?'

He grinned at her evasive tactics. 'By all means. We do not wish to get overtaken again by the dusk.'

They reached Half Moon Street still bandying words and gave the horses into Dick's care. 'If you let me have your shirt, I will mend it for you,' said Nell as they entered the house.

Hugo's eyebrows rose. 'I think Henri would be shocked.'

Nell felt her cheeks scorch at the teasing glint in his eyes. 'I meant bring it with you tomorrow.' But his well muscled chest with its fascinating whorls of fine black hairs intruded on her memory as she spoke and she couldn't prevent her breath from catching on the words.

He looked as though he knew quite well what she was thinking and thoroughly approved her thoughts. 'Thank you, I accept. Having been privileged to view your needle-work, I am confident you will make a far better job of it than my man.'

He stood aside to let her ascend the staircase. As she passed, she brushed against his body. The contact sent a shock of lightning through her veins. She looked up instantly, to see the same knowledge in the deep green warmth of his eyes that she had been fighting all the way back from the Heath. 'Hugo?' she whispered.

'Nell.' The single word set her pulse racing. He put his hand out to softly trace the line of her cheek. 'Nell, I — '

Above them the door to the drawing room opened and Tom Olivant appeared.

'Your hair is a trifle wind-blown,' said Hugo, clearing his throat and moving his hand to pat an errant curl. 'A pretty pair we must look. Your brother will wonder what has become of us.'

Where he had touched her cheek it felt as if butterflies quivered. 'Then tell him of the kite's misadventure whilst I make myself presentable. You will dine with us, you and Monsieur Dessin?'

His hand had not yet returned to his side. His eyes still held hers. 'I am sorry. We have to meet someone this evening.'

'I'll bring you up tea, Miss Nell,' said Tom. 'There's bread and butter too.'

Never had she found her footman's cheerful normality more inappropriate. There should be cathedral choirs singing at such a moment. Banks of musicians should be filling the hallway with stanzas and cadenzas. 'You will have some refreshment before you go?' she said to Hugo in a dazed voice.

He smiled at her. *His* eyes did not look uncertain at all. 'Try to prevent me.'

★ ★ ★

Nell searched her reflection wonderingly as Annie re-dressed her hair.

'Brought colour to your cheeks, the fresh air,' her maid observed.

'It was nice not to be confined. Captain Derringer scaled a tree.' Nell spoke almost at random, the words detached and faraway, nothing at all to do with the tumultuous, here-and-now rushing of her heart.

Annie tutted. 'A fine way for a gentleman to behave when he's supposed to be escorting a young lady.'

'It was to rescue a kite.' She jumped up as soon as Annie had finished, submitted to a professional twitch of the cambric dress and snatched up her shawl, almost running down the staircase in her haste to be with him again.

She opened the drawing room door on a roar of fury.

'You did *what*?' Hugo's eyes were smouldering, his eyebrows were drawn together and he was balling his fists before Kit as if about to mill him down. But even as Nell's lips formed a soundless 'oh', he caught sight of her and crossed the room in swift strides, the anger fading from his face.

'Miss Kydd, you look delightful,' said Henri Dessin, standing up and executing a little bow.

'Th-thank you.' Nell scanned Hugo's face anxiously. 'What has happened?'

He drew her hand inside his arm with a new tenderness which gave her a heart-stopping thrill. 'Your miserable brother has just seen fit to inform me in what guise he visited the solicitor this morning. Here, take the corner of the sofa closer to the fire. You will be warmer there.'

Nell felt quite heated already with the length of his forearm touching hers. He relinquished his hold only to sit next to her.

'I give you fair warning, Kit,' continued Hugo. 'If you compromise your sister's reputation with a caper like that one more time, I will bind you hand and foot and imprison you in your attic until this coil is resolved!'

'Stow it. I knew it was wrong as soon as I set foot in the street. Tweedie is to come here next time he finds anything.' Kit sighed. 'I must be getting old.'

Nell picked up the teapot and poured carefully, hoping the quiver in her hand was unnoticeable. She gave Hugo his tea. The cup rattled as his fingers brushed against hers. 'Mr Tweedie was quite as scandalized as you could wish when we were shown into his chambers this morning,' she said.

'I am glad to hear it.'

'It did convince him to take us seriously, though.'

Nell glared at her irrepressible brother and passed Monsieur Dessin the next cup.

'This is a very striking tea set, Miss Kydd,' said the agent, raising it to the light and inspecting the porcelain with a connoisseur's eye. 'So unusual, a single white star on a background of turquoise shells. Sèvres, is it?'

'Yes,' said Nell, grateful for the change in subject. 'It is unusual, is it not? My grandmama collected porcelain. We have a whole room devoted to the fruits of her labours at Kydd Court.'

Kit stretched his legs. 'Provided my uncle has not sold it.'

'If he has, we shall find out when Seth returns tomorrow.' She turned with what she hoped was an uncontrived air. 'What shall we do, Hugo, send you word by Tom when he arrives?'

His deep green eyes told her that he had not missed the use of his first name. 'Knowing your groom, he is not like to dawdle on the road. I will wait on you early.'

The few inches between them pulsed with heat. Nell was amazed the others in the room seemed not to notice. 'Are you sure? If you are too beforehand, Kit will still be abed.'

Hugo leaned back against the cushions, the

gleam in his expression indicating that he had taken her meaning. 'I will run that risk.'

A few more exchanges, and then Henri put his cup down. 'The stage from Portsmouth is due,' he reminded Hugo.

'Burn it, I suppose we should be going.' Hugo stood up and lifted Nell's hand to his lips. 'Until tomorrow.' He held her hand a moment longer than was necessary while his agent also made adieus, then nodded carelessly to Kit and followed Henri from the room.

Until tomorrow, echoed Nell silently, feeling the spreading warmth of his kiss still on her fingers. Crossing to her worktable, she swept aside the white muslin to cut instead the pieces of a joyously warm russet spencer.

★   ★   ★

As it happened, the whole household was up when Seth arrived the next morning. Nell had woken early and lain in bed savouring the new and strange sensations that chased themselves around her body whenever she thought of Hugo. Was this how he had felt when he'd caught her as she slid from Snowflake's back on Finchley Common? No wonder he had held her so close. She began to calculate how soon he could be here, how

278

long before they could talk. All she had of yesterday was that one awakening look and the subsequent pressure of his fingers and his arm. Nell wriggled out of the bedclothes and caught up her shawl. She would slip downstairs and heat some washing water. She was so piercingly happy she didn't want to share this moment with another living soul.

She was out of luck. As she set foot on the lower flight, she saw Annie approaching with a steaming jug. 'What are you doing about so early?' she said, disconcerted. 'I was sure you would still be abed.'

'Aye, and so I would be,' said her maid sourly, 'if that dratted Lily hadn't been fidgeting and fussing since I don't know when, asking if I didn't think Seth would be here soon and how she couldn't like the thought of him arriving to a cold kitchen and maybe she'd just go down and build up the fire.'

Nell stifled a giggle. 'How provoking for you.'

'I've left her singing to herself. It's my belief you'll need the rector to put up the banns for them next time we're at Hadleigh.'

'Banns?' Nell was startled. 'But Lily is too young, surely, and Seth is — Seth is not . . . '

'All the more reason,' said Annie darkly. 'Won't neither of them *intend* anything, like

279

as not, but that don't mean it won't happen. She's of age, and Seth'll be as foolish as the next man once he finds a willing maiden snuggled into his lap.'

Nell blushed at her henchwoman's forthright words, picturing herself in Hugo's lap. As she washed and dressed, shivers of anticipation chased over her skin. She went down to the drawing room to work on the spencer before he arrived, but to her dismay found her brother already at the table, being provided with coffee and toast by Tom. 'Is everyone in the house up?' she said with a strong sense of ill-usage.

'Bad head,' said Kit, wincing. 'Too much cheese for supper I daresay.'

'Or too much ale in the George & Dragon,' retorted Nell.

They were interrupted by a shout from downstairs. 'Seth!' said Kit. Headache forgotten, he hastened from the room.

Nell stayed to fold together some buttered toast and pour herself a cup of coffee. Then she too descended to the kitchen to hear her groom's tale.

Hannah's laboriously written list lay on the table. It didn't make comforting reading. The two most comprehensive sets of tableware and many of the figurines were missing from the porcelain room, as were various articles of plate, vases and other ornaments from around the Court.

'Might be some more books gone too, Miss Nell,' said Seth between draughts of ale supplied by a worshipful Lily. 'Hannah says there weren't none of them big folios out like there usually are, and she disremembers quite so many gaps in the cases.'

'I must write to Mrs Belmont and thank her for Hannah's time,' said Nell distractedly. She read the list again. 'The green Sèvres service with the garlands and the Worcester spotted fruit set . . . Where would he sell them? Would Hugo know, Kit?'

'Bound to. Have to try the bigger booksellers too. Pity we don't know which volumes we're looking for. Did anything come of those leaves of parchment, Seth?'

'I've got them here. That Walter Harvey was a-nosing around, Miss Nell. Said he wanted to know how the mistress was a-getting on at the Manor.'

'I hope you sent him off with a flea in his ear! How was everyone else? Was the harvest all in? Did the livestock look healthy?'

A great frown descended onto Seth's round face. 'Sheep are all sold. Bill Copping says Mr Jasper only got a few shillings apiece for 'em at market. And he's gone an' put all the hands on half-wages over the winter.'

Tears sprung to Nell's eyes. 'The fiend! Oh, those poor people! How will they ever manage?' She left abruptly for the coolness of the hall, endeavouring to compose herself away from the others' sympathy. A loud knock on the front door set her heart hammering. She could *not* face anyone in this disordered state. She shrank into the unused, shrouded parlour as Tom answered the summons.

'Morning, Captain,' she heard her footman say. 'Seth's back from Kydd so we're all down in the kitchen. Been terrible doings up at the Court, there have.'

'Hugo?' Nell steadied herself against the doorframe, so full of misery for the Coppings and the others that she forgot all she had been going to say to him.

He immediately caught her hand between his. 'My dear, is it very bad?'

'It is that,' said Tom. 'Master Kit said if it was you, to come down and join us and he'll tell you all.'

'Gladly,' said Hugo, waving him forward. He drew Nell's arm within his own.

Nell leaned on him thankfully. 'I beg your pardon. It was the shock of hearing what my uncle has done. I am not usually so foolish.'

'I know it. Courage, love, I do not believe we are far off an end now.'

Love? Had he truly said *love?* And what did he mean, *not far off an end?* But they were downstairs already and Kit was bent intently over some spread out pieces of parchment.

'Look at these, Hugo. What do you make of them?'

Hugo strolled forward. 'Is this the paper which fell though the study grate?'

'Aye,' said Lily, twisting her hands in her apron, thoroughly bewildered.

'Lily,' said Nell, 'would you be very kind and set the coffee on to heat up again. We have left the breakfast jug upstairs and forgot it and I daresay it has become quite cold by now.'

The little maid bustled out, glad to have something normal to do.

'They are accounts,' said Hugo, studying the pieces. 'There cannot be any doubt of it. See, a clump of dates: February 1811 . . . March 1811 . . . Here are figures: 12/9d, £1/1/7d, 18/4d. Here are descriptions: candles . . . working soap . . . These are torn up pages from ordinary household accounts.'

Nell sat down, bitterly disappointed. 'Is that all? Then we are no further forward.'

Hugo turned a serious face to her. 'On the contrary, we are a great deal further forward. I can think of no valid reason why your uncle should wish to destroy household accounts only three and four years old. There is also the powerful fact that he deemed their destruction so hazardous to himself if discovered that he dismissed Lily on the negligible chance of her recognizing the pages. Can we piece together these scraps?'

Realizing he was right, and glowing at his superior logic, Nell took heart and pulled her chair up to the table. At first glance it seemed that the pieces, singed round the edges and in some cases scorched from the fire, could none of them go together. Then, as she studied the entries and her eye became more attuned to the writing, she saw there were variations in ink colour which made matching easier, and some lines appeared to have been written in a different hand altogether.

'Not uncommon,' said Hugo. 'Ink varies from batch to batch and older entries will always be more faded than recent ones. As for the handwriting, I daresay the housekeeper or the agent changed.'

'Not at Kydd,' said Kit. 'Not since 1811 anyway. We have had the same agent for years.'

'Uncle Jasper dismissed him,' said Nell. 'Shortly after Papa died.'

'These here aren't Kydd accounts,' said Tom Olivant roundly.

All three turned startled faces on him. 'Not?' said Nell. 'How can you tell?'

Tom jabbed his forefinger at one of the entries. '*Candles — one box*. Pa never ordered a single box of candles in his life. They'd have been used up in no time. One crate, more like.'

'That's true,' said Kit, excitement colouring his tone. 'And see here, *Farmer — quarterly rent*. We don't have a tenant by the name of Farmer.'

Nell felt the blood drain from her face. 'But *I* do — Dick's father!' She scanned the next line. '*Barker* . . . . He is the tenant at Spring Hill. These are from Hadleigh — but how can they be? I have the full set of accounts in my bookroom.'

Kit and Hugo were staring at each other. 'Fraud,' breathed Kit, a hard light in his blue eyes.

'Fraud,' agreed Hugo. He turned to Nell and took both her hands in his. 'Nell, think very carefully. The ledgers you have: do the entries vary as they do here between different inks and different writing?'

'I-I don't know. I don't believe so, but I was concerned with the figures, not how they were written down. I am sorry.' She screwed up her eyes, trying to visualize the pages, wanting to help.

Hugo gave her hands a tiny squeeze. 'I daresay they were the first set of accounts you had ever seen. You cannot be expected to know how such things look in general. What of the bills? Did they look to have been altered at all?'

'Bills? There were none. Only the ledgers.'

'Destroyed,' said Kit. 'That would make it even simpler. He would only have to falsify the entries themselves.'

'What do you mean?' said Nell, bewildered. 'What good would altering the bills do?'

Hugo still had hold of her hands. 'It is an old trick. Do you remember one time showing me bills which you had collected from town for your uncle to pay? He could easily alter 25/- to 35/- on the butcher's paper for example, enter the fabricated sum in the ledger, pay the correct amount to the trader and keep the extra ten shillings for himself. A cursory examination would never pick it up. With the Hadleigh accounts having no bills available for cross-checking, false entries would be well nigh impossible to spot. There is no blame attached to you.'

Nell felt a little comforted. 'I do remember that my uncle was a considerable time in giving the books to me.'

'While he copied them out, no doubt,' said Kit with relish. 'Changing the figures as he went along. You said, did you not, that the numbers did not seem to agree with what your tenants told you they had paid?'

Nell realized suddenly what he and Hugo were implying. It was as if a great burden had been lifted from her shoulders. 'Do you mean Uncle Jasper lied about Hadleigh's true worth? He took the profit for himself and made it *seem* as if there was no surplus? But that is wonderful! It means I do not need to worry whether the Manor can support Mama and me! How stupid of him though. What could he hope to gain from such falsehoods? He must know I had only to speak to the tenants to realize the true state of affairs.'

Tom Olivant cleared his throat. 'Not him, Miss Nell. Less than dust, we are. Did you ever know him talk to anyone on the Home Farm bar that Walter Harvey?'

'We must have those books,' said Hugo with decision. 'And statements from your tenants.'

'I already have Dick's father's figures,' said Nell. 'I was keeping them to show Kit when I found him, thinking the discrepancy must be mine.'

Hugo smiled. 'Excellent girl. Seth, will the bays stand a trip back to Hadleigh today? Will you take Miss Nell and Mr Kit to fetch the accounts? It is of the first importance that we lay them, and these scraps of Lily's, in front of Mr Tweedie as soon as may be.'

'There today and back tomorrow? Aye, they'll do that. Nobbut fifteen miles each way.'

Nell's eyes were fixed on Hugo. 'Only Kit and me? Do you not go with us?'

He exchanged the merest flicker of a glance with her brother. 'I cannot. I am engaged on business for the rest of today which may not be put off.'

She fought down her disappointment. 'I understand. You have been most generous with your time on our affairs as it is.'

He smiled again. 'You had best let your maid know and pack what you need for tonight. Then you may return in good time tomorrow. I do not think it wise for you to travel after dark again.' And in a lower, more teasing voice, 'At least you will not have to spend tonight rearranging furniture.'

Nell's lips trembled. 'That is true. And it will do Mama more good than I can say to see Kit. It is just that I had hoped . . . ' She broke off.

He spoke again, still in that lowered tone. 'I must go. If I do not see you tomorrow, I will come on Thursday. Stay safe.'

'You too.' She took a steadying breath and got up from the table to find Annie and acquaint her with their change of plans.

14

Frustrated as she was at being parted from Hugo again, as soon as Nell entered the drawing room at Hadleigh Manor, she could not be sorry to have come.

Kit swiftly crossed the room to kneel before his mother, companionably darning sheets with Mrs Webb. 'I am here, Mama,' he said. 'I am sorry to have caused you so much pain.'

'Oh Kit, oh my dearest boy, such a long time as you have been,' cried Mrs Kydd, pulling his moon-bright head to her breast and rocking him, tears running down her cheeks, as if he had been four years old and not four-and-twenty.

Nell melted from the room and beckoned Mrs Webb to do likewise. 'My brother and I are to stop for the night. Will you prepare a room for him? I must warn Cook that she will have more to feed than she had expected. I only pray she did not send all the spare food to Half Moon Street with Seth this morning!'

Mrs Olivant reassuring her on that head, and Mama being taken up with Kit, Nell felt no compunction about walking to the village with Annie to pay the butcher's and fishmonger's accounts. 'For if I am to pass these books over to the solicitor as evidence, I wish them to be properly up to date first,' she said. She thought of her uncle's machinations with a shudder. 'I will transcribe all the entries since we moved here and start afresh.'

'Are we to stay then, miss? Even when Master Kit is back at Kydd?'

'I don't know, Annie. I do not feel Mama will go back to Northamptonshire now. Kydd holds too many memories of Papa. Here she has recovered her balance.' She did not say what was rather shamefully in her mind: that if Hugo were to offer for her, her home would henceforth be wherever his business took them. Her cheeks flamed to think of her presumption. She only had that one look, and the gentleness of his attentions and the tone of his voice since. For all she knew, he might have different feelings about her entirely.

When they got back, Kit was regaling the household with the tales of India which Nell had already heard. 'And how have your days passed, Mama?' she said when he stopped to refresh himself. 'Have you had any visitors?'

'A great many, my love. The dowager Lady Moncrief with one of her nieces. The rector called on two occasions. His daughter was sorry to miss you. Several other ladies have taken tea. Poor Olivant has been quite rushed off his feet.'

Nell cast a glance towards the butler, who gave a slight nod. These were real visitors then. Mama was truly recovering. 'What excuse did you make for my absence?'

'That you were passing a few days with a relative.' Her mother smiled with satisfaction. 'And it was not even a bouncer, was it?'

Kit laughed delightedly. 'No, Mama, it was not, though where you had that language from I cannot imagine.'

'But, Nell, I have had the most extraordinary letter from Lady Norland! I had no notion the poor woman was so unhinged. She is suffering from the delusion that you attended a party of hers with Cousin Jane, of all people! I feel sorry for Sir Thomas. It must be a terrible thing when a man's wife cannot separate truth from imagination.'

Nell almost choked on a slice of cake. 'A great sadness. But I did indeed go to the Norlands. And Kit dressed up as Cousin Jane to escort me as he could not go in his own right. It was all for nothing, however. Captain Derringer found out the information we went for far easier than we could have done.'

'So she is not deranged,' said Mama with disappointment. 'Though I have always said calling two of her daughters Euphemia and

Augusta does not argue an immensely well regulated intelligence.'

'Undoubtedly. Have you kept the letter? Did she mention anything else?'

'Only that a few gentlemen seemed most interested in you. But as one was that portionless youth, Gibbs, and another a married business acquaintance of Sir Thomas, I paid it no heed. The rest concerned her hopes for a brilliant match for Sophia and her expectation that Euphemia will make just as big a hit as her sister next season. Are you *sure* she is not deluded?'

'Only on the subject of her daughters,' Nell said. But her eyes met Kit's uneasily. If Mr Stapleton had 'shown an interest' to Lady Norland, he was like to be in possession of her whole history by now. She could only hope his dealings with her uncle were conducted through several intermediaries.

The evening passed tranquilly, as did the following morning. Nell had Seth pole up the cob and they drove the gig around the estate to visit her tenants. By the time she and Kit arrived back in Half Moon Street, it was in the knowledge of two days well spent, and she could look forward to Hugo's visit that evening with a clear conscience.

To her chagrin, it was not Hugo who called, but Mr Tweedie, accompanied by a younger gentleman.

'I am glad to see you dressed more seemly, Christopher,' said the solicitor. 'How did you leave Mrs Kydd? Well, I trust? Captain Derringer informs me you have evidence regarding fraud on the Hadleigh estate. I need hardly tell you that such an accusation is very serious and must be thoroughly investigated before any action is taken. I have brought my junior partner, Mr Congreve, to witness what it is you are placing in my care, Miss Kydd, and from whom you had it and under what understanding you received it. Your footman or maid can be the second witness.'

Nell blinked. 'Certainly. Tom, will you stay for a moment please?' She drew breath, ordering her words. Mr Congreve gave her an encouraging wink and seated himself at the table ready to take down her statement. 'These are the books that I had in mid-September from my uncle — '

'Mr Jasper Horatio Kydd of Windown Park, Wiltshire,' murmured Mr Tweedie.

Nell glanced nervously at Mr Congreve whose pen scratched noisily over the paper, ' . . . on the understanding that they were all the accounts pertaining to my mother's estate . . . ' another pause while Mr Tweedie intoned Mrs Kydd's full name, ' . . . of

Hadleigh Manor in the county of Hertfordshire.'

Mr Tweedie took the account books and described them for the benefit of Mr Congreve's busy quill. 'The supporting evidence of your claim from your tenants?'

'Dick's father's figures, do you mean? I have them here.'

Once again this was transcribed into legal language and then Mr Tweedie said, 'Lastly, the pieces of parchment which were raked out of the fire in the study at Kydd Court. I shall need the date, to within a few days, and also to have speech with the housemaid concerned.'

Lily, clutching Seth's arm the whole while, gave her story word for word as she had told it to Nell, made her mark on Mr Congreve's sheet and escaped like a hunted rabbit to the kitchen.

Nell could not help but sympathize with the little maid. 'I had no notion this would all be so formal.'

'It must be. These are grave charges. We need now your sworn statements that the volumes Captain Derringer bought from the bookseller came originally from Kydd Court, and Christopher's description of the items in Mr Levy's establishment.'

Tom withdrew to fetch refreshment. Kit

stretched. 'The other affair Captain Derringer is helping me with passed off all right?'

'It did. I was profoundly saddened. This is a bad business indeed.'

'Which other affair?' asked Nell. 'Kit, what have you not told me?'

'What of your office boy? Has he discovered anything?'

Mr Congreve spoke for the first time. 'Alfred has been having the time of his life,' he said with a twinkle in his eye. 'He is firmly of the opinion that he has a shining future ahead of him as a spy. To date he has discovered that your uncle is mean-mouthed and mean-spirited, that he is determined to increase the size of Windown Park by fair means or foul, and that he has an idiosyncratic attitude towards land deals. He likes to pay in cash.'

Nell sighed. 'All of which we knew already. Give Alfred our thanks anyway.'

Kit spun around. 'He pays for land in cash? Not a draft on his bank? That is singular.'

Mr Congreve met his eyes. 'Just so, Mr Kydd.'

Nell looked from one to the other. 'Is it significant?'

Kit's face was as grim as she had ever seen it. 'Only in that without access to my uncle's accounts, there is no way of knowing where the money for his purchase has come from.'

The next morning Nell was in hourly expectation of seeing Hugo. Surely he must visit them today. She could not believe his business affairs were taking up this much time. As she finished trimming the white muslin dress with knots of ribbon (the spencer had been completed at Hadleigh and she was wearing it now), she had the lowering thought that he was deliberately staying away so as not to extend hopes which he had incautiously raised, but at last one of her regular flits to the front parlour window showed his tall, infinitely desirable form in riding coat and boots striding down the street.

He is here, her heart sang, and she instantly discovered in herself a need to go downstairs.

Barely had her slippered feet touched the bottom tread when there was a commotion from the kitchen region. 'Miss Nell! Oh, Miss Nell!'

Lily and Seth were scrambling up the basement stairs, followed by a bewildered Tom Olivant. 'Miss Nell, it's Mr Jasper! I was taking Seth a bite to eat in the stable and we seen him! Seth recognized his chaise and I saw his face behind the glass. It was only for a moment, Miss Nell, as he went past the end of the mews, but it was him all right.' The little maid's voice rose. 'He knows I'm here. He's come to turn me off and send me to Cissy. What shall I do? What shall I do?'

There was no time to think. Nell's moves fell into place with the shimmering certainty of a plan that could only go one way, because if it did not, all would be lost. 'Hush, Lily, he is not here for you. He is here for me and Master Kit. You must pack up every scrap from the kitchen which would give away that we have all of us been living here and take it to the topmost attic, just as we practised the other day.'

As Lily gave a frightened gulp and ran off, there came a knock on the door. *Hugo*, remembered Nell, her heart giving a violent stutter. Was there time to get him inside before her uncle's chaise appeared in the street? She was darting towards the window to see, when from outside she heard her uncle's sharp voice.

'Derringer! What the devil are you doing on my doorstep?'

Nell and Tom looked at each other in appalled dismay. Hugo's cool reply came through the front door. 'Good day, sir. I am glad to find you at home. I had business in this neighbourhood and remembered you

297

saying your town house was available to let. I have been commissioned by my sister to find her a suitable property for next season.'

Oh, Hugo, you marvel!

'Indeed! Do I understand you have an appointment to view?'

Nell shivered. She knew that silky tone well and prayed Hugo would not fall into the trap. 'Upstairs,' she whispered to Tom. 'Tell Kit to start shrouding the furniture *immediately*!'

'An appointment? Why, no. I assumed your housekeeper would show me over the rooms.'

'There is no housekeeper,' she heard her uncle reply. 'Why would I keep a pack of servants eating their heads off in an empty house? The keys are with the agent. I sent him an express telling him to meet me here at noon.'

'Then I will wait with you if it will not inconvenience you. That is a very smart equipage you have there. Are you newly arrived in town?'

'Thank you. Yes, I am just come from Windown Park on my way to Hadleigh and am checking the house on my way through.'

Hadleigh! So he did suspect her! Mr Stapleton must have let his meeting her slip and this was the result.

'Hadleigh?' repeated Hugo with a blend of civility and bafflement.

'Where my brother's widow and daughter now reside. Were you not at Belmont when the scheme was mooted?'

'I recall some discussion or other. I was on the point of setting out for Wiltshire, so did not pay it any particular attention. My friend has an estate just outside Salisbury, you know. I believe I mentioned it at the time. I must say you were quite in the right of it when you said I should find the countryside delightful. I have never seen such fine . . . '

'Seth,' whispered Nell, 'go to the stables and pull the end doors closed on the barouche so it cannot be seen. Then sweep out all the stalls as if we had never been there and tell Dick to take the bays to the livery stables and bide with them until Tom comes. You and I will have to ride as hard as we can for Hadleigh before ever my uncle's chaise sets out.'

'What about Lily? I won't have her going to her Cissy, not no way.'

'She will hide in the top attic with Master Kit and all our effects and he will protect her until we are back again. Hurry, Seth. There is no time to lose.'

She ran up the stairs to where Kit and Tom already had the Holland covers in place and were starting to pile up the recovered books. 'Oh, well done,' she said. 'My sewing and workbox must needs go to the attic too and then the shutters may be closed. I cannot stay and help for Uncle Jasper has just told Hugo he is going straight on to Hadleigh. Seth and I must be away as soon as may be so he does not overtake us on the road. Lock yourselves into the top attic until he is gone, then Tom must retrieve Dick and the bays from the livery stables and drive him and Annie to Hadleigh in the barouche. I will tell my uncle you are marketing should he remark on your absence.'

She then fled up to where Annie was stripping beds for all she was worth, scrambled into her habit and raced back down, passing Lily going upwards with a crammed basket, her eyes big with fear.

'Seth will take care of you, miss,' the little maid said in a tremulous voice.

Nell smiled. 'I know it. And Master Kit will take care of you. Do your best to prevent him doing anything foolish whilst I am away.'

'Just as you won't, I suppose,' jeered Kit, manoeuvring his way out of the drawing room with an armload of books. He kissed her forehead swiftly. 'Stay safe, brat.'

'I will.' She paused a fleeting moment by the front door to hear Hugo now quizzing Uncle Jasper with every appearance of interest on Wiltshire society, and then slipped out of the kitchen and towards the stables.

Seth and Dick had done a good job. The barouche was hidden, the bays gone, the stalls as empty of life as when they had arrived. Whether her uncle was suspicious enough to remember where they were and check on them, Nell had no idea. Hugo, she knew, would attempt to keep his inspection to the principal rooms. If they did penetrate this far however, they would find nothing. Seth gave her a boost into Snowflake's saddle, mounted Valiant himself, and in as inconspicuous a fashion as they could manage, they trotted out of London to the first point at which they could put their horses' heads down and race for Hadleigh.

★   ★   ★

The household at the Manor were amazed to see Nell and Seth gallop up the drive, but set about aiding the deception with alacrity. Old Webb hurried to the stables to assist Seth in rubbing down the sweating horses before turning them out into the paddock. Rose bustled Nell away to dress her hair and change her into her old fawn muslin gown.

It was perhaps an hour later when the sound of carriage horses was heard outside and an autocratic knock thundered on the

301

door. Nell continued to read aloud, her voice smooth and steady, whilst Mama worked at her needlepoint and Mrs Webb darned table linen.

'Mr Jasper Kydd,' announced Olivant.

Nell broke off Lady Catherine's catechism to Elizabeth Bennet and looked up, her eyes wide with surprise. 'Uncle,' she said. 'What ever are you doing here?'

'Good day, Helena,' said her uncle, strolling forward. 'Good day, Margaret. I have come to see how you are progressing.'

Nell gestured about them with her book. 'As you see, we are very snug. I am all amazement at your arrival, sir. Could you not have written? To make such a long journey for so trifling a purpose seems remarkably singular.'

'You imagine I find your welfare trifling, niece?' His cold eyes darted about the room as he spoke, noting each patch and darn on the upholstery, curling his lip at the faded drapes. Mrs Webb bobbed a nervous curtsy and edged out of the door.

'Indeed, I have no notion of what you deem important,' returned Nell. 'It is only that you said you would no longer interfere with our concerns.'

'I see isolation from society has not improved your manners.'

'Oh, we have not been isolated, Jasper,' cut in Mrs Kydd brightly. 'The dowager Lady Moncrief has called. And Mrs Bishop from Undersley House. And we have been to the rectory, such a pleasant daughter the rector has, she and Nell have taken quite a liking to one another.'

'Spare me, Margaret. I do not stay long enough to listen to your fantasies. I am amazed any of these callers returned if they were shown the same lack of courtesy as myself. Are your affairs in such poor order that you cannot offer your visitors refreshment?'

Nell rose. 'I beg your pardon, you will naturally be in need of something after so long on the road. I shall speak to Olivant at once. But do I understand your meaning correctly? Do you not stay tonight?'

Her uncle snorted unpleasantly. 'Remembering my previous inspections, I hardly thought to find you with a fit room. There will be light enough to get me to St Albans.'

Nell hid her satisfaction at this excellent news by raising her eyebrows and saying, 'A fleeting visit indeed. We should be honoured that you have put yourself to so much trouble. Your horses, though, will they not need to rest?'

'Good God, are you addled? I would not bring my own cattle a quarter so far without a change! No doubt the post-boys are even now regaling themselves on your servants' ale whilst that lummox you call a groom does their work for them.'

Nell compressed her lips. 'Both horses and men are in safe hands then,' she said, 'and you need not fear an accident due to the team being too tired to go on.' She withdrew to give the glad tidings to Olivant and to ask whether his professional pride would stretch to offering her uncle non-decanted wine to hasten his departure still further.

When she returned, Mama was placidly enumerating all the improvements they were planning for the house and garden. Jasper was listening with such a supercilious look, Nell was quite sorry Kit wasn't there to wipe it off his face.

'I congratulate you, Helena,' he said, when Mrs Kydd's gentle loquacity faded. 'You must be turning a pretty profit to be contemplating even half these schemes. Do you have your accounts to hand?'

Nell's heart thumped with alarm. 'They are not yet made up. You said I would not have to show them until the quarter.'

He gave a mocking smile. 'I see how it is — you are afraid to let me see what a sad job you are making. I guessed how it would be.'

Nell fought to keep her temper under

control. 'It is not that at all. I simply do not perceive why you are going back on our agreement.'

'Leave them, then. It is of little consequence.' His eyes followed Olivant as the butler brought in wine followed by Mrs Webb with cold meat and fruit. 'Have you let go your footman, Margaret, or did he decide to broaden his horizons once he saw Hadleigh?'

'Neither,' said Nell, answering for her mother. 'He has driven my maid into town to execute some commissions.'

Jasper sipped the wine and made a sour face. 'You allow your servants extraordinary freedom.'

'One man's licence is another's trust.' As she spoke, Nell's ears caught the sound of wheels. Praying it was Tom and Annie, she raised her voice to cover the noise. 'I hope you left my aunt well? And my cousins?'

Jasper applied himself to the cold meat. 'They are in tolerable health.'

'And the children?'

'How the devil should I know? They keep to the nursery.'

Naturally, thought Nell. Why would his grandchildren be treated any differently than his children had been? It was a pity, though — children were generally good for at least a quarter of an hour's conversation. What else could she ask? Oh yes! She should have done it sooner. 'What of my brother? Have you had word of him?'

'I have not. Nor I think are we likely to. I do hope you were not imagining Christopher home in time for Christmas?'

'Why should I not? Much can happen in two months.'

'Certainly. Two months ago, for example, you were living at Kydd Court in expectation of an offer from Philip Belmont.'

'We should not have suited.'

Her uncle continued to eat. 'Had you accepted him however, you would not now be serving watered wine and wearing a gown quite two seasons old.'

'I beg your pardon if I offend your sense of taste, but we consider there are more essential items to spend our income on than fine vintages and personal adornment.'

'A door knocked through in the servants' quarters? New shutters for the second bedroom? The rose arch repaired? These are hardly features which will catch you a husband, Helena.'

'I told you, I have no wish to marry and until I do, these things will add greatly to our comfort here.'

Jasper poured himself out a second glass. 'You will not marry Belmont in any event,' he said. 'He is to be leg-shackled to the Caldwell fright.'

'So Mrs Belmont wrote this week. I am very pleased for them both. Emily is a particular friend of mine.'

He made another disgusted face and slammed his wine down. 'She must be, for you to have made her a present of so eligible a suitor! When I think of the trouble I took to get him to offer for you — '

'I don't believe you did any such thing. It is well known that Mrs Belmont has been entreating Philip to choose a bride these last two years.'

Mrs Kydd drifted into the conversation. 'I have never considered Emily Caldwell so very plain. She has a sweet smile and was most obliging about sorting my silks the last time she was at Kydd. I am sure she and Philip will deal very well together.'

'Enough! I have no patience with either of you. Send to the stables to wake up my post-boys.'

Nell inclined her head and went to the door, where Tom Olivant was standing to attention just as if he hadn't been on the London road a few minutes before. 'Mr Kydd is ready for his carriage, Tom.'

* * *

307

Nell watched her uncle's chaise sweep down the drive and let out a deep, pent-up breath. 'Thank goodness he did not stay. How ever did we put up with him at the Court without losing our tempers twice a day?'

'I don't believe you did, my love,' said Mama.

Nell laughed ruefully. 'I fear you are right. What a lowering thought. That sarcastic manner brings out the worst in me. Do you mind if I take a turn in the grounds? I feel I might burst else.'

'Then you should certainly stay outside,' agreed her mother.

'Miss Nell, you did oughter know that — '

'Later, Tom.' Waving away her footman, Nell strode across the stable yard to the overgrown shrubbery. As she penetrated the main path, gloom from the high bushes chilled her and she realized that in her haste to shake off the taint of her uncle's presence, she had picked up neither shawl nor cloak. She shivered and turned to take a side path back to the autumn border. Out of the corner of her eye she caught a wisp of movement.

'Who is there?' she called, her heart beating unnaturally fast.

The tallest shrub rustled. A man's form took shape beside it.

Instantly, the spectres of the highwaymen

rose up to fill Nell's mind. As she opened her mouth to scream, the man strode out from the shadows.

'Don't you ever do that again!' thundered Hugo.

'What are you doing here?' she demanded, furious at being given such a fright. 'You should be in London with Kit!'

The folds of his riding coat billowed. 'Stay tamely in Half Moon Street whilst you gallop hell for leather across the country?' he said incredulously. 'Burn it, Nell, what do you take me for? Your brother can look after himself. *You* cannot!'

'Of course I can! Not look after myself indeed! What would you have me not do?'

'Ride out of London by the most dangerous road you can find with only a groom as foolish as yourself to protect you, of course!'

Injustice rose up in her. 'Hugo, I had to do it, you know I did! You heard my uncle say he was coming on to Hadleigh! What if he had not found me here? You cannot have expected me not to make at least a push to get here before him.'

'Naturally I expected you to. But decently and sensibly in the barouche as befits a young lady, accompanied by your maid and footman as well as your groom. I strung out my inspection of the house as long as I dared to make sure of giving you a head start.'

'Vastly obliging, I'm sure, but I never thought you would do otherwise. It was what gave me the confidence to try to beat him. Even so, you do not know Uncle Jasper as I do. He was *expecting* to find me in Half Moon Street. He was looking for me. One missed pin or strand of muslin in the drawing room, one breath of scent upstairs and he would be perfectly capable of abandoning you to the agent and whipping up his horses after me.'

'In which case I would have followed him as fast as I could and put him in a ditch without the least compunction, instead of being forced to dawdle in the vanguard to ensure that cow-handed footman of yours did not overturn your maid! Do not try to deflect me with spurious reason, Nell. I *know* what speed you must have been travelling at!'

'Of course I was! For heaven's sake, it was no time to be observing decorum! Who was to see me? What does one gallop more or less matter? You have no right to define my conduct!'

Hugo's hands clenched as if he was fighting not to take her by the shoulders and shake some sense into her. 'Not your conduct, imbecilic girl, your safety! Even without the danger of highwaymen, a single stumble and you could have been thrown! Your horse could have fallen on you! You could have galloped full tilt into a chaise or the stage, not seeing it until it was too late! You could have been maimed for life or worse than that, killed!'

They were both shouting by now, each furious with the other. 'My life, my risk!' stormed Nell and whirled away from him.

White with passion, Hugo yanked her back and crushed her lips to his. His arms held her fast to his breast making escape impossible. '*My* life,' he said raggedly against her mouth. 'Good God, Nell. How can you not have known?'

15

It seemed a very long time before Nell's swimming, whirling senses brought her back to the world.

'Hugo?' She leaned back against his encircling arms to look wonderingly into his face.

His hold slackened, but not by much. Nell could feel every strong, reassuring inch of him. His eyes were dark and passionate and entrancingly possessive. 'I love you,' he said. 'I loved you in that dreadful dress at Belmont. I loved you even more in your riding habit with the wind blowing at your hair the next morning and I positively adored you in your nightgown in Half Moon Street.'

At this last reference, Nell felt herself blush from her toes to the roots of her hair. 'Hugo, you cannot have admired me that first evening,' she said to cover the delicious hammering of her heart. 'You looked appalled when Philip introduced us!'

He held her closer, beautifully secure, teasing pins out of her hair to let the cloud of it surround his fingers. 'Can you blame me? I was expecting to see the leggy, jealous-angled child you were ten years ago. I was not expecting a bewitching young woman to arrow straight into my heart.'

She blushed again. 'Did I do so?'

'You did.' He tipped up her chin and kissed her more gently than she would have believed possible for such a powerful, virile man.

Another glow rippled through her. Much more of this and she would be wax in his hands. 'You hid it well,' she managed to say.

'Not by choice, I assure you. Call it the penalties of being a spy. I was never nearer letting Kit's affairs go hang in my life.'

'But you disapprove of me. You never see me but to scold.'

His answer was to kiss her again with a thoroughness of mouth and hands which left a molten core of arousal in certain startled parts of her body. '*Because* I love you. Heaven help me, Nell, you terrify me with your daring even as I glory in every defiant step you take. How do we get out of this miserable walk? I refuse to remember the happiest moment of my life as taking place here.'

Nell swallowed, suddenly breathless. 'Turn left at the laburnum. Webb has not had the opportunity to prune along here yet; it used to be the most charmingly shaded ramble. And I have to tell you, sir, that I do not believe a single word you are saying. After our first few encounters, you were quite odiously distant.'

313

'Naturally. You told me everyone assumed me to be hanging out for a wife. Sweetheart, you're cold. Why do you not have a shawl? Does nobody in your household look after you? Here, let me wrap you in my coat. You must see I could not afford for your uncle to make enquiries about me and guess my connection with Kit.'

'I might concede that,' she said, allowing herself a lingering glance at his glorious physique as he divested himself of his coat in order to drape it about her shoulders. 'But was it also necessary to hide your intentions from me?'

He had the grace to look abashed. 'I did not set out to, but remember I was in Northamptonshire under false pretences. I did not wish you to think I was merely dallying with your affections. It was the damnedest position to be in!'

Warmth filled Nell. She had not imagined those moments of shared rapport. But she was not finished with him yet. 'And London? You were not playing a part there.'

'You were unchaperoned,' he protested in virtuous tones. 'It would have been vastly improper to declare myself!'

She turned a laughing face up at him. 'So you circumvented your conscience by teasing me disgracefully in the bookshop and then flirting with Sophia Norland under my very eyes! Poppycock, Hugo. You and Kit were engaged in being sleuths and I was an irritating distraction. Admit it.'

'Vixen,' he said tenderly. He glanced with satisfaction at the cross walk they were approaching. 'Roses. Much more appropriate.' He drew her underneath a scented arch, laid his hat by her feet and held both her hands. 'Nell, my darling, I love every wilful, spirited inch of you and I swear to protect you and provide for you all the days of my life. Will you do me the very great honour of accepting my hand in marriage?'

He looked so extraordinarily handsome standing there in the evening sun, in shirtsleeves and waistcoat with the last two or three overblown roses shedding petals on his dark hair that Nell's heart melted clean away. 'I will,' she said and stretched up on tiptoe to kiss him on the lips.

'My heart,' he breathed, and loosed her hands to gather her to him.

Some considerable time later, they strolled back to the house with her arm entwined in his. 'And now,' she said, 'tell me the real reason you were so concerned by my flight today.'

'Are highwaymen lurking behind every bush and rabbit holes strewn across your path not enough?'

The sun had not sunk so far that Nell could not meet his eyes steadily. 'Hugo, I love and revere you and there is nothing I wish more than to share your life and make you happy. I understand your desire to protect me, but concealing the facts means I am likely to stray into far worse danger through ignorance.'

She could see him struggling with himself. 'We were always going to tell you as soon as we were sure,' he said at last. 'I wish I could spare you this pain. My overwhelming worry today was what your uncle might do if he happened on you alone.'

'I don't understand.' She frowned, catching up with his words. 'Wait, what do you mean, spare me pain?'

His deep green eyes were filled with helpless compassion. 'There is no easy way to say this, sweetheart. Certainly we must never say it to your mama. Kit and I believe that your father's death was no accident.'

No accident? But that would make it . . . *murder*. For a moment, the wide lawn swam around Nell in the gathering dusk. She forced herself to breathe. 'What makes you think so? Why would you imagine such a terrible thing?'

Hugo supported her, cursing himself for his ham-fisted delivery. 'John Farley,' he said at length.

'Old John? The foreman at Kydd Court?'

'Young John. The groom your uncle hustled into the first regiment he could find regardless of whether or not it was suitable for the boy's skills.'

Nell stared. 'But he did him a favour! Johnny wanted to go.'

He started her moving towards the house again. 'My heart, did it never occur to anyone to ask *why* an inoffensive young man should be so anxious to get himself killed far away from the horses and land that he loved?'

'What are you saying? That Johnny was responsible? Hugo, he grew up with us at Kydd. He would *never* have harmed Papa. He was eaten up by guilt over the horse bolting — though how he could have prevented it I have never seen.'

'Love, he wanted to get away because he thought he was unfit to be a groom. He found thorns under your father's saddle when they captured the horse and blamed himself for not checking the tack properly. He imagined his eyesight or his mind must be failing.'

'Why did he not say something?' cried Nell, distressed. 'To torture himself like that! He must have known we would pay Dr Eversly to examine him.'

'He was not thinking rationally. It had happened before. The horse reared — and your father's broken leg was the result. The second time, your father died.'

Tears ran down Nell's cheeks. 'Poor Johnny. Oh, poor Johnny. What a terrible burden for him.'

'Hush love, for we come to the meat of the matter. Did you not tell me you occasionally met your uncle whilst on your way back from a ride?'

'Yes. He did not approve of my going out before breakfast and was forever arguing the unconventionality of it with Papa. I used to think he deliberately rose early to catch me, for in general he went nowhere near the stables.' She broke off in appalled comprehension. 'Hugo, do you mean that it was *he* who — '

'Those thorns did not get forced into the horse's leather by accident. We cannot prove anything. All we can do is show the opportunity existed. It is suspicious enough that the trouble only occurred during your uncle's visits, and those visits did not begin with any regularity until after Kit had gone to India.'

'And Kit had thorns under his saddle there too! But my uncle planted these. He planted them and let Johnny take the blame! He smiled and sympathized and stole our money and turned away our servants and — ' Nell pulled away from Hugo, looking wildly around as rage poured into her. 'I'll kill him! I'll kill him myself! Why did you let him go? I'll saddle Snowflake. I'll race after him and — '

Hugo restrained her, gripping her in his arms until she ceased to struggle and her angry sobs quieted. 'Hush. Hush, love. I understand. I understand very well.'

Nell lay against his chest, wrung out and helpless. 'Such a termagant as you will think me.'

He gave a low laugh and passed her a handkerchief. 'It will come about, Nell. We will make it so. And *now* I have full right to act for you.'

She quickened at his possessive tone and tucked her hand once more into his arm. 'Hugo, how do you know all this about Papa and Johnny?'

'Because, my darling, your uncle is not the only person hereabouts with connections in the Army of Occupation.'

'Oh, your useful friend, I remember. Has he located Johnny then and had speech with him?'

He smiled down at her with a trace of smugness. 'Better than that. I put Henri Dessin on to it. He traced the 28th to Paris, procured Johnny's discharge and arranged for him to be shipped home. That was the reason we had to meet the Portsmouth stage. I got the boy and his testimony safely to Mr Tweedie two days ago and then smuggled him by night to his family at Belmont.'

'Hugo!'

'I will accept a kiss as a reward . . . '

She blushed. 'Hugo, we are near at the door!' Her mind continued to resolve puzzles. 'That is why we did not see you yesterday! You were at Belmont! And you came straight to Half Moon Street this morning and then on here. You must be exhausted!'

He caught her in an opportunistic hug a fraction of a second before Olivant opened the front door to them. 'On the contrary, for some reason I find myself wonderfully replenished.'

Not by a blink of an eyelid, did Olivant show that he had registered their hasty separation. 'Good evening, sir. The mistress is in the drawing room.' He divested Nell of Hugo's coat, giving it a practised shake and brushing it down before restoring it to its owner. 'May I be the first to wish you joy?'

Nell blushed in confusion but Hugo grinned broadly and said,' You may indeed,' with such heartiness and such disinclination to keep their new-found love private that she found herself in her mother and housekeeper's presence in a turmoil of unsettled spirits long before she was ready to make a declaration.

'Mama,' she said, her fingers gripping Hugo's arm. 'Hugo and I are — ' The enormous word 'engaged' trembled on her breath.

Her swain gave her a laughing look. 'Indian manners, ma'am,' he said, settling Nell masterfully on the sofa and bending low over Mrs Kydd's hand. 'I have committed the unpardonable solecism of offering for your daughter before inquiring as to whether my suit is acceptable to you. What is to be done?'

'Foolish boy,' said Mrs Kydd placidly. 'As if I could be anything but pleased. I had not thought it would take you so long. Ah, Olivant, how timely. A toast is certainly required. Mrs Webb, you will join us? And the rest of you?'

At the edge of her vision, Nell saw the rich gleam of Madeira being poured into the best glasses. Grinning all over his face, Tom lit more candles. She was aware of Cook in the doorway, of the other servants crowding behind. Panic filled her. It was too public, too soon. Her instinctive flight was halted by Hugo who put a glass into her hand and met her agitated gaze with loving understanding.

'To us,' he said softly.

'To my daughter and my new son,' said Mama.

'To Miss Nell and the Captain,' murmured the staff. Mrs Webb gave a happy sob.

In a dream, Nell raised the glass to her lips and felt the amber wine tingle along her veins.

'No going back now, sweetheart,' said Hugo, his eyes never leaving hers. 'We've been witnessed by your entire household.'

Nell swallowed. 'Why would I want to?' She took another sip and realized that only now did Hugo drink as well. The knowledge slid the world back into focus. 'I wish Kit was here.'

'An' I wish Lily was,' said Seth loudly. 'What if Mr Jasper goes back to town and finds her?'

'He won't, Seth. He is to lie at St Albans tonight. He said so.'

'Aye, an' he said to solicitor as how he'd look after you. I don't trust'n. When are we going back?'

Nell opened her mouth to reply, then looked uncertainly at Hugo.

He smiled wryly at this change in his status. 'Tomorrow,' he said. And as the servants filtered away to the back premises, 'Not that I would not prefer you safe here, but we have china warehouses to inspect and only you can identify the Kydd possessions. I would have this business settled as soon as may be.'

'Oh, of course. With every passing day, the tableware may be sold.'

His eyes teased her. 'I was thinking rather that we cannot be married before Kit is restored to life and free to give you away.'

Nell's mouth dried without warning. 'There is another reason for going back tomorrow,' she said quickly. 'The only modish outfits I possess are in town. I am losing count of the number of times I find myself ill-dressed in your company.'

'We are a pair tonight then, for I must dine in riding clothes.' He turned to Mrs Kydd. 'Will you forgive us, ma'am?'

'Engaged couples are known to be eccentric. Your father once escorted me to a picnic in full evening dress, Nell.'

'No, did he?' An involuntary giggle escaped her before she was struck by a most satisfactory consequence of her engagement. 'I will have to make no more insipid gowns! The *Ladies' Monthly Museum* says it is only unmarried girls who must stick to white in their first season.'

Hugo turned his dark head to look at her quizzically. 'You still want a London season, then?'

'Do you not trust me with the town beaux?'

'That depends. Do you trust me with the Vienna beauties?'

She sat up in shock. 'Vienna? Why do you go to Vienna?'

He grinned. 'I have a business to catch up with, love. And I would introduce you to my sister. And my guardian.'

'Oh, you meant *together!*' Relief that he was not leaving flooded her, startling her with its vehemence. 'That was most unhandsome of you!'

'I admit it. I apologize.'

A frisson of excitement shivered through her, born of his teasing look and the faint male scent of him. 'When — when do you wish to go?'

A wicked gleam danced at the back of his eyes. 'I would say before Christmas, except the sea crossing that time of year is hardly appropriate for a bridal journey.'

He was desirous of marrying her this soon? She darted a startled look at his face and felt her own cheeks flame at the unmistakable warmth in his expression. 'I daresay I could endure the discomfort if your business needs are so urgent,' she said with creditable calm.

Hugo bent to prod one of the logs in the grate. 'It is not my business needs that are urgent,' he murmured.

Nell gave a small gasp, marvelling that she could preserve a decorous facade when every brush of his sleeve against hers, every nuance of his voice was suddenly setting her on fire.

'Oh dear, should I be inquiring into your prospects, Hugo?' asked Mrs Kydd, folding her embroidery away as Olivant announced dinner.

'Of course you should,' said Nell, seeking revenge for the effect her betrothed was having on her. 'All he will tell me is that he has money in Funds, a tendency to boredom and various agents to do all his work.'

He tucked her arm in his as they went through to the dining room. 'My wife will not want, I assure you. I shall have to make changes in my lifestyle, though. At the moment, I cannot even offer her a home.'

'I knew it,' said Nell with satisfaction. 'He intends to live here and sponge off us, Mama. I should have foreseen it when he was professing such an interest in Hadleigh the other day.'

Hugo inspected the dishes on the table and carved both her and her mother a portion of duck. 'Which is precisely why your uncle pressed you to wed Philip. A happy-go-lucky young man fond of hunting and dancing, with his own manor to run, is unlikely to have the time to look into his bride's dowry two counties away.'

'Unlike a down-at-heel, half-pay officer with an eye to future rents,' agreed Nell. 'Say what you like, Uncle Jasper is a shrewd judge of character.'

The banter continued in a similar vein throughout dinner and the hands of piquet which followed. 'Every single rubber to me,' said Hugo when Mrs Kydd had withdrawn in a most irresponsible manner to bed, giving the engaged couple a few minutes alone to say goodnight. 'But as I am feeling mellow, a kiss will suffice in lieu of payment.'

Nell moved into his arms, all her senses heightened. 'You took unfair advantage. I never *have* been able to count cards, which I think you knew full well. Wait until I play you at chess and then we will see who has the better grasp of strategy.'

He traced her lips lightly with his finger, then stroked her throat and let his hand linger on her bodice until she trembled. 'If you move your pawns as recklessly as you lay down discards, I shall look forward to it. I know a most enjoyable variation on the normal rules of taking pieces which I learnt in Portugal.'

'And can this variation be played in company?' said Nell breathlessly. From the way his hand was caressing her, she had no doubt at all about which sex had taught him.

'Hmm, on reflection, we had better leave it until after we are married.' He bent his head to hers.

Nell surrendered wholly to his embrace. It seemed that she had been waiting more than just this one evening for the continued declaration of his love. She was aware of his body pressed against hers, of his hands sliding over the thin muslin of her gown. She had a sudden vision of herself in oyster satin and him in tight-fitting pantaloons and how his hands and body would feel to her then.

As she arched against him involuntarily, he groaned and pulled away, his eyes green and rueful, his breathing ragged. 'You had best go to bed, sweetheart, else you are like to wake a fallen woman. Do you happen to know if the pump in the yard is in working order?'

'I — yes — why?' She gazed at him, bewildered, as he steered her to the stairs. Had he not enjoyed their embrace? Why had he broken it off?

'Something else I learned in Portugal. I shall ask Tom Olivant to hold me under it.'

She looked at him uncertainly, her hand on the newel. 'Goodnight, then.'

'Sweet dreams, my love. Be ready to start in good time tomorrow. Believe me, the sooner we have evidence against your uncle, the better.'

★ ★ ★

Kit received the news of their engagement with irritating aplomb. 'Knew something was in the wind. Hugo's been like a rutting stag for days.'

Fortunately, before her betrothed could express his opinion of this highly uncomplimentary description, Annie interrupted with a request that Nell come and change. 'It'll have to be the primrose,' the maid said with a pointed look at Kit. 'Being as how *someone* let the cambric get crushed behind all manner of boxes while we was away.'

'It would have to be anyway,' said Nell peaceably. 'I still do not have a pelisse to go with the green dress. But,' she said, suddenly struck, 'it is no longer my problem. At the first hint of rain, Captain Derringer will feel obliged to leap up and shield me with his umbrella. Really, there is no end to the advantages of being engaged.'

They had no luck in their search for Kydd china that day, though they learnt a good deal about each other's tastes and Nell discovered that in the early days of an engagement, a hackney carriage was a far more convenient mode of transport than a curricle.

'It is an odd courtship,' mused Hugo, kissing her lips lingeringly as they were jolted over cobbles slick with rain once again the following morning. 'Escorting you to warehouses and booksellers instead of to balls and the theatre.'

'It is unconventional, certainly,' agreed Nell. She rescued her bonnet just as it was about to tumble to the floor and twitched her detested black cloak (a concession to the dismal weather) out of the way. 'Hugo, what if we do not find enough evidence to confront my uncle?'

'Then Kit comes out of hiding, we create a huge scandal about the state of his inheritance and I marry you regardless,' he said.

She nestled against him. 'When we are married, you can escort me to as many balls as you like. Annie and I are designing the most improper dress in oyster satin and sea-green gauze. She has lost all her scruples over what I may wear now that we are engaged.'

Hugo gave an odd groan and eased a finger around his neckcloth.

Nell looked at him inquiringly.

He shook his head. 'Sorry, I was endeavouring to think about pumps. You do not have to fashion your own clothes, love. I have money enough to commission you a wardrobe.'

'But I like to. You may save your fortune to buy me a sumptuous emerald necklace. Showier than Sophia Norland's garnets for preference.'

Hugo grinned, then glancing out of the window, suddenly rapped on the glass. 'Hi, driver, stop a moment.' He turned to Nell. 'Stay there.' He dived out into the slanting rain and into a blank-faced building. In less than five minutes he was back, thrusting a soft parcel into her arms. 'Not emeralds, I'm afraid.'

Curious, Nell unwrapped one corner and peeped in. 'Better,' she cried, her eyes shining. It was a length of deep green wool, fine and soft, the very stuff she had wanted for a pelisse and coincidentally the exact colour of Hugo's eyes. She kissed his cheek impetuously. 'It is perfect! Thank you! I can throw this dreadful cloak away and make a start tonight. How ever did you find the time to look with all the other tasks you have been doing?'

Hugo's expression was complacent. 'The benefit of organizational experience. I put a mercantile contact on to it. He has a russet velvet you may view another day, if you wish.'

'If I wish!' Nell sat up eagerly. 'Oh Hugo,

can we not go back there now?'

But they were clattering to a halt before yet another china warehouse. 'Business first, pleasure later,' scolded Hugo, preparing to alight and casting an appraising look at a group of ragged boys as he fished out coins to pay the jarvey.

As they were accompanied into the first of the rooms by a fawning assistant, all Nell's thoughts about russet velvet vanished. 'Hugo,' she whispered, her hand flying to her breast, 'that Chinese jardinière. I'll swear it is ours.'

As they walked from table to table, it was evident why they had not found anything at the previous establishments. Nell identified item after item. She turned from the Worcester tableware depicting a different fruit on each setting, with tears in her eyes. 'Papa's favourite,' she whispered.

Hugo turned to the obsequious assistant. 'Have everything we have indicated packed up and conveyed to the manager's office, if you please. For a purchase of this size, I would prefer to deal with him. I will, of course, mention how helpful you have been.'

The assistant bowed and hurried off, snapping his fingers at lesser mortals on the way.

'Listen, my darling,' said Hugo in a low voice. 'I am going outside to send one of those urchins for Mr Tweedie. I do not want the people here to be aware of our actions before we have an official witness. Stolen property, no matter that it was bought in good faith, carries no commission.'

So Nell strolled about the room, pretending to admire a macabre depiction of dead game-birds on a ewer intended for washing water. It seemed no time at all before Hugo was back at her side.

'Ugh,' he said, glancing at the ewer with a shudder, and they made their way in as dawdling a fashion as they could contrive towards the manager's office.

Nell could only admire what she privately called Hugo's diplomatic manner as he spun out the interval before Mr Tweedie's arrival with fulsome compliments on the stock, praise for the manager's most recent additions and congratulations on the calibre of the agents who had discovered the various treasures. Long before it was over, however, she felt the beginnings of a headache, and when the solicitor fussed in, flanked by his partner, and the atmosphere in the office descended from awkwardly unpleasant to distinctly hostile, she became truly ill.

'Hugo,' she whispered in desperation. 'Might I sign my identification of the pieces and wait for you in the bookseller's opposite?

I cannot abide this wrangling much longer.'

He looked at her in quick concern, glanced out of the grimy window to where the rain had stopped and weak sunlight was filtering through the clouds, and had the matter organized within minutes. 'Wait for me here,' he said, escorting her into the cool, quiet bookstore. 'I shall finish the business with as much dispatch as possible.'

She gave him a wan smile. 'I will do very well, I assure you. A Milton sonnet will soothe me in no time.'

'Send you to sleep, more like,' riposted Hugo. He caught the proprietor's inquisitive eye and grimaced. 'Burn it, I cannot even give you a parting kiss in here.' He raised her gloved hand to his lips instead and strode hastily back to the warehouse.

Nell pulled out a volume at random, saw that it was indeed Milton and put it back with a smile. Her eye fell on a stack of lithographs at the back of a recess. She moved towards them and realized with astonishment that the topmost was *The Lamb* by William Blake. Mr Blake had been an acquaintance of Papa's and she knew he had made very few copies of his early poetry because the work was so time-consuming. So few indeed, that she was certain this was Papa's own engraving. What could be more likely? She had ample proof that Uncle Jasper had disposed of the Kydd china collection at the warehouse. Small inconvenience for him to sell what remained of her father's library just across the road. She went through the rest of the engravings with gathering anger and then turned her attention to the folios, transferring everything from Kydd to the proprietor's counter to await Hugo's return.

Concentrating fiercely, she did not notice the clatter and bustle outside, the calls for assistance with unloading boxes from the roof of a chaise. Even when the door to the bookseller's opened and a greatcoated figure stalked in carrying two heavy portmanteaux, she only registered the disturbance as a draught of damp air circling her ankles. This was a much more prosperous shop than the previous one she and Hugo had visited. Nell had found some of her father's most cherished possessions around the shelves and was burning with such a rage it was doubtful whether she would have given the Regent himself the time of day had he popped up in front of her at that moment.

Fortunately for her future position in society, the newcomer was not the Prince Regent. Unfortunately, he was the one person in the world who constituted a threat to that future.

'Good day,' said a cold, cutting voice behind Nell's stack of shelves. 'As you see, I return earlier than expected. I trust this will not prevent you advancing me a sum of money on my latest acquisitions?'

Nell froze, her heart jumping with fear. She looked around frantically, but the recess was packed tight with books. There was no hiding place, no way of escape.

'Good day, sir. No, no, delighted, I assure you. It *is* rather short notice . . . '

There was a snap and a series of thuds as of a portmanteau being opened and its contents tipped onto the counter. 'I have no time to waste. If you are not prepared to handle my business, say so at once and I will dispose of these elsewhere. I must conclude the matter and be on my way today, for I have no wish to travel on a Sunday.' A second set of thuds followed the first.

'No indeed, sir.' Nell heard the bookseller's indrawn breath as he lifted a volume. 'Dante's *Divinia commedia*,' he breathed in reverential tones.

'What will you give me for it?' said her uncle's curt voice. Then the timbre of his words changed. 'What are those doing still out? You assured me they would go into your stock straight away.' There was a sound of a fist crashing down on the counter.

'They did, sir,' said the proprietor nervously. 'It is the young lady's purchases. Picked out near everything you brought in, she has.'

'*Which young lady?*' And the next second a looming shadow darkened Nell's alcove. Her uncle stood there, radiating hatred. 'So, Helena,' he said, 'Stapleton was *not* mistaken.'

A moment before, Nell had been sure she was paralysed. Now rage and adrenalin between them brought cool words to her lips. 'How extraordinary to see you, Uncle Jasper,' she said clearly. 'I had thought you back at Windown Park with my aunt and cousins. As you see, your comments on my attire have not gone unheeded. Annie and I have been in the cloth emporium along the way.' She indicated the parcel dangling from her wrist. 'But she felt unwell so is lying down in the inn with the rest of our purchases whilst I await Seth here.'

He gave a thin, unpleasant smile. 'How . . . unfortunate . . . for you.'

She raised her eyebrows. 'He will not be many minutes, I assure you.'

'That gapseed? Alone in London? He has likely walked the horses down the wrong street and mistaken his road entirely. You had best wait in my chaise.'

'I am in no difficulty here. Ladies often visit libraries and suchlike alone.'

'The more fool they.' He took her wrist in a grip of iron and forced her into the main part of the shop. 'My money, sir? Or do I take the books elsewhere?'

The proprietor hastily counted out a large roll of notes. His mouth opened as Jasper Kydd snatched up the empty portmanteaux, hauled Nell unceremoniously out through the door and thrust her into his coach. It was raining again. There was no one on the street. Nell could only hope the man had not been too immersed in his new treasures to hear the words 'Uncle Jasper' and 'Windown Park' and would report them to Hugo along with her pile of evidence when he came to fetch her.

'Back!' Her uncle snarled the order to the post-boys. 'Back the way we came! Spring 'em!'

'Back where?' said Nell. 'What of my — ?'

Jasper Kydd's fist crashed into the side of her jaw. 'Silence!' His face was a livid mask of calculation. 'All is not lost,' he muttered to himself as the chaise jolted forward. 'I can collect the money for the porcelain when I return. Aye and more besides. The ability to turn adversity to advantage, that is the mark of the victor.'

Nell huddled herself into the corner of the carriage, tears standing in her eyes, her hands clamped to her pain-filled cheekbone. She was rigid with shock and wildly, fiercely angry.

Her uncle was still muttering. 'Yes, yes, that's the course to take. Sooner than I would have liked, but no help for that now. It will settle Stapleton's hash once and for all. The nerve, holding out against me when all Wiltshire knows it is bellows to mend with him. Bad judge of investments, and lives beyond his income. He will not be proof against what I have to offer.'

The rain lashed down. Half-familiar streets swam and bulged in Nell's vision. This was not the road to the west. 'Where — where are we going?' she said, forcing the words through the agony in her jaw.

He turned to her. She saw the glitter of madness in his eyes. 'Why, to Kydd Court, God rot the place. Where else but to Kydd?'

16

This could not be happening. It was impossible that Nell was imprisoned in a bouncing, swaying coach nursing a hideously swollen jaw and listening to an embittered uncle tell over the slights and insults of a lifetime. His vitriol against the whole human race would have made her vomit had she not encased herself in this horrified disbelief for protection.

'I always hated your father,' he said at one point. 'The favourite child. Older, stronger, cleverer, comelier. Popular.' He spat the last word. 'I hated the way he excelled at everything without even trying. The way he thought himself too damned superior to use his talents and frittered away his inheritance on hot-air philosophers and no-hope writers. I hated our parents too. Showering the world on him and giving me a beggarly allowance and patting me condescendingly on the head when I worked like blazes to raise the money for Windown Park. *I'll* be the one who is remembered though. My estate is my own, not handed to me on a silver platter. It was bigger than Kydd once — and will be again.'

He lapsed into a brooding silence. Nell began to think the devil himself was driving him when they stopped to change the sweating horses and she heard him flay the ostlers and grooms unceasingly until the new team was hitched. He bought a bottle of brandy but no food and sat sipping it and staring out at the hurtling countryside whilst Nell's stomach growled and her hopes that Hugo would overtake them grew ever harder to cling on to.

After the next change he began calculating again. 'I only left this morning. I'll tell the staff I forgot something and send the post-boys to the Cross Keys so they don't gossip. You will have to remain in the chaise until I can get you in at the library door. Fortunately I have trained your tiresome servants to stay out of my way whilst I am in residence.'

Daylight waned. The miles into Northamptonshire were eaten up under flying hoofs and blurred wheels. Jasper still had not eaten. Nell was unsurprised his mind had turned if he had been travelling at this pace for nigh on three days and starving himself into the bargain. She herself was achingly hungry. What had he meant by getting her in through the library door? What did he intend?

'Yes,' he was musing, 'they will be at

church in the morning (how fortunate that you have drilled piety into them, Helena) and I shall give them the rest of the day to themselves so they will not hurry back. That will be ample time. Servants always take advantage. And by then I will be long gone.'

Ample time for what? In desperation, Nell tried to reckon how far behind her Hugo might be. Provided he was behind her. Provided he had not gone chasing into Wiltshire. Frantically, she reminded herself of his *organizational experience*. Of course he was behind her. He would not trust to a single overheard phrase. He would have contacts checking all the roads out of London. Once assured of their destination, he would know of this devil-ridden progress through the turnpikes and staging posts almost as soon as it happened. Any minute now she would see Conqueror's rangy brown flanks pulling past the window.

They stopped to change horses yet again. Jasper pulled the blinds down. She would have to be very careful, she realized, noticing the mad glitter back in her uncle's eyes. She must not enrage him. She would have to buy Hugo time.

'I am afraid you are going to be uncomfortable for a while, Helena,' he said conversationally. He rummaged in his valise, drawing out a crumpled neckcloth. 'This subservience you are affecting does not convince me at all.' And before she knew what he was about, he had twisted her arm sharply behind her back causing her to cry out in pain and making it quite impossible for her to prevent him from capturing the other wrist and tying them both together with shocking efficiency. 'I cannot have you sidling to the stables for assistance once we arrive, or blundering down to the Home Farm.' His low, unpleasant laugh made the hairs on Nell's skin stand up. 'Not that it would serve you. There isn't a mount left on the estate that would get you even as far as the village. Kydd is all but a shell. My revenge shapes nicely.'

'Shells can be refilled,' said Nell, struggling futilely against her bindings. 'There is nothing wrong that hard work and sound management cannot put right. When Kit returns to the Court, he will make Kydd as profitable as ever.'

Jasper pulled a second cravat out of his bag. 'I told your father years ago that his habit of encouraging you to argue with your elders would lead to your downfall. See how right I was.' With a quick movement he pinned her hard against the squabs with his knee and wound the neckcloth viciously twice around her mouth. 'I have always found silent women to be vastly more agreeable companions,' he said, tying it. 'Ask your aunt if it is not so. As for your brother, on whom you place such touching reliance, the last information I received from India put Christopher under several fathoms of water in Bombay harbour. Typical of him, thwarting me even in death. Having no body as proof has put me to a great deal of trouble, with the fool executors pronouncing him only 'missing' and refusing to grant probate. I have had to employ considerable subterfuge to get what is rightfully mine. Were it not for that, I could have raised the money easily.'

Nell's gag distorted her words into an angry swelling of sound. 'Why did you need the money? Why *now*?'

'Because Stapleton's affairs are exigent enough for him to be selling now of course!' He paused and went on more softly. 'But it serves. The longer I spend in Northamptonshire, the more I want to witness the ruination of Kydd Court. I want to squeeze it dry. I want the whole estate reduced to a mere memory. Ground to dust and its owners' names with it. Then my humiliation will be salved. *My* dynasty will be the one that lives on: the Kydds of Window Park. There will be no others left.'

He was going to kill her. The knowledge numbed Nell's mind. She had found out he was selling Kydd effects to finance his own estate and she must therefore be removed as he had already removed her father and Kit.

Pushing aside the throbbing of her jaw and the discomfort of her bound wrists, Nell desperately considered her options. If he was going to take her in via the library he would first have to go through the house and open the door. There would be a space of perhaps five minutes when she would be in the coach alone. She could feel behind her back for the door handle, swing round and down, and edge around the house to the kitchen. Clarrie could hide her in the cellar whilst the pantry boy ran to Belmont for help.

Opening her eyes, she saw her uncle studying her coldly. 'No, you are altogether too mobile still,' he murmured and although she struggled fiercely he got her legs up onto the seat, sat his full weight on them and bound her ankles. 'That should settle any ideas you might be harbouring about escape,' he said.

She glared at him with loathing. He laughed and swigged his brandy.

At the Court, Jasper directed the post-boys to continue on the sweep until they reached the side of the house, then instructed them to unhitch the horses and take them to the Cross Keys. 'Be back at ten in the morning,' he said.

'But it's Sunday tomorrow!'

'I feel sure an additional fee will take care of your conscience.' He strode towards the main door. 'I find I forgot something,' Nell heard him say calmly. 'Lay a fire in the library, leave plenty of logs and candles and bring food and wine to me there. Then do not disturb me unless I ring for you.'

Trussed helplessly on the seat with the gag tight around her mouth, Nell was unable to get free. She was furious with both herself and her uncle by the time he opened the door on her.

'You may walk, Helena,' he said, 'but I warn you that at the first sign of disobedience I will tie your feet again.' He cut the knot away and pulled her upright.

Nell's eyes fastened with horror on the blade in his hand.

Her uncle smiled maliciously. 'I always carry a knife in case of footpads, my dear. You surely didn't think I would travel on England's roads unarmed.' From his coat pocket, he drew out a silver-mounted pistol. 'I have this too,' he said, and stroked its muzzle along her swollen jaw. 'You would do well to remember it.'

It was only having had nothing to eat all day that prevented Nell from choking there and then on her own vomit. As it was, she hobbled up the steps to the terrace and in through the library door with sweat standing on her brow and her heart thumping twice as fast as usual.

Jasper pushed her roughly into a chair. 'One sound — one movement — and I bind your legs again.'

He need not have worried. He had chosen one of the wing chairs, deep and soft. It would be impossible for Nell to struggle out of it without him seeing her. She was appalled at the number of missing volumes in the library — many more than she had discovered in the bookshops.

Her uncle followed the direction of her gaze. 'They have been good for something after all,' he said sardonically. 'Who would have believed it?' He pulled out what Nell recognized as the catalogue she had helped Papa's secretary to compile two summers ago. He hadn't been making a new one at all. That had been a fabrication to explain his continued presence at Kydd. Working methodically along the shelves, he transferred volumes to his first portmanteau, ticking entries as he went. 'Did you know this used to be a drawing room when I was a child? It was your father's notion to move the library in here as it had so much more pleasant an aspect than the original room. Naturally my father thought it a wonderful scheme. I hated them for it at the time — this door had long been my private exit from the house, you understand — but it has made my life very much easier these past weeks.'

These past weeks? The words startled Nell. Was it really that short a time since she and Mama had left Kydd Court? How much had happened since then. Reviewing it in a scatter of rushed scenes, Nell wondered that she had found time to sleep. The only thing she truly regretted was going to the Norland party with Kit. If she had held out against his persuasion, Mr Stapleton would not have seen her, would not have mentioned her presence in London to her uncle. Jasper in turn would not have come to Half Moon Street and then on to Hadleigh to check up on her. From there he would not have gone up to plunder Kydd again and thus would not have been in the bookshop at the fatal moment.

Nell gave herself a mental shake. What nonsense. Given her uncle's obsession, he might have uncovered their deception at any time. She should be glad to have survived this long.

There was a hesitant knock at the door. 'Your supper, sir,' came the young footman's muffled voice.

Jasper instantly slammed her chair around to face the wall. 'One word,' he reminded her in a hiss, 'and it will be the worse for him as well as for you.'

Nell remembered the silver-mounted gun and sat motionless. Behind her she heard plates being set on the table, the chink of a decanter and glasses. The aroma of stewed mushrooms, something in a wine sauce, something else sharply citrus and a potato and turnip mash with herb-butter set her mouth salivating.

'Clarrie says as she's sorry there's no fish, but we didn't expect you back you see, sir, and — '

'The woman is clearly as disorganized as she is incompetent and totally unfit to have charge of a kitchen. I shall require shaving water at eight in the morning and a substantial breakfast. Is she capable of understanding that? Do not come back to clear up tonight. I am working on a particularly delicate matter and do not wish to have the slightest paper disturbed, not today or tomorrow. Indeed, tell the staff that you may all have tomorrow off after church to spare me your presence. I shall not be attending. Where is the brandy?'

'S-sir?'

'Brandy, fool. To make palatable what passes for a repast in this miserable pile. Bring two bottles immediately.'

'Yes, sir. Will — will you not require a nuncheon tomorrow?'

Her uncle's voice could have chipped stone. 'Imbecile! You will, naturally, see that it is set out in the dining room before you leave for church!'

Nell heard the footman back out and imagined the poor lad wiping his brow as soon as he was safe behind the door. She did not blame him for returning with the brandy mere minutes later. Anything to keep contact with her uncle to a minimum.

Jasper locked the door and then turned around the chair in which she was imprisoned. 'Dear me, Helena,' he said. 'You look quite pale. How remiss of me not to have ordered enough food for two.' With deliberate malice, he arranged himself opposite her where she could see every mouthful, tossed down one glass of wine, poured another and began to eat.

Nell watched him in silent fury. Her face throbbed, her arms ached abominably and her stomach creeled with hunger. Behind his left shoulder the clock ticked on. Nell concentrated on it. What time had they arrived here? Forty minutes ago? Which made it how long since they had left London? Nowhere near as many hours as her original journey had taken, since they had travelled so fast and with so many changes. Five perhaps? Then where would Hugo be now? How much longer would she have to hold out? As her uncle ate, stoking his depleted body with single-minded intensity, Nell began to calculate.

She remembered that Jasper had unloaded more porcelain before coming into the bookshop. Hugo had, at that moment, been in the warehouse manager's office with the solicitors. She wondered what had been in the consignment. The Meissen perhaps? The Kakiemon with its delicate asymmetric flowers? Either would have been too valuable for the fawning assistant to handle alone; both together, definitely so. He would have sent a boy to fetch his superior so that even had Hugo not heard the commotion of unloading, he would have been speedily appraised by the messenger of her uncle's arrival with more stolen goods.

Nell's brow furrowed. That would have taken fifteen minutes at the most. Mr Tweedie must have been ecstatic, thinking he would be able to catch Jasper at first hand admitting the items were his to sell. They would have hidden themselves within earshot and waited. But meanwhile her uncle had taken the remainder of his night's labours to the bookshop, and that they could not have known. How long before his absence made them uneasy? Half an hour? Three-quarters? Say an hour before Hugo discovered her own disappearance, then a further hour to make the inquiries which would determine the direction of their flight.

He was at least two hours behind her then, three if she was being realistic. Nell withdrew her gaze from the clock and tried to imagine what her uncle's plans for her might be. He wouldn't want her back in the coach, that was for sure. Her eyes went to the spare clusters of unlit candles, to the full log-basket, to the second bottle of brandy . . .

I want Kydd Court ground to dust and all your family with it.

He was going to set a fire! Nell gasped and jumped as the realization hit her.

Jasper looked up from his meal. She moaned in her throat, accompanying the sound with a retching movement. His lips twisted with gratification. 'Do continue, my dear. It is most diverting. You should know by now that I am quite impervious to other people's suffering. Indeed, the fainter and weaker you are, the better it will suit me.'

At his words, Nell knew she had guessed right. The only question remaining was — when?

He had ordered breakfast for eight o'clock and the chaise for ten, half an hour after the servants left for church. How long did a fire need to take hold? Nell remembered a wing of the Grainger mansion had been nearly destroyed by fire in her childhood. It had started in the study, she recalled, and burned all night, sealed in stone and thick doors until it was a veritable furnace. The housemaid who had opened up first thing in the morning to rake out the grate hadn't stood a chance.

Nell grew cold with horror. Her uncle had forbidden any more entry into this room. And here were drapes and wooden bookcases and paper in abundance for fuel. He would spend the night loading the chaise with everything of value left in the house, then start the fire first thing tomorrow. Maybe even tonight if his nerve held out. When the servants came in here in the evening to air and clean, it would be too late.

Nell half closed her eyes and let her head loll. At some point her uncle would have to leave the room to collect what remained of the china. He would need to make three or four journeys at least. She must plan her actions during those absences well.

Jasper drank down the wine, finished every scrap of food and mopped up the sauces with the last hunks of bread. He scraped orange syllabub from the glass as if he hardly tasted it. Nell had gone beyond hunger now; she was conserving every ounce of energy. When he carried the first bulging portmanteau out to the chaise, she fastened her gaze on the clock, timing how long it took him.

Three minutes! Nell shut her eyes, appalled, as the door reopened. What could she do in three minutes? As much as possible, she thought grimly. So on her uncle's second trip she struggled out of the chair and crossed to the branch of candles on the table. By the time she had reached backwards, grasped the base to pull it to her, twisted to look over her shoulder, stretched again and manoeuvred it behind her back to a position where she could raised her bound wrists to the flames, she had only thirty seconds left in which to totter back to her chair. She collapsed into it, sweating. Her uncle didn't notice a thing.

On his third absence, books stuffed into a sack which he had brought in from the chaise, she was faster. She burnt through half the cravat near fainting with pain, before throwing herself back into the chair, suffocating the flames with her own body and praying he wouldn't notice the smell of charred linen.

During his fourth trip she managed to free herself. The agony in her shoulders as her wrists came apart was worse even than the blisters and long shooting burns under her ruined sleeves. She staggered to the chair with her arms behind her as if still bound, tears overflowing and soaking into her gag, unable to bring her hands round to wipe her eyes even if she had dared risk smearing soot on her face.

Her uncle by this time was barely glancing at her. She spent his fifth absence moving her arms forward in tiny agonizing stages and trying to flex some life back into her fingers. Fortunately, kid gloves had protected the hands themselves from the flames. Kydd gloves. She remembered the quip she had made to Hugo all those weeks ago, and had to clamp down fiercely on a bubble of hysteria.

Jasper seemed to have run out of sacks and was thus finished with looting books. 'Invaluable,' he said, returning the list to his pocket. He put a new log on the fire and turned to scrutinize Nell who was slumped in an exhausted doze.

She did not have to feign her scream of pain when he shook her roughly by the shoulder.

'I have things to do in the house,' he said. 'I

shall be locking both these doors. It will be of little use your attempting to escape.'

She made an inarticulate sound and rolled heavy-lidded eyes which appeared to satisfy him. He went out. She heard the key turn in the lock. She stayed where she was, eyes closed, head against the wing of the chair, not trusting him. She was right to be cautious. Within two minutes he was back, surveying her supine form. This time after he turned the key, she heard him walk away.

Nell did not waste time on doors or windows. Turning gingerly, she found the parcel of green woollen cloth which she had dropped into the chair on arrival. She opened one end of it, crossed to the jug of water which was the only thing her uncle had left untouched at supper, and emptied the whole lot as slowly as she dared into the parcel until the cloth was completely soaked through. Many a time she had seen foresters dip mufflers into streams and wrap them around their noses and mouths in order to breathe that bit longer and easier when fighting blazes in the woods. Copying the foresters should buy her precious minutes in which to escape. The cloth might dry out between now and then, but she couldn't run the risk of her uncle drinking the water after all. She stowed the parcel carefully behind a cushion and resumed her position.

It was now over four hours since they had arrived at Kydd. The servants had long gone to bed. Her uncle made regular trips through the library door with items both bulky and small wrapped in a variety of coverings, from articles of clothing to torn sheets and blankets. Every time he went out, Nell strained to hear noises in the night. Every time she was frustrated. Why was Hugo delaying? She brought to mind his passionate kisses and avowals of love in the shrubbery, the way their embraces engulfed him as well as her, and refused to believe that he wasn't outside, immobile in the darkness, waiting. He was leaving it a mite late, she thought crossly, and wondered for an incredulous moment if he had chosen this one time to allow her to rescue herself.

No, she realized, as her uncle came back in, cursing because he had tripped on the steps in the dark. She hadn't taken into account the conditions out-of-doors. The moon was on the wane and the sky was overcast. There was hardly light even for Jasper to see by, and Hugo was far less familiar with Kydd and its environs than her uncle. He had been three hours behind them and would not have been able to travel near so fast as they as the daylight ebbed, not daring to do anything that

356

might risk an accident to himself or his horse and so lessen the chances of getting her away. He was coming for her steadily and without mishap. Her tension dissolved.

Another hour ticked by. Nell really did doze. She started awake to leaping flames from the fireplace, ripped books scattered about the hearth and her uncle's knife by her ear.

'Just to make sure,' he said silkily, and to her terror she felt the point slide down the line of her jaw.

The gag fell away, stiff with sweat and dried tears. Her uncle's lips stretched in a mirthless smile seeing the unconcealed fear in her eyes. In stupefaction at still being alive she could only goggle at him, her mouth hanging open.

'Excellent,' he murmured, and tipped the contents of the brandy bottle down her throat.

It was only by a super-human effort that Nell kept her hands behind her back. As she spluttered and gasped, she saw the door into the hall open the tiniest crack. Her heart leapt. It was a lifeline. She forced her parched mouth and swollen lips to spit out the fiery liquid, so that her uncle was obliged to wrench her mouth open with one hand whilst continuing to pour with the other. The crack inched wider.

'I'm doing you a favour, my dear,' Jasper said. 'Raw spirit on a starved stomach will cause you to pass out in no time. You won't even feel the flames.'

Nell gagged and spat out more brandy, shaking her head from side to side, keeping his attention focused on her.

He hit her hard, making her cry out with pain. The door behind him jerked wide open. 'Scream away, niece,' he said, not noticing. 'No one will hear you.' He forced her bruised jaw down once again.

And found himself lifted high off his feet and sent clear across the room by the most punishing right hook that ever graced the boxing rings of the Dragoons.

'Hugo,' croaked Nell weakly, and with her hand on his sleeve, tried to pull herself upright.

'Later,' said her beloved, his face murderous, 'after I've finished with — '

There was the most almighty explosion. Flames burst from the fireplace in an eruption of green and blue and red and orange. Shards of glass and splinters of burning log rained outwards. Only the fact that Nell had grasped Hugo's arm to help her stand and he was therefore bent over her with his back to the fire, saved them both from horrific injury. As it was, the force of the explosion pushed them flat against the chair. At the same time there was a high, animal shriek of pain from Jasper Kydd.

'The brandy bottle!' cried Nell as she and Hugo struggled upright. 'He was holding it when you hit him! It must have fallen into the fire!'

She gasped when she saw the room. Smouldering pieces of wood had been hurled indiscriminately. Flames were licking hungrily across the carpet and there were a myriad more around the shelves. Jasper was scrabbling frantically at the outside door, blood pouring from his face. Everything was overlaid with the glitter of glass and the stink of spirits.

'No, you fool,' roared Hugo. 'Don't let the — '

But he was too late. Jasper stumbled out onto the terrace and the flames leapt up sevenfold with the surge of cold air.

Nell didn't stop to think. Even as Hugo shouted 'Tally Ho, Kit — the fox is away!' in a positively enormous voice through the terrace door, she dragged out her soaked cloth, wrapped it twice around her head and hauled down the first of the curtains to begin smothering the fire.

The night outside, from being quiet, was suddenly violent with men's voices. What sounded like half a hundred pairs of feet and a whole company of horses thundered across terrace and grounds.

'Get out, Nell,' yelled Hugo.

'No,' said Nell, pulling down another curtain.

He slammed the door shut. 'God help me, I haven't got time to make you!'

'Then help me instead,' gasped Nell from inside her damp cowl, frantically beating at a burning chair. 'Who's outside? Where have you *been*?'

'Kit let me into the scullery then rode to Belmont,' grunted Hugo as if it was obvious. He turned the hearthrug upside down on the books nearest the fire and stamped the flames to death. 'Philip will have sent grooms to the Graingers and the Caldwells. As long as you were unharmed, I was supposed to wait until they were in place outside.'

He dragged the hearthrug over the floor to douse another area of carpet. Nell swept smouldering books off shelves and smothered them. They worked fast, necessity giving them wings. Eventually, the last rogue flames expired. The air was greasy with acrid soot and ruined damask. Nell let her tattered curtain fall and looked at Hugo across the flickering, smoke-filled room. 'I'm glad you didn't wait,' she said.

He reached out blindly for her. 'God, sweetheart, when I heard you . . . I couldn't have stood by if the realm itself had depended on it.'

Nell dissolved into his kiss, feeling the pain come back into her burned arms, wincing as his unshaven cheek met her bruised mouth.

'I knew you'd look good in green,' he murmured, pushing the still-damp cloth aside.

'Probably the most useful present you'll ever give me,' she said with a watery smile. She felt his fingers stop as they found the swelling on her jaw.

'What the — !' He tilted her face to the nearest candle, took a proper look at her and whirled furiously for the terrace door. 'KIT!' he yelled.

'Don't you dare give that hell-born scum into charge before I get my hands on him!'

A gaunt young man caught himself against the doorframe, panting. 'Mr Kit's giving chase, Captain,' he said. 'Looked like death, did Mr Jasper, when he saw Mr Kit a-running towards him through the darkness. Scared him something terrible. Howled like one of them mad dogs fair to turn your stomach. Forgot there weren't no horses to his chaise and then when he saw Mr Belmont and all a-waiting for him by it, he upped and grabbed your Conqueror from where you'd tethered him and rode off across the fields like he was possessed. Mr Kit's ridden after him. The others are following.'

'Johnny?' said Nell, barely recognizing the man. 'John Farley, is that you?'

'Aye, Miss Nell. I — ' The young man stopped, his eyes widening as he took in Nell's injuries. 'Spare horses down below, Captain,' he said to Hugo.

'Thank you, I — ' But Hugo too broke off, as first a shot, then horses neighing, then an unearthly scream pierced the night air to be followed by absolute silence.

'Oh no, not Kit. Please, not Kit,' whispered Nell. She burrowed into Hugo's chest, trembling.

After an eon of waiting — during which Hugo simply held her and all there was in the world was their rasping breath and the double thump of their heartbeats — she heard the murmur of men's voices and the tramping of shod feet, human and animal, coming up the lawn. The arms around her tensed. Then, 'It's all right, sweetheart! It's all right! Kit's in front leading Valiant.' Hugo's voice faltered. 'He's leading Conqueror too.'

Nell raised her head, unable to see through her tears, thanking God with her whole soul and everything she possessed that both her men had come safely through this night.

Kit had lost his hat. His moon-bright hair had been pushed in bedraggled, sweaty locks away from his face. He met Hugo's eyes first, then Nell's. 'It's over,' he said in a drained, exhausted voice. 'God help us all, it's over. Seeing me in front of him when he'd thought me dead must have wholly unhinged my uncle's mind. He took Conqueror. Stupid of him, he couldn't hope to get away. As I closed, he turned and loosed off a shot at me over his shoulder. Both horses reared.' His voice shook. 'Both of them, Hugo — Conqueror and Valiant. He didn't stand a chance. I only just managed to hang on, myself.' He swallowed. 'They'd trampled him to death before I could do anything about it. It was horrible.'

'Oh, Kit.' Nell let go of Hugo and fell on her brother's neck to comfort him as best she could.

Kit held her tightly. 'Peace, brat. I'll survive.' He shot a look at his friend. 'I promise I'll never roast you again about resigning your commission.'

Philip Belmont rode up. 'What ho, Nell,' he said cheerfully. 'Bad business, eh? Just wanted to say no need to worry about the body, Kit. M'future father-in-law's seeing to it. Justice of the Peace and all that. Dashed useful.' He frowned. 'You know, Hugo, I don't believe that horse of yours was ever in the Dragoons. Rearing up at a single shot like that? Ball didn't even graze him!'

'No,' said Hugo, a tremor in his voice. 'No, I bought him after I sold out.'

Philip's face cleared. 'Knew it had to be something like that. Marvellous goer, though. Let me know if you ever want to get rid of him. Daresay he'd ride to hounds a treat.' He peered past them at the library. 'Looks the devil of a mess in there. Want to come to Belmont? M'mother'd love it. Adores company. Make you up beds in a trice.'

This time it was Nell who struggled to keep a straight face. 'No thank you, Philip. It is very kind of you to ask but we'll stay here at Kydd. Kit has — Kit has missed it.'

'Ah, yes, forgot. Want to start setting things to rights straight away, eh, Kit? That's the stuff. Said you weren't one to be sticking your spoon in the wall, didn't I? I'll ride over tomorrow with a couple of the men to see what needs doing. Tell you what, Nell, I'll bring Emily. Have a comfortable coze. You'll like that.'

John Farley eased the reins from Kit's hand and led the horses around the lawn to the stables as if he'd never been away. Nell could hear scandalized voices from the servants indoors exclaiming at the state of the library. She, Hugo and Kit watched as Philip rode jauntily off, followed by his men.

Kit gave a weak laugh. 'Never changes, does he?'

Nell shook her head. 'No.' She leant against Hugo's side. His arm came round her, safe and strong and wonderful. 'I don't believe I will ever regret not marrying him.'

'I should hope not,' said Hugo. He searched her face. 'All right now?'

She nodded. 'I am just so glad it is finally over.' And in a whisper, 'I knew you would come.'

His deep green eyes gazed into hers. 'Always.'

A tremor ran through Nell. She raised parted lips to him.

He turned her in his arms and bent his head to kiss her, then checked. 'Kit,' he said, glancing across to where his friend was watching dawn come up over his ill-used demesne. 'Be a good fellow and tell your people to heat hot baths and roast fatted calves or something, would you?' His eyes returned to Nell. 'I have some interrupted business with your sister that cannot wait a single moment longer . . . '

We do hope that you have enjoyed reading this large print book.

Did you know that all of our titles are available for purchase?

We publish a wide range of high quality large print books including:
Romances, Mysteries, Classics
General Fiction
Non Fiction and Westerns

Special interest titles available in large print are:
The Little Oxford Dictionary
Music Book
Song Book
Hymn Book
Service Book

Also available from us courtesy of Oxford University Press:
Young Readers' Dictionary
(large print edition)
Young Readers' Thesaurus
(large print edition)

For further information or a free brochure, please contact us at:
Ulverscroft Large Print Books Ltd.,
The Green, Bradgate Road, Anstey,
Leicester, LE7 7FU, England.
Tel: (00 44) 0116 236 4325
Fax: (00 44) 0116 234 0205

Other titles published by
The House of Ulverscroft:

FORTUNATE WAGER

Jan Jones

Secrets and subterfuge abound in Regency Newmarket . . . Caroline Fortune wants only to train horses and to continue her progress towards independence. So she projects a cheerfully argumentative persona in order that the suitors, dredged up by her mother, will leave her alone. Lord Alexander Rothwell is happy to do so. He's in Newmarket purely to fulfil an obligation; irritable because he believes he's investigating a mare's nest, he wants to return to his political career in London as soon as possible. So, when Caroline finds Alexander left for dead at her brother's racing stables, they are both considerably disconcerted . . .

FAIR DECEPTION

Jan Jones

Fate seems to intervene when Kit Kydd rescues Susanna Fair from abduction. Kit must appear settled to be made his great-aunt's heir, and Susanna is an actress. By pretending to be engaged during a visit to Lady Penfold, Kit can protect Susanna from further danger. But Lady Penfold lives in the horse-racing town of New-market, which holds the secret of Susanna's scandalous past. And the dishonourable Rafe Warwick has wagered two thousand guineas on making Susanna his mistress. Now how will she cope with her theatre company's request to make a final public performance . . . and falling in love with Kit?